VAMPIRE
Crush

VAMPIRE Crush

A. M. ROBINSON

HARPER TEEN

An Imprint of HarperCollinsPublishers

HarperTeen is an imprint of HarperCollins Publishers.

Vampire Crush
Copyright © 2010 by A. M. Robinson
HarperCollins Children's Books, a division of HarperCollins Publishers,
10 East 53rd Street, New York, NY 10022.
www.harperteen.com

Library of Congress Cataloging-in-Publication Data
Robinson, A. M. (Andrea M.), 1982–
    Vampire crush / A.M. Robinson. — 1st ed.
        p.   cm.
    Summary: Sixteen-year-old journalist Sophie McGee's junior year is
filled with unexpected drama—and romance—when she discovers that her
new classmates are hiding a dark secret, while the boy next door from her
childhood re-enters her life.
    ISBN 978-0-06-198971-1
    [1. High schools—Fiction. 2. Schools—Fiction. 3. Vampires—
Fiction. 4. Stepsisters—Fiction. 5. Newspapers—Fiction. 6. Dating
(Social customs)—Fiction. 7. Family life—Michigan—Fiction. 8. Michigan—Fiction.] I. Title.
PZ7.R557Vam 2011   2010009397
[Fic]—dc22   CIP
                                                                AC

Typography by Alison Klapthor
11 12 13 14 15   CG/BV   10 9 8 7 6 5 4 3 2 1
❖
First Edition

For Mom and Dad

Chapter One

"Sophie McGee, Editor in Chief."

I have to say, it has a nice ring to it. I say it again just for kicks, only this time I use a whimsically French accent, the kind you only see in zee bad comedies. Then, since I'm on a roll, I launch into a few others—Southern (great), Australian (hot), Swiss (breezy and natural, but a person from Switzerland should probably be the judge). Mr. Amado, my journalism teacher, should really give the position to me now. I'm just about to attempt Human Who Is Secretly a Robot accent when someone knocks on my bedroom door.

"What are you doing? Are you talking to yourself?"

asks a muffled voice that's curious and impatient all at once—a trademark of my stepsister, Caroline.

"I'm on the phone," I say loudly, before remembering that last night I left my phone on the coffee table downstairs. I add "Lie Better" to this year's to-do list.

"You're doing the name thing again, aren't you?" she asks. "I don't think your teacher will make you editor in chief if you are crazy."

It's a fair point. Still . . .

"What do you want?" I ask.

"Mom says she's going to eat your first-day French toast if you don't come downstairs for breakfast now."

Not wanting to waste time when there's powdered sugar involved, I thank Caroline for warning me and return to packing my bag as I hear her skip down the stairs. Pens? Check. Schedule? Check. Journalism notebook with article ideas for this year? Triple check. Name perfection aside, there are a lot of reasons that I deserve to be editor in chief. I've done everything I can to make sure that it's me—writing filler articles, taking extracurricular photography courses, and even going to a summer journalism camp where we were all forced to wear lime green T-shirts and work on a fake newspaper called *Teen Issues Today*.

After checking to make sure that my hair isn't doing anything too experimental, I clomp downstairs to the kitchen to find my family halfway through the McGee breakfast routine.

Caroline sits at our round table, dressed to the tens as she picks suspiciously at the remains of her fruit plate. Marcie gave her three slices of cantaloupe again, and as usual, one sits smiling and abandoned on the place-mat while she taps her grapes as if they might be tiny purple grenades. They don't pass the test. Abandoning the fruit altogether, she crosses her tan legs and sets to picking invisible lint off of her outfit. Today it is a short denim skirt and a series of layered candy-colored tank tops, all beneath a wispy excuse for a cardigan that's designed to make our matronly principal's head spin. Caroline won't admit it, but her favorite hobby—after watching reality television—is flirting with wardrobe malfunction.

My father sits across from her in a banker-blue suit. For the first nine years of my life, I steadfastly believed that he wore a tie to bed. This morning's selection is red, striped, and currently peeking out from beneath the local business section. Every so often his head shakes as he mutters something about the NASDAQ and the depressed real estate market.

The only thing missing is my stepmother, Marcie, eating my food (lies!) and asking when I'm going to try out for tennis to fulfill her vicarious need for high school sports. Instead she's peering out the window that faces our neighbor's house, or what used to be their house until they moved out six months ago. I slide into the last empty seat and drag some French toast onto my plate with as much stealth as possible; no need to attract her attention.

"I think the house next door finally sold," Marcie announces to no one in particular. "There's a light on upstairs . . . but I haven't seen any moving trucks."

She leans over the sink, not caring that the pink belt of her silk robe is dangling down the drain. If there's one thing Marcie likes more than being our family's judge, jury, and cruise director, it's keeping tabs on the neighbors.

"It's probably an early morning reflection," my father says.

"The sign's gone."

"Then they moved in late last night."

Marcie looks doubtful, probably because she was spying last night at dinner, too, but she drops the curtain and takes her place at the table next to Caroline.

"I wish it were the Hallowells," she says sadly, reaching over to steal Caroline's neglected cantaloupe slice. "Sophie got along so well with their son."

I shove a bite of French toast in my mouth so I will be saved from responding. Marcie used to think that their son, James, was my soul mate because one time we managed to get through a picnic without starting a ketchup war or calling each other "snotbucket." In reality our relationship consisted of hair pulling (age six), doll vandalism (age eight), and relentless teasing about my freckles (age eleven). Not exactly Romeo and Juliet, but try telling Marcie that. Luckily he moved away to New York before either one of us had to drink poison or kill a cousin.

"I hope they have a teenage son," says Caroline, who's gone back to scraping the seeds off of her strawberries. "A cute one," she adds before glancing up to study my outfit. "Seriously? That's what you've decided to wear on the first day of school?"

I look down at my faded green T-shirt, low-rise jeans, and classic Converse sneakers. No reason to go cry in a corner. "What?" I ask. "Is my butt supposed to have something written on it?"

She ignores my joke. "If you want to borrow something, just ask. You know, like a skirt. Or something not made out of cotton."

"I'll keep that in mind," I say, shrugging it off. It might sound mean-spirited, but Caroline's concern for the fashion victims of the world is genuine. I once caught her sniffling over *People*'s "Worst Dressed" list. She claimed it was allergies, but I suspect she was momentarily overcome by a star's debilitating case of quadra-boob.

After Caroline returns to inspecting her fruit, my father lowers the corner of his newspaper and winks at me, his traditional bonding gesture. Before I can wink back, Marcie leans across the table and taps me on the wrist with a manicured index finger, waiting for my full attention before she asks her question.

"Have you given any more thought to tennis this year?"

And with that, I know that it's time to grab my backpack and leave for school.

Thomas Jefferson High is on the edge of town, a location normally reserved for insane asylums and industrial plants that leak hazardous waste. I arrive in plenty of time to snag my usual parking spot at the far end of the lot, right next to the woods that border it to the west. The towering pine trees ensure that the sun does not make my Jeep a sauna, which in turn makes sure that I won't have to kill myself in the afternoon because the car is too hot. For this reason, I like the woods. My classmates also like the woods, but more because they can sneak off and kiss behind the trees.

As for the building itself, nothing has changed since last May; it could still double as a penitentiary, albeit a penitentiary with a lot of jail spirit and a streamer budget. The narrow windows are more suited to a castle turret than a place of learning, and on a gray day it's difficult to distinguish brick from sky. Unless it benefited from a surprise makeover this summer, the inside isn't any less gloomy.

The front sidewalk is peppered with clumps of students

desperate to soak up the final seconds before the last bell spurs a mad stampede toward the front door. Usually I cut through the gauntlet of chatter and make my way to class, but today I'm not hearing the normal buzz about summer pool parties, new cars, and mean bosses at Dairy Queen. Instead it's about a group of new students who tried to shake everyone's hands in the hallways.

"I heard they were foreign exchange students," says Danny Baumann, his sunny, all-American head towering above the cluster of football players to my right. "From Bulgaria, or someplace else in South America."

No one would be surprised to learn that Danny Baumann spent the entire semester of World Geography planning his fantasy football league. I know this because I spent the entire semester studying Danny Baumann. Ours is a secret love. I lean in to hear more, but Lindsay Allen cuts my eavesdropping short by hopping in front of me.

"Hey! Good to see you again," she says, startling me with a hug. Five-foot-nothing, she's a red-haired dynamo who reigns over Student Council and anything involving wind instruments. She gives a mean rendition of Lady Macbeth's soliloquy at Speech meets, and the rumor is that it once made the drama teacher cry. More frightening? She moved here less than a year ago, but she's my competition for editor in chief. When she pulls away, she's already talking a mile a minute.

"So Mr. Amado wants to see you before the bell if you have a chance. He thinks we should get a head start on the welcome-back issue of the paper," she says and then readjusts her thick-framed glasses.

Great. She's beaten me to the newsroom, aka Mr. Amado's journalism classroom. Her glasses also look very editorial. I'm losing this thing already.

"What does he want us to handle?" I ask, dreading the answer.

"The new student profile thing," she says. "It's gonna be fun! And a little annoying. Hey, I called you a few times over the summer, but you never got back to me."

"Oh. Right. I was . . . busy." As excuses go, it's fairly lame, so I try to make it better by explaining that the leader of the journalism camp was in love with homework. The truth is that I meant to call her—I did—but something always seemed more important. Thankfully the ten-minute bell rings, and Lindsay makes panicked noises about having three more teachers to see before running off and saving me from digging a deeper hole.

When I get to the journalism room, Mr. Amado's busy writing his name and an "inspirational" quote in small, spiky letters on the whiteboard. The room is a haphazard jumble of desks, article clippings, and computers, many of which are so old that their keys have only the ghosting of letters. I love this place. I take in a deep breath and then start to cough. It also smells like rubber cement, even though they switched to electronic layout years ago.

Mr. Amado drops the marker in the tray and turns around. "Sophie! Nice to see you."

"Lindsay said that you wanted to discuss the welcome-back issue?" I say when I've recovered.

"Right!" he says, clapping once as he moves behind his desk. "But first, have a seat in the front row and let's go over what our goals are for this year."

He points toward a desk in the front row. I sit, taking a moment to study the deranged art scratched across its top, including a sketch of what is either Mr. Amado in drag or an attractive female Bigfoot. I'm still debating when he rolls over in his chair, brow furrowed like he's going to tell me I have brain cancer.

"I hope that you know what a great journalist and writer I think you are," he says. "Your work last year was exceptional. If my grade book didn't tell me otherwise, I would have thought you were a senior. I'm honored to have you back on my staff."

Well, this is a step up from cancer. "I know that you want me on the new-student thing, but I actually had a great article idea for the first issue," I say, tugging at my backpack's zipper and pulling out my story notebook. "Have you ever wondered how many of our library's books have never been checked out? I bet if we compare our percentages to the state average you'll see just how illiterate the student body really is. I mean, you can already see it, but just think—"

"Sophie," Mr. Amado interrupts gently and then tells me to listen. "Like I said, I love everything you're doing, but our school paper is generally supposed to be less investigative and more . . ."

"Fluff?"

"Celebratory."

"Oh."

"It's not that your article on the health code violations committed by lunch ladies in the cafeteria wasn't stellar—it was—but I think we are ruffling too many feathers. I also think they spit in my soup when I'm not looking."

I have a snappy comment ready about progress and how it can't happen if you're afraid of lunch ladies, but I swallow it. Seeing that no response is forthcoming, Mr. Amado sighs, rolls over to his desk to grab a folder, and rolls back.

"We have a lot of new students this year. Eight in the junior and senior class alone," he says, handing over the folder. "I want you and Lindsay to handle them for the 'Getting to Know Our New Tigers' feature. You have four; she has four. Frame the profiles however you like, but just make sure it's a human interest piece." The corners of his mustache lift in amusement. "You're not trying to get them to confess their innermost secrets. If they shot a man in Reno just to watch him die, good for them. We don't want to know about it."

This assignment sounds about as fun as naked paintball. A part of me thought being a junior would mean that I could stop scouting out the mall's best frozen yogurt or asking random students if they liked the new *Saw* movie.

"Everything okay?" Mr. Amado asks.

"So we're talking favorite foods, hobbies, colors, movies, pets, and hair products, right?" I ask, doing my best to stop sulking and fake excitement.

"It's up to you," he says just as the warning bell rings. As he walks me to the door, he tries to be reassuring. "You'll do great, don't worry. And hey—I promise that your next story can be about how the members of the Green Team don't recycle."

One can only hope.

Chapter Two

A few years ago the administration suddenly realized that forty-five minutes isn't enough time to teach the history of Roman civilization or complex math. Now we still have eight classes, but we only go to four of them in a day. This means that savvy planners can finagle days without vectors, formulas, equations, decimals, or any other mathematical things designed to crush one's spirit. This year I've arranged it so that I have two art classes in a row, then English, then back to Journalism with Mr. Amado. First up is Drawing II with Mrs. Levine, a perpetually unhappy woman who is rumored to have dated all three of the gym teachers at once. No one knows the whereabouts of Mr. Levine. Some say that she ate him.

She gives us the usual first-day speech—don't eat, don't shout, and don't knock over any of the expensive paints or your parents will pay—before she plops bowls of pinecones on our tables.

"Still Life with Pine Cones. Go," she barks and then slams her office door.

Not surprisingly, the glamour of drawing pinecones wears off quickly. After glancing back to check that Mrs. Levine is still hiding, I slip out the folder from Mr. Amado and find a list of the new students' names and a copy of their schedules inside.

Marisabel Jones
Violet Martin
Neville Smith
Vlad Smithson

Drunken baby naming is a very serious problem, I think as I flip to their schedules. I half expect to find them signed up for Defense Against the Dark Arts, but their classes are normal. I have English with Vlad and Violet, and

French with Marisabel. It's a start. The schedule I'm sketching is just starting to take shape when a shadow falls over my page.

"Pinecones, Miss McGee?" asks Mrs. Levine.

"Yep. Abstract ones."

"Cute. But this one's a realistic still life, okay?" she says before wandering back into her cave.

Five minutes before class is scheduled to end, the intercom begins to crackle, and Principal Morgan's voice reminds us that next period will be replaced by First Day Assembly. When the bell rings, I grudgingly gather my things and trudge to the auditorium.

By the time I push my way through the heavy wooden doors, most of the seats are taken. The back rows are dominated by the students in oversized band T-shirts who try without much success to hide earbuds beneath their shaggy hair; Caroline and crew hold court in the front. Usually they are the center of attention, laughing about nothing and jumping back and forth over the rows while the rest of us watch.

Today, however, their heads are turned to the side. I follow their gaze to the auditorium's right wing, where a tall blond boy is leaning against the stage. His features are sharp—a long nose, highly arched eyebrows, and slicing sideburns. Every so often he uncrosses his arms to tug fastidiously at the cuffs of his tailored black shirt. It's a strange gesture, as is the way he tilts his head whenever someone in the front row speaks to him. He must hear the whispers, now at a fever pitch, and yet he keeps his gaze trained on the row of students before him, seemingly oblivious to the five hundred pairs of eyes dissecting his every move. But now and then the corner of his mouth twitches as though he's fighting off a smirk.

Ten to one he's a new student—hopefully one of my new students. Editor in chief, here I come.

The heavy curtain begins to ripple, and Principal Morgan backs onto the stage, still barking commands at a helpless AV Club hopeful. Realizing that the show is about to begin, I slip into the nearest open seat a few rows back before anyone can point me out to Ms. Kate, the terrifying teachers' aide, who may or may not be 137 years old. I still have nightmares about the day she stood behind me in the lunchroom until I finished all of my peas.

The seat happens to be next to Neal Garrett, who's

nice enough in an "I went to space camp this summer" way, but who brings his hamster to school at least once per year. The way he's murmuring to the left pocket of his khakis right now makes me think that today is the day.

"Good morning, students," Principal Morgan says from on high, and then sets to smoothing her hair as she waits for the microphone to cease whining. Satisfied her bun is scraped high enough to pull the edges of her eyebrows up demonically, she continues. "I'd like to welcome you to another year at Thomas Jefferson High and to remind you that it's time to put away your summer brains and bring out your thinking caps." She mimes putting on a hat. I hope that Neal's hamster bites me and gives me a strain of rabies that will kill me quickly.

The rest is familiar stuff: our sports teams are great, good grades are great, cleavage is bad, short skirts should be burned immediately. By the time she gets to the evils of graphic tees, most of her audience has checked out, either staring blankly ahead or studying their crotches with great interest. I glance at the new kid to see how he's taking it, expecting to find the same glassy-eyed condition that has infected everyone else around me, but instead he's bravely sitting on the arm of an aisle seat and scribbling furiously in a small bound notebook. Every so often he looks up as though afraid he's missed a stray word. One of the teachers tasked with policing the crowd approaches, face stern, and says something in his ear, but he just waves her away impatiently. The teacher tries again, and this time he turns to look at her directly. I can't see what he says, but after a few seconds she backs off.

"So, in conclusion," Principal Morgan drones on, causing my ears to perk up in the misguided hope that she's reaching the end of her speech, "pointy shoes will no longer be allowed due to an unfortunate incident at the end of last year. I will determine what is pointy and what is not." She clears her throat and shuffles a stack of note cards. "Now, please be aware that we have a bumper crop of new students this year, and I hope you will welcome them and help them learn our rules." She moves on to the next card and announces that she will be recapping proper lunchroom decorum, but stops when something in the front row catches her eye. The new boy is taking large, purposeful strides up the staircase onto the stage.

The auditorium groans. Last year's assembly ran over two hours because of a skit where a student pretended to need the principal's help reading Thomas Jeff's code of conduct. Some people get annoying pop songs stuck in their heads; I get dialogue from "The Code and You." ("Gee, but is copying off Wikipedia really plagiarism, Principal Morgan?") She's obviously recruiting the new students early.

But Principal Morgan doesn't seem to be in on the skit. "What are you doing? Go back to your seat this instant!" she snaps, clutching the head of the microphone, but the boy doesn't stop until he reaches the podium. Ignoring the principal's stuttering, he covers her death grip on the microphone and catches her gaze with a smile.

"May I have the floor?" he asks, the microphone picking up enough that the question echoes. There's a precise quality to his speech that sharpens each word.

Principal Morgan sputters something about this being First Day Assembly, and the boy smiles encouragingly. Disconcerted, I look to Neal to see if he is registering the weirdness, but he is occupied with taming the wiggling bump in his lower pocket.

"Everything's fine," Principal Morgan says suddenly, and the few teachers who had pushed forward in anticipation of being backup retreat as she folds her hands in front of her and gives him the floor.

The boy's lips quirk as he eases behind the microphone. "I'd like to introduce myself," he says smoothly before another echoing rap of footsteps comes from the side stairs. His smile falters when he sees that a willowy girl has taken the stage and is now crossing to stand by his side. She is gorgeous in a dark, moody way, with thin black brows and long chestnut hair that breaks into a natural wave at her shoulders. If ever there were a girl meant to sit in a smoky café and tell you about the guinea pig that died tragically when she was four, it's her.

The boy clears his throat. "Yes, well," he begins, but then stops to glare at her when she tugs on his sleeve. His jaw tightens as he turns back to the microphone. "We'd like to introduce ourselves. My name is Vlad, and this is my . . ." He pauses and tilts his head to the side. "This is my stepsister, Marisabel. We hope that you'll welcome us to your charming state of Michigan.

—21—

I know some of us will become fast friends."

Vlad and Marisabel—two of my interviewees. I confirm it with my list just as he winks at the front row, executes a stiff bow, and hops off the stage. Marisabel follows a few seconds later, looking suddenly glum. At first no one is sure how to react. There is a surge of whispers, a smattering of applause, and then, finally, a few admiring whoops. When he gets back to his seat, two guys in football jerseys lean over and pat him on the back like he's just pulled off the ultimate prank. At first he seems affronted, but when he sees that they are smiling at him, he matches it with a sly grin.

"Well, yes. Okay. Thank you," Principal Morgan says, her voice shaky as she moves back behind the podium. She clears her throat a few times as her hands flit around the microphone. "Assembly is dismissed," she says finally. "No running in the halls."

"That was weird," Neal remarks from beside me, his hand on the pocket of his khakis to calm the creature that is now visibly doing a wiggle dance, most likely agitated by the din of five hundred student bodies barreling toward the cafeteria.

"I think he broke her," I say, my eyes still on Principal Morgan. Teachers have surrounded her in a protective circle. She's shaking her head and waving them away, and while I can't tell what she's saying, she still looks a little vacant.

"That's not a totally bad thing," Neal muses. "Maybe we're due for a kinder, gentler regime at Thomas Jeff. Pointy shoes for all!"

"Maybe," I say and start to ask him what he thought of Vlad's performance when I see a pink nose emerge from beneath a khaki flap. "Your, um, friend is escaping."

"Oh crap, he's hungry. Check ya later," Neal says, and scoots out the back auditorium doors in an awkward run.

Figuring out where to sit for lunch is always a tricky process. Sometimes I sit with Lindsay, but most of the time she's saving the whales or forests or last season's winter coats. Caroline will always make room for me, but only on the condition that I don't speak to anyone. She doesn't like it when I ask her friends questions like "Don't you think wearing a shirt that says 'I Brake for Boys' is laying it on a little thick?" and follow it up with "I think it's generally illegal not to." Most of the time, I end up picking a quiet corner to read or work on upcoming articles.

But after the assembly weirdness, insider access is too good to pass up. I make my way to the sea of school colors that signifies Caroline's table, where she immediately scoots over to make room for me. Her eyes are glued across the middle aisle, where Vlad, Marisabel, and a few other students I don't recognize huddle around one of the central tables. *Is this new-kid solidarity, or do they all know one another?* Before I can mention it, Caroline demands my attention.

"Oh. My. God. Sophie, he winked at me! I mean it was at me, right?" Caroline looks around the table with an appraising eye. "Yeah. It was totally me. It was, like, so electric. I've never felt anything like it before in my life, not even when Tommy gave me his jersey after the homecoming game."

"I imagine that felt sweaty."

"You know what I mean. Amanda, tell her."

I look at Caroline's three best friends, sitting in a row across the table. They all look like the same person with different haircuts.

"Oh yeah, electric," the middle one says, bobbing her head until her dangly earrings swing in agreement.

That adds nothing, Amanda. Before I can ask for clarification, or even decide if I want clarification, Caroline grabs my arm and hisses my name.

Vlad is making his way across the cafeteria. He moves silently and with an easy grace, an achievement when you take into account the cheap tile that makes everyone in sneakers sound like farting mice. When he stops at the end of our table, his handsomeness is more apparent, even if my discount view only gives me a direct shot of nicely defined nostrils. Reaching across my chest, he picks up Caroline's hand.

"May I have your name?" he says, bending over and kissing a knuckle.

Caroline's close to hyperventilating, but she manages to croak it out.

"A lovely name for a lovely girl," he says, politely ignoring the fact that his "lovely girl" is acting lobotomized. "I wonder if you would do me the honor of showing me around your school."

The lines are corny and dated, like excerpts from the failed script of *Pride & Prejudice: The High School Years,* but that doesn't seem to bother Caroline.

"Yes," she blurts. "I would be delighted to chauffeur you around."

My sister has a tendency to lose her powers of vocabulary when nervous. I'm guessing she was going for "escort," but the rest of it's strangely formal, too, even for someone who's not her.

"Wonderful," Vlad says, and then probably follows it with something else ridiculous ("Your hair is like sunlight in space" or "Let's greet the dawn with kisses"), but I'm distracted by a loud huff, followed by a smacking sound and the swing of a lunchroom door. I sneak a peek at Vlad's table. Marisabel has disappeared. Either she thought too hard about the "Surprise!" part of "Lunchmeat Surprise!" or she does not approve of Vlad wooing Caroline.

I want to ask Vlad about his stepsister, but the bell rings, sadly bringing an end to our twitterpated weird-fest. After another strange little bow, Vlad strides back to his table, and I realize that this is probably as good a time as any to talk to him about getting that interview, which I have to admit is looking more interesting. After grabbing my stuff, I dump my tray and approach, annoyed to find that he's already in the middle of a group conversation with two beefy, athletic-looking guys and a boy with coppery hair who can't seem to decide whether or not to put his hands in his pockets. I slip into a seat at a nearby table and pretend to be searching for a worksheet as I wait for an opportunity to jump in.

"They already like me, Neville," Vlad says. "Did you see how many of them congratulated me afterward? Look, this is called a 'fist bump.' It is more accepted now than a handshake."

Neville—or, as I like to call him, "Interview Subject Three"—ignores Vlad's proffered fist. "I still think that it is unnecessary attention," he says and then pulls a crumpled schedule out of his khaki pocket. "What do you think one studies in 'Basic Skills'? I do not think I will attend that."

"You must go to everything," Vlad snaps. "Everyone goes to everything."

For a moment Neville looks as though he might protest, but then thinks better of it. "Very well," he says, looking around the cafeteria. "Where is—"

"I do not know. I will deal with him later. Go to class."

Neville's mouth tightens, but he complies, and I'm a little disappointed that I won't get the chance to knock two interviews off at once. After he's disappeared through the cafeteria doors, Vlad turns to the two quarterbackesque boys with a look that suggests he finds Neville's attitude unbelievable. They say nothing, just respond with matching smiles. Except for a chin dimple and their hair color—one black, one a dirty blond—they're almost identical.

This is officially the creepiest clique ever. Not only do the new kids all seem to know one another, they—

No, I tell myself. *No*. According to Mr. Amado, my job is not to suspect, just to interview. Before Vlad has a chance to turn and talk to the other two guys, I walk up and tap his shoulder. He whips around, the suave grace from before replaced by a wary alertness. When his eyes flick down to meet mine, I notice that they are a dark gray.

"Hey! I'm Sophie," I say, holding out my hand, but he stares at it like I've just hauled my pet fish out of my pocket and suggested he touch it. When it becomes clear that he's not going to shake it, I let it go limp at my side. "Okay. Anyway, I work on our school paper, and we like to do features on all of the new students. You know, the traditional stuff: where you're from, favorite bands, what dead person you'd like to have dinner with . . ."

He snorts at this last one. God, this is embarrassing.

". . . that sort of stuff. I know it sounds boring, but if you want to pick a time, we can get it over with."

I wait. For the first time since I started this appalling introduction, he looks at me, really looks at me, from the crown of my head to the tips of my sneakers before meeting my eyes.

"No."

"What?"

"No, I think not," he says politely, and gives me a cool smile before turning his back and walking toward the exit. The two giants lumber after him wordlessly.

"I'm Caroline's sister!" I call out, and then make a mental note to punch myself in the face for making the humiliation worse. But it doesn't matter; the swinging door marks this conversation as over.

My next class is around the corner, so I allow myself a few moments of post-snubbing indignation before heading for the classroom. As I'm walking to the door

I give my ego a reassuring pat by telling it that I don't have to see him again. And I don't, at least not until two seconds later, when he's sitting in the front row of my English class with his long legs extended. I steel myself for a smirk, an arrogant chuckle, or some sort of recognition, but he's leaning back in his chair, alternating between absently studying his fingernails and writing in the small black journal I first saw in the auditorium. (My guess? "Today I was a total douche for no reason. The End.")

Even though I'm one of the last ones in, there's still an empty spot in the back row. It doesn't take long to figure out why. A wave of floral perfume hits me like a truck before I'm even halfway there. It's coming from the diminutive blond girl I saw leaving the cafeteria earlier, who is now sitting primly in the corner seat like the poster child for perfect posture. Of all the newbies, she wins the award for strangest outfit, having chosen a lavender floor-length skirt with a flouncing layer of gossamer ruffles and a fitted velvet jacket.

I check my chart. Good morning, Violet Martin. After Ms. Walpole passes out our semester syllabus, I make a bid for her attention. "Psst, Violet."

She continues to stare ahead, idly twisting one of her blond curls. I wait until Ms. Walpole turns to write the five steps to a good thesis statement on the board and then tap Violet's shoulder.

"Yes?" Violet says, her voice strange and airy. First-day lectures are never anything to make you stand on your desk and thump your chest, but she's achieved a new level of spaced out.

"My name is Sophie," I whisper to her cheek, "and I'm doing profiles of all the new students for the school paper. If you have a second after class maybe I could ask you a few questions?" I notice that her boots have hundreds of little black buttons and an intricate tangle of laces. "I know I'm eager to hear your fashion philosophy."

I get no response, unless you count how she fiddles with her hair and the locket around her neck. I try another tactic. "So . . . is that locket from your boyfriend?"

"No, it's not," she hisses, and then collapses into a few dainty sniffles before pulling a lace handkerchief from her bodice to dab at nonexistent tears. A few people in front of me turn around to glare, worried that the noise will get them in trouble. I am about to tell them to mind their own business when Violet's fingers clamp around my wrist.

"Can I ask you a question?" Violet asks, finally looking at me as she jerks me toward her and starts rambling in a breathy rush. "Let us say that you liked this boy. You liked him so much that you didn't care that your family and friends said that it would end badly. You think he admires you as well, so you give him everything that he could ever want. But what does he do? Does he stay with you forever? No! He ignores you and goes off to live who knows where." Her voice cracks, and she lets go of my arm to flounce back into her seat. "I am at a loss," she hiccups, holding the handkerchief to her mouth. "Do you think I should give him a lock of my hair? Maybe he is unaware that I still care."

I look up from studying the little pink crescents that her nails have left tattooed on my arm. "No, that would probably freak him out."

"Then what should I do? What should I do?"

"Um, here." I hastily pick up the wilting copy of *Seventeen* that someone left under my chair. Pointing to a headline on the cover, I say, "Look! 'How to Tell if Your Crush Likes You.'"

She grabs it out of my hands and flips through it wildly, mouthing the words as she reads.

"Yes, this may work," she mutters after a few seconds. "'Drool-worthy'? How repulsive. I may need some assistance with the language. Will you give me your address?" She lowers the magazine and looks at me expectantly.

"What about my cell number?"

"No. Address, please."

I'm torn—giving it to her might mean I end up with half of a "BFF" necklace and my fingers superglued into a pinkie swear. Neal, who has the desk in front of her, takes advantage of my hesitation and turns around.

"You can have my address," he says, wiggling his eyebrows in a way that is more Charlie Chaplin than leering creep, especially when you take into account that the back of his sandy hair is threatening to cowlick.

"Pardon me?" Violet says.

"My address."

"I am not entirely sure that would be proper."

"Neal, stop it," I hiss, scared that I'm going to lose all of my previous progress if we continue down this road.

He ignores me. "Has anyone ever told you that you look like an anime character?" he asks Violet. "I kind of dig it."

"Neal!"

"*Cowboy Bebop.* Come over sometime and check it out."

Violet looks to me, helpless, as if genuinely confused as to what the proper response is.

"Neal, if you don't stop I will kick your pocket," I threaten.

"But—"

"I will."

Looking more befuddled than scared, Neal turns around. Partly relieved—and yet partly offended that Neal so readily accepted me as a hamster kicker—I scribble my address on a slip of paper. Really, what's the downside? If I can lure her to my house, I may be able to get her to concentrate enough to answer one or two questions.

My last class of the day is journalism, and while it's usually my favorite, the nonexistent progress on the interview front has me worried. Sure enough, Lindsay's already at Mr. Amado's desk when I get there.

"I've talked to three of them already," she boasts as Mr. Amado listens with bemused patience. She's about to say something else when she spots me lingering at the door. "Isn't this project great?"

Sure, if you're a sucker for torture. Why didn't I get the chatty ones? I slump into the front row just as Mr. Amado shoos Lindsay away from his desk to address the class.

"Most of you stopped by to see me this morning, and I think we all have a good idea of our individual responsibilities for the first issue. We go to press in two weeks, so I'm not going to bore you with my classroom rules or make you share what you did last summer. Let's get started." He points to Neal, who is busy drawing something on the back of his binder. Neal does the monthly comic strip for the paper and thinks that his class participation should end there. Mr. Amado, on the other hand, insists that he should try his hand at articles as well. Sometimes I think that their power struggles are the highlight of my life.

Mr. Amado walks over and takes a place in front of Neal's desk, tapping the corner when His Boy Friday fails to look up. "Neal, what have you found out about the missing donated blood from the Back-to-School festival?" He shoots a glance toward Lindsay. "Students worked hard to make sure there was a volunteer component this year."

"Well, there was blood . . . ," Neal starts.

Mr. Amado's eyes light up with hope. "Yes?"

". . . and now there is less blood."

Mr. Amado gives a tight smile. "You're going to need more than that for your article," he says, straining to keep his voice encouraging rather than frustrated.

Neal goes back to shading the complex design he's sketched on the back of his folder. "Isn't this something for the police?" he asks, distracted.

"I wanted you to look at it from the student's perspective, talk to the girls who manned the booth. They were there until eight that night."

"I did."

"Great!"

"They don't know what happened."

Mr. Amado sighs. "Just do me a favor, Neal, and dig a little deeper. Please."

Neal salutes. "Righto, Mr. Amado."

Unappeased, Mr. Amado bends down to Neal's level and starts to whisper encouraging threats, or possibly threatening encouragement. Lindsay takes the opportunity to lean over and study my closed notebook. Hers is already covered in scribbles. Editor-in-chiefly scribbles.

"So, what's your angle going to be?" she whispers. I can spot the competitive edge through the friendliness.

"Why the new students hate me."

"What?"

"Never mind." The least I can do is act like I might have something to write down. I flip open my notebook and try to make conversation. "Have you met all of yours yet?"

"Almost," she says and turns the page. "Everyone except for James. Hey, do you want to maybe see a movie on Friday? There's that indie cinema on Main Street that always plays cool stuff."

"I can't," I say, still annoyed that she is beating me.

"Oh, okay. Well, maybe—"

"Mr. Amado's on his way over."

Lindsay straightens in her seat while Mr. Amado strides toward us as purposefully as one can in loafers.

Crouching down, he peeks at what we've written. I put up my hand as a shield.

"So," he starts, and then holds up a finger before Lindsay can speak. "I think I have a good idea about Lindsay's progress; I'm interested in what the other half thinks."

The other half has no idea what to say. Put on the spot, I ask some of my actual questions. "Don't you think it's strange that they all seem to know one another? And think Michigan is charming?"

Mr. Amado doesn't respond at first, just gives me a look akin to the one you'd give the homeless person who stands outside the grocery store shouting that there are aliens in the bread. If his mustache had fingers, it would be wagging one at me right now. "Sophie," he says. "I thought we talked about this."

Out of the corner of my eye, I see Lindsay shooting me covert sideways glances like she was once warned not to stare directly at a loser eclipse.

"I know," I say, "but—"

"We're not investigating," he says. "We're celebrating. Try it again tomorrow."

He raps the desk and walks away, leaving me to wonder why Neal's curiosity is encouraged while mine is smashed into tiny little bits. I sink into my chair and draw circles in my notebook for the rest of the period while Lindsay rattles off all the juicy tidbits she's collected about the two boys who were hanging around Vlad in the cafeteria. Their names are Devon and Ashley—a slap in the face to their obvious aspirations to be brick walls.

"They don't speak all that much, but we managed," she says. "Do you know that they were in the circus when they were little?"

"Wait. You're telling me that they're mute circus people?" I ask, wondering if this is some great cosmic experiment: See how long it takes Sophie's head to explode if we drop her in a vat of weirdness and continue to tell her that no, the soup she's in is perfectly normal.

"Well, okay," Lindsay admits, "it's sort of different. But it's going to make a great article. Unlike Andrew Archer, who doesn't want to talk about anything but dirt bikes." She closes her notebook. "What about

Vlad? He's yours, right? He seems interesting at least. A little show-offy. I can't believe Morgan let him get away with that this morning."

Me either, Lindsay. Me either.

Chapter Three

At dinner that night I am treated to "The Vlad Show." Vlad is hot. Vlad is cool. Vlad has a silver Hummer with tinted windows and he offered to drive Caroline around in it. Vlad is rich. Vlad's parents are away on business in Europe, so he has the house to himself. And yes, he's delighted that they let his friends come stay with him this semester so he wouldn't be lonely. Caroline's so excited, she's shoveling vegetables into her mouth without inspecting them first.

"And get this," she bubbles, holding her fork aloft. "He wants to know everything, absolutely everything about me. When I was born, where I was born, what my plans are after high school, if I have any birthmarks . . . everything! How cool is that?"

If I were a less petty person, I'd thank Caroline for plopping all this information at my feet, albeit coated in the slime of infatuation. Instead, I try to steer the conversation to other subjects. But when Caroline starts to reenact their good-bye scene by her locker, I can't take it anymore.

"He's weird," I say. "What's with all the bowing?"

Caroline colors. "He's European," she says defensively.

"No, you said his parents were in Europe."

"Same thing."

"Okay, that makes absolutely no sense at all. *None* of this makes any sense at—"

"Did you meet any of the new students, Sophie?" Marcie interrupts, attuned to stopping sibling fires before they start.

"Violet. I think she's crazy," I say and then pause, remembering our earlier address swap. "She, uh, might be coming over."

A childhood of saying things meant to shock Marcie has made it tricky for her to tell when I'm serious. Her lips twitch before finally deciding on an indulgent grin.

"Okay," she says. "Just let me know. I'll put the knives away."

She's still smiling at me, proud of her joke, so I smile back. She'll understand when Violet shows up looking like she just rolled around in her great-grandmother's suitcase. Thankfully, my dad dominates the rest of dinner with talk of bankish things. After I help do the dishes, I beat a hasty retreat to my room before Caroline can corner me with more Vlad babble.

Our house is a renovated Victorian that still retains a few creaks. My room is on the very top floor in what used to be the attic, and I'm in love with it, even though the ceilings are low and slanted and eau de mothball lingers in the air. When I was twelve I painted the walls a deep, dark red. Marcie once said that makes it look like a bordello, but if so, it's an inactive one—the only boy who's ever been in my room is James. (When we were nine and played doctor, I tried to give him an appendectomy with a plastic fork. He chickened out mid-surgery.) My favorite part is the two small windows that jut out and create little pockets of space. I have a padded window seat in one, and I've squeezed my desk in the other. When I take a break from doing homework, I like the cramped, cozy feeling of tucking my feet up on the chair and staring across at the house next door.

Tonight, however, I don't have time to waste. The info Caroline dropped at dinner at least gives me something to work with before the next class. I jot down what I know so far.

Vlad
Likes: Expensive cars, being the center of attention, my sister
Dislikes: Common courtesy, me

Marisabel
Likes: N/A
Dislikes: Vlad talking to Caroline

Violet
Likes: Mystery boy, showering in perfume, teen magazines
Dislikes: Listening, making sense

Neville
Likes: N/A
Dislikes: Basic Skills, going to it

And I'm tapped. I throw my pencil down in frustration and end up staring out the window anyway. At first all I see is the reflection of my room—the light behind me, my daybed, and a darker version of my frustrated face—but then, beyond all that in the window across the way, a little halo of light.

Déjà vu comes swift and cold. Since our parents were cheap and lame, James and I used to use flashlights in lieu of walkie-talkies. We even had our own Morse code, uncrackable by Caroline or Nazis. Two long flashes and one short meant "I'm so bored that I want you to come over"; one long and two short meant "Go to bed and stop bothering me"; and three short dashes meant "Please close your window, weirdo exhibitionist." Needless to say, that one got a lot of play during his sixth-grade, I'm-going-to-play-basketball-in-the-park-with-my-loser-friends-every-evening phase.

I press my face to the glass to get a clear view of the neighboring house. True, there are no cars, but Marcie did say that she thought someone had moved in, and she has a sixth sense about that sort of thing. When another dot of light flickers to life, I smoosh in closer, letting my cheek grow cool against the glass. Breath held, I wait to see if this is the beginning of an old pattern. But when it flickers out and doesn't repeat, I feel foolish for hoping . . . hoping what?

I'm not Veronica Mars or Nancy Drew. I'm too paranoid to sneak into someone's house to steal confidential files, and the old clocks and hidden staircases of the world can keep their secrets. But checking on that light isn't investigative rocket science. A quick peek should do it. I promise myself I'll come back up here afterward to stare at what remains of my high school journalism career.

That decided, I formulate my plan of attack. The easy thing to do would be to ring the doorbell, but what would I say if someone answered? "I was spying on you from my bedroom window and thought I should introduce myself at night and without cake." Not likely. I could peek in the front windows, but that might attract the attention of our neighborhood's resident cat lady, Mrs. Sims, who has a habit of calling the police if she sees anyone she doesn't recognize out and about after seven thirty. And since she's half blind, there are very few people she recognizes from more than five feet away. I'll have to cut through the back.

After tiptoeing downstairs, I ease past the living room where Caroline and the parents are watching some incarnation of *CSI*, head through the kitchen, and then slip out the back door into the summer heat. Our back-yard is small and mostly taken up by Marcie's garden of pale tomato and cucumber plants. It is surrounded by a wooden fence that's older than me; whatever paint it once had has long since chipped away, and the wood is turning gray. But this is good—if someone had ever decided to paint it, they would have noticed the two missing planks that make a secret superhighway to the yard next door.

The gap is hidden by overgrown lilac bushes on both sides. I discovered it when I was ten and desperate to find the missing shoe that James had thrown over the fence in retaliation for my spraying him with water when Marcie wasn't looking. I said the hose had acci-dentally gotten away from me; he said my *Little Mer-maid* flip-flop had accidentally flung itself into his yard;

and Marcie told us both to be quiet, she was watching *Oprah*. James's clothes dried out, but I never recovered the flip-flop, even after several covert scouting missions. When I push away the bush's scratchy branches and duck through the gap, a part of me still hopes, irrationally, that I'll find it.

The yard is a mess. The remains of a rusting swing set lurk in the far corner, and the smell of urine emanating from the collapsed shed suggests that it's the new home of the local strays. James's mother's old, crumbling birdbath still stands in a small circle of defeated geraniums, and I wonder if it attracts only robins, like it used to. For a while the harried Realtor had attempted to keep up with the maintenance, but if the grass is any indication, he lost hope a couple of months ago. It's high enough to tickle my knees. If I were really dedicated, I could crawl on my belly and be invisible.

Settling on the half crouch of the semi-determined, I sneak onto the rickety back porch. There are no curtains hanging in the family room window, so I waddle up and peek over the sill. From this spot I can see down the hallway, all the way to the front door. Not much moonlight makes its way into the house, but there's enough to realize that, other than dust and a few snaking cable wires, the family room is empty.

I sit back on my heels; there must be some sort of limit to how many times I can be wrong in one day. I'm just about to start my return creep across the yard when a figure darts through the far hallway. For a second my shocked brain scans for a "Stop, drop, and roll" sort of acronym that explains what to do when you're about to be caught spying. I decide on RLH—Run Like Hell.

I take a flying leap off the porch and hit the ground sprinting, resisting the urge to look behind me, even when I hear the quick creak of a screen door opening and closing again. The tall grass slows me down, and I'm so panicked that my breath is coming in short, jagged little bursts. The lilac bush is only ten feet away when a heavy weight tackles me from behind. My attacker lets out a startled curse as we both fall to the ground.

My side hits first, but the weight of a person on top of me rolls me to my back. I know I should have my eyes open so I can defend myself, but fear is keeping them squeezed shut, and my brain is shouting *stupidstupidstupidstupidstupid*. I'm flinging my fists up wildly, but they bounce off my attacker's shoulders. It finally registers that I should be screaming, so I suck in a deep breath and start to wail. But it's soon smothered by the hand that clamps across my mouth.

"Sophie."

It's a male voice, but soft and exasperated whereas you would think a potential murderer's would be hard and menacing. All my concentration is currently occupied with trying to jerk my knee up where he has my legs pinned, so it takes a moment to realize that he's said my name. I open my eyes.

His features haven't changed, but they're sharper somehow, and squarer. He still has the hint of a scar on his forehead from the rock I lobbed at him from over the fence, and even though it's night out I can tell that his hair is still black. It's shaggier than I remember, but back when I knew him his mother was always dragging him off for haircuts twice a month.

Seeing that I recognize him, he lifts his hand away from my mouth.

"James? James Hallowell?" I yell in disbelief, causing him to clamp his hand back over my mouth. I scream a few other things into his palm, most of it not fit for my own ears, let alone children's. As my tirade rolls on, he starts to smile, his teeth glinting in the darkness. It only enrages me further.

When it comes to anything involving a ball or special shoes, I'm not very athletic, but once upon a time I attended a weekly karate class with the same fervor as a nun attending Mass. It was three years before my sensei told Marcie that he was afraid I was there for the wrong reasons. I believe the word "bloodthirsty" was used. Right before the phrase "I think you should get her checked out."

Now I channel all of my anger and lingering fear into one mighty upward chop to the nose. When he covers his face, I bend my knees up and use my legs to pop him off of me before rolling sideways and scrambling to my feet, my legs still shaky from the adrenaline. All the action has made me dizzy, and I bend over to catch my breath as I wait for the ringing in my ears to pass. When I look up, he's hauling himself off the ground. Now that he's standing, I should add about a foot and a half to my list of things that have changed.

Some people (Caroline) think that I am immune to boys. Not true. The boys of the world may ignore me, but that does not mean that I ignore the boys. I've had giggly crushes along with every other girl; after all, the only reason I like summer is that it makes Danny Baumann wear shorts. So James's attractiveness is not lost on me. But I know from experience that he is a pain in the neck.

"I guess this rules out a neighborly casserole," he snarks, touching his nose one last time before shoving his hands in his pockets. "Although, since all of the things you used to make me had dog food mashed up in them, maybe I should be grateful."

He looks at me expectantly. If he thinks I'm about to whip out a "Welcome Back" banner and tiny hats, he's going to be disappointed. "I'm sorry, were you expecting a parade?"

"Some people might say that it's the least you can do for the guy who gave you your first kiss."

"First kiss? I woke up in my family's hammock to find you slobbering over my cheek," I say and then cut to the chase. "What are you doing here?"

"I live here," he says, and then gestures back at the house just in case I thought he was talking about the lawn. "Again."

"And you couldn't have told me this without jumping me from behind?"

"In hindsight, it's possible that my plan had a few kinks," he says, but when he's met with only my irate incredulity, he drops the swagger. "I didn't mean to tackle you. I just had to catch you before you made it back to your house and told people that I was here." He gives me a long, considering look. "You know, you don't run very fast—maybe you should practice."

"Practice being assaulted? I'll try and remember to jot that down." My breathing has at least returned to a recognizable pattern of in and out, and my muscles have stopped trembling. "Why does it matter if other people know that you're here? They're going to find out tomorrow."

"What's tomorrow?"

"School."

James gives a short laugh. "Considering that I'm not going, I think my secret's safe."

That surprises me. James always loved school, mainly because around sixth grade, the popularity fairy visited. By the time he moved away the summer before freshman year, there wasn't a team roster or MASH list that didn't have his name on it. He had even dated Caroline's friend Amanda, in that they went to school dances and sometimes her dad drove them to the mall. I, on the other hand, only cared that when someone pointed me out to a friend in the library, they responded with, "Oh, that girl" instead of "Oh . . . *that* girl."

"Your public will be disappointed," I say.

"I doubt it," he says. "A lot of things have changed." James pulls a lighter out of his pocket and starts to flick it on and off. I recognize the source of the flickering halo in the upstairs window. He looks at me with a small smile. "Turns out messages are a lot trickier with a lighter," he says as though reading my mind. "What was the signal for 'come over'? Two long and three short?"

"Two long and one short."

"Nice memory," he says with a distinct hint of teasing, as though me remembering our long-ago code means something more than it does.

"Don't get cocky," I warn even as he continues to grin. Flustered, I try to change the subject back to school. "What about your parents? How do they feel about you skipping?"

His smile vanishes immediately, and I realize what

I've said. While my memory may hold on to stupid things from childhood, it doesn't hold on to the important information. Like the fact that one day toward the end of my freshman year, I came home to find Marcie sitting at the kitchen table with a pen and a card. She wasn't writing anything, just staring at the wall with a shattered expression. When I asked what was wrong, she told me that she had just found out that the Hallowells had been killed in a house fire a few months earlier. "I wanted to write James a letter," she said. "But then I realized that I have no idea where to send it."

Now James flicks off the lighter, his face dispassionate. "My parents are dead," he says, and then stalks back toward the house to sit on the porch's first step and stare down through his knees like he's going to be sick.

I don't know what to do, so I just stand in the middle of the yard, my mind flooded with images of the Hallowells—his mother bending down to give us both red popsicles on a hot day; his father wearing a fisherman hat at the many barbecues they hosted; the glow of the candlelight on his parents' faces when they set the birthday cake in front of James at all those parties I was forced to attend. Finally, I take a place next to him, wrapping my arms around my knees even though it's far from chilly. "I'm sorry," I say softly.

"Not your fault," he says after a short pause. "I shouldn't have snapped."

No, it wasn't my fault, but I could have tried harder to contact him. After he moved, I used to check his Facebook page every so often, looking at all the unfamiliar names on his wall and wondering what his new life was like. As soon as we learned what had happened, I searched for him again, with every intention of sending him some sort of message, but his profile had disappeared.

"How?" I finally ask. "I mean, I know that there was a fire, but—" I cut myself off, realizing that the last thing he probably wants to do is answer a bunch of my nosy questions. "You know what? Never mind."

We sit in silence for a few moments, listening to the night bugs. He starts to pull absently at the tall grass creeping up alongside the stairs. "I wasn't there," he says suddenly. "When it happened. I was playing video games at a friend's house."

"Was it an accident?"

"That's what the fire chief said. Faulty wiring. I was

just lucky to be out of the house. Or unlucky," he notes darkly.

I don't know how to respond to that. I want to ask him another question, but I tell myself it's not the right time. Still, he must see something on my face.

"Just ask."

"How can you live here then? I mean, by yourself?"

"I turned eighteen in August. There was a lot of insurance money."

"Yeah, but a house? Doesn't that take some sort of credit history?"

He waves a hand in the air. "Look around, Sophie. It was on the market for six months—I could have told them that I wanted it because my old one was full of dead bodies, and they still would have asked me when I could sign."

We fall into another uncomfortable silence. "So you're not going to school?" I finally ask.

"Nope."

"Why?"

"Like it even matters anymore."

"What does that mean?"

He starts to say something, but then thinks better of

it. "Who's going to care?" he asks after a few seconds, less impassioned.

"The future people who have to talk to you." The jab rolls off my tongue before I can stop it, and I'm immediately wracked with guilt for my insensitivity.

"You're just the same, you know," he says, and I am relieved to see that he's smiling.

"Mean and a slow runner?"

"No."

"Then what?"

"Honest," he says, giving me a look I can't decipher before pointing at my nose. "And you still have three freckles right there."

Caught off guard, I bring my hand up to my nose without thinking. Suddenly, I'm desperate to fill the silence with something that's not my misbehaving heartbeat. "It's late," I blurt.

James looks amused. "It's nine o'clock."

I check my watch. "Nine-oh-seven," I say, starting to feel foolish. In my scramble to think of a topic of conversation that's not my recent transformation into a giant spaz, my mind stumbles across a legitimate question. "Hey, if you're not going to school, why are you registered?"

"I'm not," he says.

"Yes, you are," I insist. "My friend is supposed to interview the new students, and your name is on her list. Unless there's another James that hasn't been showing up."

He doesn't answer for a few beats longer than natural. "It's a popular name," he says.

"Yeah, with pilgrims."

He stands up abruptly. "It's getting late. You should probably get back."

I stare up at him, baffled by this sudden about-face. He holds out a hand to help me up, and I take it without thinking. He pulls me forward quickly enough that I bump into his chest. When he apologizes, he sounds so frustrated that my only response is to mumble that it's okay. I open my mouth to ask him if he's sure he didn't just register one day and then get sudden amnesia, but I catch myself when I see how serious his expression has gotten. Maybe he deserves his secrets.

"Please don't tell your family that I'm here," he says softly. "I want to keep a low profile."

"Done," I say, knowing that the story of how I got caught peeping in his back window like a weirdo will be an easy secret to keep. After an awkward good night, I turn and head for the gap.

His voice calls out when I'm halfway there. "It's good to see you again, Sophie."

When I turn around, he's already back on the porch step, watching me.

"You too, James," I say, surprised at how much I mean it, and then duck through the bushes.

❋
Chapter Four

True to his word, James isn't at school the next day, or the next, or the day after that. I know I should be planning some sort of antitruancy PSA for his benefit, but right now my time is occupied elsewhere. Since Vlad and his friends arrive early in the morning and linger in the halls until late at night, one would think that I'd have plenty of time to corner them, extract a few mundane details, and then call it a day.

One would be wrong.

That's why I'm spending my precious after-school time crouched in front of the room where the speech team practices. Lindsay told me that Neville joined their club on the first day and has since been laying waste to everyone in competition. At this point, I will drag him into the girls' restroom and corner him in a stall if it means I can start this stupid project. The excited laughter coming from behind the door tells me that it's going to be a while, so I camp out on the floor and try to recap what I've learned these past few days about my other targets.

Violet has been the easiest nut to crack, but that's not saying much. She volunteered for the French club on day two, bringing our total membership to five. I'm president, but she's nearly fluent. When I asked her if she had studied in France, she just blinked and said, "Governesses." While it's been nice to have someone advanced enough to talk about more than the weather and the physical characteristics of our classmates, she won't stop harping on her inattentive crush. She's found her own source of magazines, and in nearly every English class she hands me a rippled copy of *Glamour* with most of the corners folded down and then asks for my opinion. I don't know how she got the idea that I'm a wellspring of boy knowledge, but I'm afraid to reveal my inexperience in case she decides to stop answering the personal questions I manage to sneak in. So far I know that her favorite color is purple, she used to ride horses in a park, and she and her friends moved here from upstate New York.

"Look here," she said one day before English, deflecting my question about her dream vacation and pointing a finger at an article in the dating section. "This implies that kissing on the first date is appropriate. Is that true?"

"Sure."

"Then I have been going about this topsy-turvy for so many years," she said, seemingly close to tears.

"Have you ever thought about dating someone else?"

She just shook her head. "No, I can't give up on him. He owes everything to me. I refuse to let this happen again, do you hear? I refuse."

I decided to save the battle for another day, possibly armed with self-help books. Considering I've never seen her eat, I'm halfway convinced that she runs entirely on relationship advice.

Marisabel has been a more difficult target. While her schedule puts her in French with me, she has yet to show up to *repetez, s'il vous plaît.* I hear she spends most of her time in the bathroom, sulking and commiserating with any girl who skips class. Most of the time they're the ones who dress in black, favor combat boots, and carry around battered copies of *The Bell Jar* in oversized messenger bags. Because I am scared of them, I've been waiting to catch her without her posse. So far, no luck.

And then there's James. I shouldn't even be thinking about him. James is not my problem, he's Lindsay's. In fact, he's her biggest problem.

"I pestered the attendance aide today," she fumed in journalism, flipping through her papers. "He hasn't been here at all! I told Mr. Amado so he would let me take him off my list, but he says that sometimes a journalist has to put a little work into finding her subject."

I just smiled nervously and told her that I understood. Even now, I feel guilty for keeping mum about James's whereabouts, especially since I suspect my silence is more because I want to prevent Lindsay from one-upping me than because of my promise to James. There's no reason I can't tell her something that will convince Mr. Amado to strike him from the list. I should do it. I will do it.

I'm frowning into my notebook, wondering how long I can legitimately stall without falling into the "bitchy" zone, when two voices float around the corner—one male, one female, and both angry. I scoot behind the door of an open classroom; they'll most likely be gone in a second, and I can still maintain surveillance on the speech practice.

"Marisabel, I told you. This is politics," growls a voice that I now recognize as Vlad's. So far, most of what know about him I've gotten secondhand from Caroline, who's still overflowing with giddiness at having snagged the mysterious new guy. The only thing that I, personally, have determined is that I would like to punch him. Hard. And not just because he refuses to give me my interview. I've watched him with Caroline. When her eyes are on him, he's relaxed and charming, but the second she turns away, his face grows cold and strangely . . . resolute.

Unable to resist the possibility of seeing Vlad uncensored, I peek around the edge of the door. They are by the far wall, Marisabel leaning against a locker with a knee up and Vlad looming over her. Devon and Ashley loiter to one side, silent as usual.

"But it's been a week," Marisabel says, "and you're getting nowhere. All I've seen you do is whisk around that blond girl."

"It's been three days. If you are so concerned, you might try helping instead of flitting around with that pack of harpies."

"They're not harpies—they're nice." When Vlad gives a dismissive snort, she changes tack, reaching out as though to brush his face. "Why don't we go away? Just the two of us, like before."

He smacks her hand away and then slams his fists into the locker, one on each side of her head. "I am sick of living like we don't exist," he spits as the clang echoes down the hallway. "If you want to traipse off and remain in obscurity, fine. I am staying here."

Marisabel doesn't respond, just rubs her arms and stares at the worn blue carpet. I check to see if Devon and Ashley are finding this as frightening as I am, but they are staring off into the distance.

"I am waiting for your answer," Vlad says, straightening but not allowing Marisabel any more space to breathe. I can hear the tick of the classroom clock that hangs over the doorway.

"I don't want to go anywhere without you," she finally murmurs.

"Excellent. Then I believe we can leave," Vlad says, and then he pivots so quickly that I barely have time to tuck my head back behind the door. I hold my breath as they stride past. When their voices echo enough to signal that they've reached the main lobby, I emerge from my hiding spot with a new plan. First I am going to convince Caroline that she needs to drop Vlad, and then, no matter what Mr. Amado says, I will be getting to the bottom of what these people are doing here. Because one thing's for sure: He and Marisabel are not stepsiblings and they're not just here because Vlad's parents are "off in Europe."

As if on cue, the door to the speech room bangs open, and students start to trickle out. When Neville emerges, I jump in front of him and rush through my boilerplate proposal: interviews, new students, embarrassing icebreaker questions, please help me. I leave out the part where, after I know his favorite B-movie, I am going to grill him senseless.

"Of course," he says, placing a hand on my back to usher me into the nearest empty classroom—health class, if the mutant ovaries on the board are any indication. Once we're seated he looks at me expectantly. Not wanting to scare him off too early, I start out with questions that I consider boring. But when I ask if he likes it here at Thomas Jeff, his face lights up.

"I do! Everything is so lawless," he says. "Yesterday I fought with a young man who said that I was staring at his girlfriend. And I was, but not for the reasons he believed." He points to his earlobe. "She had a hole as big as a button, right here."

It's hard to imagine a place that could make Principal Morgan's reign seem like anarchy. "Where did you go to school before?"

He hesitates a second too long. "Here and there."

"Where was here and where was there?"

"Oh, I don't remember," he says before leaning over to peek at my notepad. "What other questions do you have?"

I back off for the moment, and we chat about hobbies. He's not much into sports, although he knows enough about boxing to punch you in the nose if you trap him in a corner; he's always loved acting but it has been a while since he has had the opportunity; the speech meets have been wonderful because they've given him a reason to dust off his old monologues. Since things have been going so well, I decide to ease back into more sensitive topics.

"So, you're staying with Vlad, right?"

Neville has been the perfect interviewee, receptive to all my questions and nice enough to phrase all his replies in neat little sound bites. But now I see a wall go up behind his eyes, and he does nothing other than give a sharp little nod.

"How long have you known each other?"

"A few years."

"How did you meet?"

His eyes slide to the side like a senator who's just been asked that same question about the new intern. "The usual."

"Which is?"

"Class," he says quickly.

"What class?

"Music class."

I hope he is a better actor than improviser. "That's interesting," I say. "What do you play? I can't wait to get Vlad's side of the story. Oh, maybe we could take pictures of you both with your instruments!" I threaten, knowing that a person would have to be crazy to have something like that published in a high school newspaper.

"No, I don't want that!" he panics. "Don't write that."

I hide my smile in my notebook. "I'm sorry?"

"No, I was thinking of . . . another friend. George. Yes, George."

"How did you meet Vlad then?"

He leans back, his eyes flicking toward the door. After a discreet cough, he pushes his sleeves up, revealing a small, strangely iridescent tattoo on the inside of his forearm. Considering he got in a fight after ogling some girl's ear gauge, I would never have pegged Neville as someone who had even a dot of ink. It's a star with eight points, light in the middle and darkening to a shimmering blue as it approaches the tips. A swirl sits in the center—no, wait, not a swirl, an ornate letter "D."

"That's an interesting tattoo," I say. "What does the 'D' stand for?"

Neville follows my gaze and stares at the tattoo as though it's a scorpion perched on his arm.

"Ex-girlfriend?" I ask.

He snorts. "Hardly. There must be something else

we can discuss. I will tell you about the time I played Oberon in *A Midsummer Night's Dream*."

"What's the significance of the star?" I ask, refusing to be deterred, but then try to soften the question. "I'm sorry; I'm just really into tattoos. I'm thinking of getting one, but I really want it to, you know, mean something."

"There is no significance," he says with a new edge to his voice. "I would be rid of it if I could, but the damned thing won't come off. *They* make sure of that."

His inflection makes me pause. "You mean tattoo artists?" I ask innocently. "Because that's sort of the point."

"No, I mean the—" Neville stops, his mouth compressing as though he's trying to bite something back. He covers it up with an easy smile, but I can tell he's annoyed with himself. When my eyes flick to his tattoo again, he shoves his sleeve down. "Are we done? I should be heading home."

"No," I say, deciding that it's time to attack while he's rattled. "What's the real relationship between Vlad and Marisabel?"

His eyes widen. "That's not . . . I don't . . . they're

siblings," he finishes lamely.

"Right. Then what sort of company do Vlad's parents work for that sends them on an extended business trip to Europe? And how are your parents okay with six teenagers living together? And what does Vlad mean when he says that he's—"

He stands up so quickly that the student desk crashes forward. Before I can react, he leans toward me and grabs my hand, his grip crushing. "It was wonderful chatting with you," he says. "I mean it; I enjoyed our talk. But you should stop asking so many questions," he says. "Please."

And then he's out the door before I can even ask him to wait.

I replay the interview on the drive home, cursing myself for being too aggressive and wondering about the tattoo and Neville's mysterious "they." I think back to the tiny snippet I overheard that first day in the cafeteria, when they were at odds over the importance of going to Basic Skills; Vlad definitely acts as though he is the boss of something and an organization of some sort would explain why they all arrived knowing one another. As

I pull into the driveway behind Caroline's silver VW Bug, I brainstorm possibilities—a cult? A social experiment? A new low for MTV reality shows?—but all of them seem preposterous and none of them explain why his number-one priority upon arriving was to make a beeline for Caroline.

Which reminds me: The first order of business is to convince my sister to dump Vlad. Normally I try to avoid discussing guys with Caroline. When we were eight, I told her that the boy she had a crush on picked his nose and she punched me. But considering that dating Vlad seems far more dangerous than a few stray boogers, I'm going to have to try again. Still, I wish I could delay the talk until later, like after she's eaten a tub of ice cream. Or better yet, after she's been accidentally hit with a tranquilizer dart while on African safari.

Caroline's bedroom is on the second floor. The door is already open when I get there, and I catch her standing in the middle of the beige carpet, trying on a pink sundress that matches the walls and makes her look like the ballerina in a jewelry box. A tag still dangles beneath the armpit, and she tugs at it while sucking in her cheeks and examining herself in the full-length mirror. After a few deep, calming breaths, I knock lightly on the jamb.

"Sophie! Okay, so what do you think?" she asks as she whirls to face me, holding out the skirt of her sun-dress. "I think it makes me look like a cupcake."

"Do you want to look like a cupcake?"

"Sure." She twists around to check out her butt in the mirror. "I want Vlad to bite."

Thank you, segue gods. "I wanted to talk to you about him, actually," I say as I take a seat on the edge of her daybed. "I overheard something that made me uncomfortable."

"Like what? Sometimes he can get a little nosy with the questions," she says, alternating between a series of little flouncing hops and rocking onto the balls of her feet like she's wearing invisible heels. "I just ignore him."

"I heard him talking to Marisabel in the hallway, talking about you. I think he's hiding something, and I think he's dangerous." Out loud it sounds melodra-matic, like I'm starring in a Lifetime movie. I would call this one *He's Crazy and Has a Fake Sister.*

She waves a hand in my general direction. "Don't be ridiculous. Do my calves look fat to you?"

I should have spent more time breathing outside the door. "Caroline, I'm serious. There's something weird about this whole situation."

Caroline stops twisting in front of the mirror to catch my gaze in the reflection. "You know, I'm surprised," she says. "I don't think I've ever seen you jealous before."

"You can't be serious."

"You never go for the guys at school, but Vlad's sophisticated enough that I should have known you'd be interested. I'm sorry he ignores you, but it's not my fault that he likes me. I told you that this was the year to embrace lip gloss." She whips around to face me, and I can practically see the lightbulb dinging over her head. "Amanda's brother, Jason, needs a date to homecoming. I could set you up. He likes writing and stuff."

"You mean the Jason who tells everyone that he's an elf from Middle Earth? I'll pass." I need to stop her before she tries more matchmaking. "And that's not even the point. The point is that you should ditch Vlad."

"Let's see," Caroline says, holding up her fingers and

starting to count. "He's smart, sexy, a good dresser, doesn't spend half of his time on the computer playing Warcraft like Tommy, and is genuinely interested in my life. So . . . no. Find your own boyfriend." She swipes a tube of lipstick off her vanity and turns back to the mirror. "I'll talk to Jason about you."

"Caroline—"

"We're done here. Go away."

When I don't make any move to leave, she picks a stuffed bear off an armchair and throws it at me.

"You know what? Fine. Date him. Have rude little babies," I say and walk out the door, slamming it for good measure and stomping up to my room. When I reach the top of the stairs I'm still holding the bear, whose embroidered smirk mocks me. I send it on a header down the stairs. That will show her. Or something.

That did not go well, I think as I collapse on my bed. Why couldn't I have started with an easier intervention, like credit cards or caffeine pills? Obviously, I need to be armed with proof in order to shake Caroline away from Vlad. I grab my MacBook off the floor and haul it onto my lap. On a whim I type "Eight-pointed black star tattoo arm thing" into Google Image and get an assortment of people showing off their new tattoos as well as a handful of academic explanations about how eight-pointed stars normally represent chaos. Appropriate, but certainly not helpful. There's nothing with a "D" in the center and nothing that looks remotely like what Neville has on his arm.

Well, crap. I'm wondering why fiction gives you unrealistic expectations about the powers of the internet when something pops at my window. It's followed by three lesser pops and a loud crack. Rocks.

The window sticks, showering paint chips when I finally manage to wrestle it up. When the coast proves clear of further pebbly messages, I lift the screen and stick my head out to find James staring up at me with an expression that asks what took me so long.

"I don't think rock throwing is considered acceptable until after midnight," I say. "Next time try the doorbell."

"Yeah. I'm not positive, but that might be a good clue that I'm here."

"And why is that a problem exactly?"

He ignores my question. "You know, I'm surprised

that you haven't come to see me yet. You used to always show up at my door to bug me. Remember when I wouldn't try out your 'Death Drop' magic trick?"

I do remember. Honestly, I can't fault him for not wanting to jump off the roof into a kiddie pool, and now that I think about it, that trick wasn't even very magical. But all of this is beside the point.

"I think your memories are skewed," I tell him. "You were the pesterer."

"It's sad that you live such a delusional life," he says and then nods toward the fence before I can deliver what I am sure would be a devastating retort. "Come outside. We can discuss how wrong you are."

"Tempting."

"Very tempting," James says with a smile so angelic that it's not anymore. He's wearing a long-sleeved gray T-shirt and jeans that could use a tango with a washing machine, but the rumpled look is definitely working in his favor. Still, I'm a little wary of how I'll react with my guard torn down by exhaustion, frustration, and the fact that my sister now hates me. Not to mention that I think I've had my fill of veils and secrecy for the day, and James's strange new hermit act will only add more questions.

"Tell you what," I propose, leaning as far over the sill as possible without taking a header into the bushes. "Come to school tomorrow and we'll talk."

Whatever James was expecting, it wasn't a refusal. "But—"

"Night," I singsong, shutting the window before any more rumble-voiced persuasion can float through. Without the night air, my room suddenly feels stuffy and claustrophobic. Worse, my heart's fluttering around in a disconcerting manner. I decide to chalk it up to the thrill of leaning out the window. Besides, I think, as I slip under the covers and flip off my lamp, his new antischool bit should keep me safe from ever having to cash in that promise.

Chapter Five

The next morning I wait for Violet at her locker. When she bustles around the corner, I attack her with another round of questions, including one asking whether or not she has any body art. If they are all in a group of some sort, it stands to reason that they would all have the same tattoo, or at least a variation. I think I am very clever.

"Body art?" she says, pulling a thread off the hem of her dress, a floral cotton baby doll accessorized by blue tights and her multibuttoned boots. Her outfits are getting more and more avant-garde.

"A tattoo," I say. "Or a piercing. Or a tattoo."

She continues to look confused, and I feel my cleverness deflating. Nevertheless, I point at the wobbly-looking butterfly on the exposed ankle of someone who is digging a book out of her locker. "Like that."

"Oh no," she says. "I would never paint insects on myself."

"It doesn't have to be insects, it can be anything. Like a star, for example."

She brightens. "Neville has something like that!"

My heart starts beating faster. "Anyone else you know?"

"Yes!" she says, and then turns to furiously open her locker and pull out a magazine. She flips to a picture of Rihanna. "Right there," she says, pointing to a spot below her ear. "I think it is very tasteful."

"I was talking about anyone else you know personally. Marisabel, maybe?"

She shakes her head. "No, no one. But that was a very informative article; I feel as though I know Rihanna," she insists before wandering off in the direction of her next class. She's left her locker door wide open. Thinking that there may be a clue, I peek inside, only to find that it's full of magazines and nothing else. *At least I have quadruple confirmation that they're not here for academic reasons,* I think as I shut it in frustration. So they aren't all in a Tattoo-of-the-Month club, but Neville definitely acted weird when I asked him about it. What's the connection?

I spend the next two periods trying to come up with at least one theory that's not stupid, but come lunchtime I have other things to focus on. It's Friday, which means that Mr. Amado wants the rough drafts of our articles, and I still don't have anything to show for Marisabel or Vlad. I decide to go over my questions for the umpteenth time in an effort to build up enough courage to approach him again. Once I've found a clean seat in a back corner of the cafeteria, I pull out my notebook and flip it open to the questions I've compiled, like "What book would you take to a desert island?" and "What are the top five songs in your playlist?" I debate adding the ones that are really running through my mind, like "Are you or are you not the leader of a cult?" and "If you were to rate your level of psychosis on a scale from one to ten, what would you be? Ten?"

Chewing on my pen cap, I stare at the lined paper, trying to think of euphemisms for "psychosis." A person-shaped shadow eclipses the table. My usual plan of action in these situations is to feign ignorance until the intruder goes away, but this proves impossible when they sit down and start drumming their fingers on the fake wood.

"Do you mind?" I ask without looking up.

"Considering you said I had to come here to talk to you, yeah, I do," the voice says, and then punctuates his sentence with one last tap. "Why are you sitting back here, anyway? It smells like Windex and ketchup."

My head snaps up. James sits across from me wearing a dark green T-shirt and a smirk. His dark bangs swoop rakishly over one eyebrow.

"The pen-in-mouth thing is very attractive, by the way," he says.

I pull it from between my teeth hard enough that they rattle. "What are you doing here?"

"Gives orders and then forgets them. Classy."

"I didn't think you'd take me seriously."

"It turns out that sitting in a house all day is kind of boring." He leans across the table to spy on my notebook. "What are you writing?"

"Journalism project. An important one," I say, hoping that will be the end of it. I'm still trying to get over the nostalgia that comes from sitting at a lunch table with James Hallowell again.

"Cool," he says, and then makes a point of peering at the empty seats around us. "I see you're still a loner."

"I was never a loner."

"Sure," James says, "you had plenty of friends. They just happened to be invisible—invisible friends that you ordered to sit on the other side of the sandbox."

I have a vague memory of ordering Pete the Pickle to give me more space, but I shove it to the side. "Maybe I did. Whatever," I say. "Can I please go back to what I'm working on?"

"Right. The journalism project." He twists his head to read the fourth question out loud. "'If you were an animal, what type of animal would you be?' Wow. Someone should tell Katie Couric to watch her back."

I knew I was scraping the bottom of the barrel with that one. I scratch the animal question out and tell James to shut up. "I have to interview the new students, and these guys are the only ones left." I point my pen at him. "There's someone looking to interview you, too, you know."

He pulls a crumpled wad of Post-it Notes from his

pocket. "So that's what these are. They were shoved in my locker."

He drops them on the table. I immediately recognize Lindsay's loopy handwriting. The blue one on my notebook is a very polite "James, please let me know a good time for us to meet. I have some questions to ask you." The hot pink one on my folders screams "PLEASE TALK TO ME" in black marker. Looks like Lindsay's sliding down the same slippery academic slope as me. At least she's also struggling to find her last interview subject, I think, and then freeze.

James is here, at school. Which means the end of interviews for Lindsay, and the end of interviews for Lindsay means a lead in Mr. Amado's polls. I've orchestrated my own downfall. Scanning the lunchroom for bright red hair, I spot her at one of the round central tables, leaning over a stack of poster board with a fat red marker. If we can just get through this lunch period without her looking my way, I'll be golden.

"Dude!" someone yells. "You're back!"

When I turn my head, James and Danny Baumann are in the middle of a complicated series of fist bumps. After one final flourish, Danny plops down on the bench across from me. It's been a while since I've sat this close to him; the caramel color of his neck still has the power to mesmerize.

"What are you doing here?" Danny asks James. "You moved away in, like, fourth grade or something."

"Eighth," James says. "But close. What's up?"

Back in the day he and Danny were on all of the same teams, and at least three times a week I would come home to find them in the backyard throwing some sort of ball at each other—or trying to take a ball from each other. It was never entirely clear. What is clear, however, is that James doesn't seem all that happy to see his long-lost friend.

"Not much," Danny says. "I totally beat that campaign in Halo 2. On Legendary."

"That's awesome."

Danny nods proudly. "Yeah, I know. Why are you sitting over here all by yourself? Everyone knows it smells funky in this corner. Hey, Amanda! Guess who's here?" he yells across the cafeteria, and then turns back to James. "She'd totally go out with you again."

"Cool," James says. "I'm actually talking with Sophie right now, but I might come by later."

There's an awkward silence as Danny notices me for the first time. He blinks. I smile dorkily and give a little salute that I will regret for the rest of my life.

"Well, okay man," he says, standing up. "But we should hang out. Play some Halo for old times' sake."

"Sure."

They do another hand dance. I wait until Danny's safely ensconced back at his table to speak. "You could have gone to sit with them," I say, even though a part of me is ridiculously pleased that he is staying put.

"I came here to talk to you, not Danny Baumann," he says. Our eyes catch, and my chest suddenly feels too tight. I look away for a moment, only to spot something that makes it feel even tighter: Lindsay Allen, striding toward us, ecstatic.

Snatching up my notebook, I frantically brush all of the Post-it Notes she left in James's locker beneath it. "Help me," I plead.

"What—"

"Hey! Who's this?" Lindsay asks eagerly. She holds out her hand, already a tiny ambassador. "I'm Lindsay. Let me know if you want a tour. Student Council is in charge of them."

"Ted," I blurt before James can answer. "His name is Ted. Comes from Tennessee. Hates tours."

Two pairs of eyes study me, but James's green ones hold mine the longest. Finally, he reaches to shake her hand.

"I'm Ted," he says, affecting a slight twang. "And tours give me hives."

Either Lindsay's pissed that her offer to show him the Wall of Mathletes has been rebuffed, or she's not buying it.

"Really? I've been spending a lot of time in the attendance office lately, and I haven't seen your name on any of the incoming new-student forms."

"It was a very sudden move. One day my parents are happy nestled in the hills of Appalachia, and the next day they want to go work for Google." James gives an exaggerated shrug. "What can you do?"

"I see. What city did you say you were from?"

"Uh, Columbus."

Lindsay squints, and I can tell that she's trying to remember if there really is a Columbus, Tennessee. *Nashville*, I want to yell. *Why didn't you pick Nashville? Or Memphis? Dammit, James, know your capitals!* Not that it would have made this plan any less transparent.

"Ted wouldn't be short for 'James,' would it?" she asks.

"Nope."

It's obvious that Lindsay doesn't know how to confront an unwilling interview subject. She frowns at the tile and then looks at me, her eyes filled with confusion, betrayal, and a glimmer of anger.

"See you in Journalism, Sophie. Mr. Amado will be surprised to hear that he missed a new student," she says, her voice so cold that it kills me, and then walks away.

I am a ball of slime, the giant kind that families in minivans pull over to see on their summer vacation. Up until now I've been picking at my lunch, but now I shove it away, sending a few fries sailing off the edge.

"So what was that about?" James asks with a practiced casualness.

"Nothing," I mutter.

"You just gave me an alternate identity. Not that I mind that much, but you gave me a bad one. Ted, Sophie. From Tennessee."

Might as well admit it. "She's the girl who wants to interview you."

"I got that much," James says and then arches into a proud stretch. "It's cute how protective you are of me."

"You wish," I say, but it's halfhearted. "Here's the deal. She's my competition to be editor in chief, and you're her last interviewee. If she has hers finished by today while I'm still missing two, I might as well give up now. It's stupid and childish and petty. I know. But it wouldn't be a problem if Vlad and Marisabel would just talk to me," I finish, slamming my fists down on the table in frustration.

James says nothing. I try to gauge his expression, nervous that he's going to think I've turned into a horrible person. This unnerves me almost as much as my recent Mean Girl impression. When he finally speaks, it's not a question that I was expecting.

"Your last two interviewees are Vlad and Marisabel?"

My relief at not being judged brings out the whole enchilada. "Yes. But not only won't they talk to me, they scare the crap out of me. They're not normal students. I overheard a very strange conversation yesterday. And Vlad's dating my sister. And possibly dating his sister, too."

James looks at me, alarmed. "Sophie, stay away from them. Tell Caroline to steer clear, too."

His vehemence startles me. "Why?"

"Never mind why," he snaps. Before I can express my outrage at being bullied, he drops the heavy-handed act and leans forward. "What if I get them to answer the questions? You already have them written down."

"That's nice of you to offer," I say. "But why are they going to pay any more attention to you than they gave to me?"

There is another long pause. "Because I know them."

"You mean you met them this morning?"

"No, I mean they went to my last school," he says quickly—too quickly—while looking everywhere other than straight at me.

For a second I can only blink at him stupidly. "Are you telling me that they're your friends?" I ask.

"No!" he snaps. "I don't want anything to do with them."

"But I don't understand," I insist. "Six people from your old school follow another boy to your hometown, and it's not connected? That's ridiculous. It's too much of a coincidence. And they're up to something; I know it. The other day—"

James grabs my hand, surprising me enough that I stop talking. I can feel his fingers, firm but cool, against the underside of my palm.

"Sophie," he says, his voice low and insistent. "I need you to trust me when I tell you to stop. I mean it. I don't want you drawn into this. I want to let what's going to happen happen, and then I just want to try to go back. Back to like it was before. Before I moved, before my parents . . ."

"James, what are you doing? Why are you touching her?"

Violet's voice cuts through the din of cafeteria laughter. It's always been prone to squeaking, but now there's an edge to it, a tension and a disbelief that threatens to crack it right down the middle. She's clutching at the fabric of her dress with both hands. I tear my own hand away from James's and stuff it beneath the table in a rush of embarrassment.

"Violet," I start, but she rambles over me, growing more and more distressed.

"They said that if I gave you space you would come to your senses," she cries, her eyes skittering wildly back and forth. "They said that if I found my own activities, you would be attracted to my new and confident self. They said it. They *said* it. And now you are making eyes at a girl who dresses like a peasant—a male peasant—and kisses on the first date. She is a hussy, James."

The word "hussy" draws some attention, but I don't care. So James is Violet's mystery boy. Swinging my gaze to James, I join the forces waiting for an answer. He waits a beat before running his hands through his hair and letting out an exasperated sigh.

"Violet, I told you. I'm sorry that I hurt you. Believe me, if I could take it all back—and I do mean all of it—I would. But you have to let this go."

"But I can't," she cries, covering her heart with her hands. "I love you."

Nothing good can come from going down this path, so I try to intercede again. "Violet," I say softly, "James and I weren't—"

"Stop it," she hisses. "You are the reason I'm in this muddle. You and your bad advice."

The malice in her face makes my heart stop cold, and I eye her clenched fists, wondering if I am going to get into an honest-to-God cafeteria fight. But instead of launching herself at me, Violet suddenly puts a hand to her forehead and starts to sway. "I think I feel faint," she says, and then collapses on the ground.

The crowd that's gathered around us gives a little gasp. Sighing, James bends down over her prostrate form and lightly smacks one of her cheeks. "Violet, get up. You know you can't faint."

Her eyelids flutter. He is about to try the other cheek when Ms. Kate, now on lunchroom duty, barrels her way through the crowd.

"What's going on here?" she booms. "Stand back, people, and give the girl some room. The bell's about to ring." She points to the ceiling, and the bell obliges her, most likely too scared to disobey. "See? Go to your class. Stop gawking."

The ring of onlookers begins to break up, students shuffling off in twos and threes. When Ms. Kate crouches down to look at Violet, James stands up and comes back toward me. Still a little shaken, I gather my things and turn to ask one of my many, many new questions, but he nudges me toward the door.

"Let's go."

"But Violet—"

"Is fine. Well, physically at least. You should get out of here." When we're in the hallway, he lets go of my arm and looks at the notebook I am holding to my chest like a bulletproof vest. "Do you still need those questions answered?"

"Well, yes."

"Great." He grabs it from me, tears out the two pages with my questions for Vlad and Marisabel, and then shoves it back into my hands. "I'll have it to you by next period," he says, starting to walk away.

"But—"

"You can pay me back by giving me a ride home today," he calls down the hall. "I'll meet you by your car. When do you leave?"

"Six," I say, still half-dazed.

"Good. See you then." He stops for a second and gives me a look I can't decipher. "We'll talk," he says shortly and then disappears around a corner.

❊

Chapter Six

y concentration is shot for the rest of the day. When I'm not trying to figure out what James is caught up in, I'm watching the door for Violet. It opens halfway through Ms. Walpole's lecture on body paragraphs, and my spine goes rigid. For once I am actually relieved when it is only Vlad, late to class again. After a few excuses about losing himself in a library book and a round of awkward staring, she waves him to his seat. From my spot at the back of the room, I can see his wavy blond head, the tops of his shoulders, and one lean, muscular arm. Every time Ms. Walpole turns around, he slips out a ragged piece of lined paper and hunches over. He's writing something, and for once it's not in that little journal he slips in and out of his back pocket.

When the bell rings, Vlad scoops up his belongings in one arm and weaves through the departing students to stand in front of my desk. I blink up at him through the fluorescent light.

"You are Sophie, correct?" he asks, sounding bored with the question. He pulls out the wilting piece of paper he scribbled on all period and flicks it at me. "This is for you."

I look down to find my list of questions, which are now accompanied by answers written in a tight, florid hand.

"Thank you," I say, trying to keep my voice even despite my boiling hatred. Now is probably not the time to tell him he writes like a girl.

"I did it as a favor to James, nothing more," Vlad says and then arches one pale eyebrow. "Anything else that you would like to know? My favorite rainy day activity, perhaps?"

"No, that's it." *Jerkface.* "Thanks again." Standing up, I start to brush by him, but where a normal human being would twist to avoid a butt bump, he stays rooted in place. Sucking in my stomach, I refuse to let him fluster me. I smile, a bit of bravado he acknowledges with a surprised quirk of his pale eyebrows. Ha. I'm almost in the clear when my bag catches on the back of a chair.

Damn. As I'm working on untangling it, my neck begins to tingle like I've been sitting too long in the sun. I look up to find Vlad eyeing it, nostrils flared, with more interest than he's ever given any other part of my anatomy. This is the last straw.

"Could you move?"

His gaze snaps up to meet my eyes before he gives a smile that's part sardonic, part self-mocking, and no parts apologetic.

"My apologies," he says, his voice so full of laughter that I'm surprised he doesn't bust a gut right there. When I walk out, I don't turn around.

The bell rings before I make it to my locker, so when I get there I'm so rushed that I almost miss the folded piece of paper that falls at my feet. There's something chicken-scratched on the front.

Sophie,

Do you know how many people I had to ask before I found

someone who knew where your locker was? I told you—

loner. Here are Marisabel's answers to your questions.

See you at 6.

—James

Well, I have my answers. Now I just wish I had a better idea of what possible connection he could have to all of this.

I stuff the questions in my folder since I'm already late to journalism. Luckily, Mr. Amado is already in full newspaper mode and doesn't seem to care. After making an offhand comment about being glad that I could join the class, he tells me that he's about to start the progress check. I slide into my seat next to Lindsay, who is studying her folders with a queasy expression.

"Since your finished articles are due next Tuesday," Mr. Amado says, "you should have all of your fact-gathering done. Lindsay and Sophie, I'm starting with you. Let's see it."

We pull out our info. I make a hasty excuse for the state of Vlad and Marisabel's interviews.

"That's okay," he says. "Today we just want the info. Lindsay?"

Lindsay hands over her typed responses, still silent. Mr. Amado flips through them and then frowns. "There are only three here. Have you talked to all of your subjects?"

She clears her throat. "I still . . . I still haven't been able to find James."

"He hasn't come to school yet?"

"The attendance records show that he was here today. But he wasn't in my math class like his schedule said he should be." She turns my way. "The only new person was Ted."

"Ted?" Mr. Amado asks. "I must have missed him. I'll look into it. But you should know that this might set you behind schedule. Good work, Sophie."

We both watch as he walks over to Neal and asks him whether or not he's managed to expand on the fact that yes, blood had been stolen. I shoot Lindsay an apologetic look that she won't return. Instead she concentrates on cleaning out her folders, lining up her papers with the precision of a drill sergeant before slipping them back in.

"Lindsay, I—"

"I'm going to work in back today," she says quickly, abandoning me to set up shop next to the computers.

I spend the rest of the period thinking of ways to apologize, working out elaborate fantasies where I play the Good Samaritan, the best of which is where I give a five-hundred-dollar donation to Greenpeace in her name and then let her know by spelling it out in cupcakes across her lawn. Deep down, however, I know that the only way to make this right is to admit that I lied, direct her to James, and let her yell at me. Five minutes before the bell rings, I ready myself to catch her as she exits the classroom, but she heads to Mr. Amado's desk early. He scribbles something on a pink hall pass, and she's out the door. I guess this giant rock of guilt will be camping out in my gut for a little while longer.

I stay in the journalism room after school lets out to work on my articles, spreading the responses from Vlad and Marisabel out on the table next to my computer.

Full name: *Vladimir Roman Smithson*

Age: *The common age for one at this school*

How many brothers and sisters do you have? What are their ages? *Seven. Deceased.*

Favorite Color: *Gray*

Favorite Animal: *Wolf*

Favorite Hangout: *This is a stupid question.*

What are the top five songs on your playlist? *This is a nonsensical question.*

Scar you're most proud of and where it came from? *Left arm, swordfight with my father.*

If you were a car, what car would you be and why? *I am not a car, nor do I wish to be one.*

If you could only have one book on a deserted island, what would it be? *The Prince and The Lost Daughter.*

When you were little, who was your favorite superhero? *Casanova.*

Are you a morning or night person? *Night.*

What's the weirdest thing you eat at home?
No comment.

What is the greatest problem in the United
States? *Elitist groups.*

What one word would you put on your
gravestone? *Impossible.*

What do people like best about you?
Whatever I tell them to like.

These bogus answers hardly seem worth the trouble, not to mention that I didn't ask the dumbface what *two* books he'd take to a desert island. Marisabel's are even worse. She answered most of the questions with "I don't know" and the rest with doodled flowers. That's it, I think, crumpling the pages into one tiny ball of suck. I'm done banging my head against this stone wall; I don't care if I have to begin my article, "Vlad likes three things: fencing, himself, and killing off his siblings." I don't care if I have to lie and—oops—report that Vlad likes finger painting with dolphin blood in his spare time. We're now entering full investigative mode.

I spend the next few hours tweaking my data, fleshing out Vlad's non-answers with anything I've heard floating around the hallways, not caring at this point how accurate this information is. By the time I look up from my computer, it's already a quarter to six, so I shut down my documents and head to the front exit. The sun is still bright enough that the windshields of the few remaining cars in the lot wink light back at me. One of them is Vlad's Hummer, its shadowy bulk looming behind my Jeep like a closet monster.

I've got ten minutes before James is set to show up—time to figure out who these people are, once and for all. After checking to make sure that the parking lot is deserted, I peer through the Hummer's windows, but the tinting means I can't see anything except for the light shining in from the opposite side. I tug at the handle in frustration, astonished when the door pops open. Unlocked. An invitation to snoop.

The first thing I find is a shopping bag full of clothes with the security tags still attached; some of them have rips down the side as though someone had tugged too hard while trying to remove them. Whatever else they might be, they're definitely A-plus shoplifters, but that still doesn't tell me enough. I need names; I need dates; I need anything that could pass as a cold, hard fact. I shove the dresses and pants back in the bag and check the glove compartment, but it's empty; there's not even a car registration.

I move to the back, cursing when the movement causes the heavy door to creak shut behind me. I find a week's worth of unfinished worksheets on the floor and a small cooler nestled behind the driver's seat. I've hardly seen any of them eat lunch, so it's odd that they'd be packing snacks. I wrestle off the top, but it's empty.

"Who's with me?" says a dim voice. Vlad's voice.

My blood turns to ice. I hit the ground and lie as flat as possible, praying that the tinted windows and large seats will shield me from view. There's the scrape of feet against gravel and the soft thud of someone leaning against the car only inches from my head.

"The more we stand outside in the light, the worse it will be," Neville says impatiently, his voice vibrating through the metal behind me and making it hum.

"The car stays here as long as I do. Crack a window

and wait in the vehicle or walk home. You choose."

My breath hitches. *Don't wait in the car. Please, don't wait in the car.*

"We'll walk," Neville says, and I almost choke on the relief. "This is not wise. Especially if you think you are close."

"Close?" Vlad gives a short, strangled laugh. "Hardly. At this point we are close to starting over."

"What do you mean?"

"I mean," Vlad says darkly, "I chose incorrectly. It's not Caroline."

A weighty silence surrounds the Hummer on all sides. Caroline's not what? The girl of his dreams? America's Next Top Mob Member?

"Not her?" Neville says, and unlike Vlad, his voice is downright chipper. "Well, then perhaps this is the perfect time to rethink what we're doing here. I, for one, think that you might be better off forgetting the Danae and staying here. People seem to rather like you," he says, "and there are so many things to do. Do you know that there is a club devoted entirely to the creation of little walking machines that fight one another? Amazing. I'm almost tempted to—"

A growl splits the air. The car tips from the force of someone being slammed against it, and the movement causes the passenger-side door to creak open. If anyone walks around to the other side, they will see me. I tuck my feet as close to my body as possible and bite my tongue to stay silent.

"I apologize if I gave the impression that this is a group decision," Vlad says with threatening precision. "We are not here to join organizations or socialize with lonely girls in the washroom. If I find that you are doing so, you will be out. And I would like to see you all take care of yourself, I really—"

He stops sharply when the car starts to ding, warning that there is an open door. Oh God. Blood rushes into my ears, thrumming so loudly that for second I don't hear anything. I look up, but all I can see is the swirl of Neville's reddish hair pressed against the window.

"What is that?" Vlad asks.

"It is the Humdinger. Violet left the door ajar again," Neville says. The car rocks as he pushes away from Vlad and walks around the back. I'm trying to think of excuses, but my mind goes blank as he pulls open the door enough to shut it. I can see his arm up to the elbow, the tattoo on his forearm standing out in stark relief to his pale skin. If he moves forward three more inches, I'm done for.

"Oh, I do not care about the Danae, or the girl, or this horrible place!" says a tremulous voice that I recognize as Violet's. I look at Neville's tattoo, the central "D" staring at me like an ominous eye. "D." Danae. It's a possibility. Now I just have to get out of here.

"I am sorry that I left the door open," Violet continues, "but it has been such a horrific day and I would very much like to go home."

Neville shuts the door without looking inside. "Then let's go."

There's a lull, and then the fading crunch of gravel as they walk away.

"Where were we?" Vlad says smoothly when we can no longer hear anything. "Ah yes, into the woods."

The foliage crashes as several people plunge into the trees, followed by the snapping of twigs. I wait for all sounds to cease before screwing up enough courage to sit up and check that the coast is clear. When it is, I scramble out of the car and gulp down the fresh air. Leaning against the bumper of my Jeep, I try to process what I've overheard. A quick check of my watch tells me that it's 6:05. James is late, and to be completely honest, I'm a little iffy now about giving him a ride home. I should peel out of here now, grateful that I've survived one close call.

I should.

Before I have time to second-guess myself, I step into the brush. Midwestern woods are many things, but scary is not one of them—they're about as intimidating as your grandmother's afghan. The predominance of pine trees gives them a nice scent, and even though that means you come out able to freshen a car, it's nice not to worry about big, slavering animals that want to chew on your face. That's why I'm caught off guard by the sudden chill that eclipses me the second I move out of the evening sun. The trees are top heavy enough to smother most of the evening light, casting their thick trunks into gloom.

Voices echo in front of me. "Ingrate" cuts through the murmur, and I stop—individual words mean that I'm too close. We walk this way until the pale orange light shining out of the leaves in front of me suggests that they've reached the central clearing. I stretch my ears as far as they will go. When it sounds like Vlad is no longer moving, I crouch behind the largest bush I can find, located about ten feet to the left of the make-shift trail. Trying not to make any noise, I peer through the branches.

Vlad is pacing back and forth, pausing every so often to kick at rocks and twigs on the ground. "Can you believe him?" he seethes. "He said that he wanted to help, and then what do I hear today? Maybe I should forget about the Danae and stay here because people like me, as if that is so difficult to believe."

"I told you from the beginning that I thought he was weird," Marisabel says from where she's stretched across a pitted picnic table.

"And I told you it was fine!" Vlad snaps.

Marisabel just shrugs, rolling on her back to stare up at an open copy of *Twilight*. Her long brown hair cascades over the edge. It sways as she shakes her head back and forth.

"This is not right at all," she says. "Edward is dreamy, though. Maybe you could get some tips."

"Oh, could I?" Vlad asks, playful, before stalking into view and twisting the book out of her hands. Pages flapping, it sails over her head and crashes into the trees behind her.

Marisabel pushes herself up and frowns at the spot where it disappeared. "Hey! That was Jennifer Pierson's."

Vlad dips into a mocking bow. "Do offer her my condolences. Tell her I will provide her with a new one should we ever achieve our main objective," he says and then starts to pace. "Can you believe them? Neville does nothing but attach himself to any organization that will have him, and Violet . . . yesterday Violet asked if I wanted to participate in a 'quiz' that will tell me what my 'best fall look' is," he says. "What does that even mean?"

"Mine is eggplant," Marisabel offers absently. "And scarves."

"So what if I need a little real refreshment?" Vlad continues. "It's the least I deserve after everything I've done to make this work. Do you know how difficult it was to get everyone registered? How much power it took out of me?" he insists. "Not to mention the constant questions from the attendance office. Despite the vacant expressions on their faces, the adults here are not nearly as dull as I would like. Today one of the old crones in the office started asking questions. I had to stare into her shriveled eyes for five minutes before she went back to her work." He stops to kick a clod of dirt, hard enough that it shatters against a tree. "I felt drained all day. It took all of my willpower not to tear into that girl in English."

My spine stiffens. He's talking about me. He's talking about tearing into me. As refreshment. I can't tell if it's my building sense of unease that's making it hard to comprehend this, or if he's really saying what I think he's saying. But that would mean . . . No. No more *Buffy* reruns. Ever. I try to force my mind back to the conversation, determined to come up with a non-insane explanation.

"What girl?" Marisabel asks. So far she's been mostly silent, but now he has her full attention.

"Oh, you know," Vlad says. "The unadorned, forthright one who dresses like she is preparing to slaughter a pig." After Marisabel's blank look, he adds, "The one James trailed after all day. The one with all the ridiculous questions."

The insult seems to appease her; she settles back on

the table like a content tiger. "If the blond one isn't it, who's next?"

"I do not know," Vlad says, kicking a stick this time. "Perhaps one of the friends. I will start again tomorrow. But for now—dinner!" he says, his voice suddenly bright. "Try that bush; I thought I saw something earlier."

He claps his hands and fixes his gaze across the clearing. I peer around the lowest branch just in time to spot Devon and Ashley hefting two large branches from the scattered leaves. When they start to thrash the bushes, my stomach lurches; the chance that they're beating the brush in the hopes that chicken nuggets will emerge, screaming and running for their lives, is slim to none. It makes sense, my brain insists, and starts to fill in the pieces. The weirdness. The strange staring contests. The lack of parents. The wonder that is Violet. James's warnings. The empty cooler. And the missing blood. Oh God, the missing blood. How could I be so stupid? They're vampires, or at least under a number of severe delusions.

Jesus, Sophie, the guy's name is Vlad.

I bite my tongue to stop from giving a hysterical little laugh, and tell myself that when I get home I'll be able to work out a far more rational explanation. But right now? I need to leave. Fast. Devon and Ashley are only a quarter of the way around the clearing, so there's time. Boosting myself into a crouch, I glance backward. Twenty more feet and I'll be out of immediate hearing range, at which point I will sprint back to my car.

Suddenly I hear a rustle, followed by an excited cry. The leaves crunch as a small ball of fur makes a startled beeline for my bush. The rabbit bursts between the leaves and then crouches at its base, terrified and trembling. Before I can react, I hear the sound of two very large men barreling in my direction. If I run now, they will see me. No question. I stare into the rabbit's glassy eyes, hypnotized by fear. Think, think, think. "Here's my contact!" I will say. "That will teach me to stop making out so much after school." Insert nervous chuckle; try not to faint dead at their feet.

Devon and Ashley bend down to peer under the hanging leaves of the bush, and the rabbit darts to the side, running for better cover. Their shadows move, and I hear a shrill squeak, followed by a sickening snap and Vlad's shout that he wasn't supposed to kill it yet. Even though I want to vomit, the rabbit's flight has given me my chance to escape. I ready my legs to launch myself forward just as a swish of footsteps sounds to my right.

"Hello?"

Lindsay's voice echoes in the startled silence. Launching myself back at the bush, I frantically shove branches out of the way so I can see clearly. Crap, crap, crap. What is she doing here?

Lindsay stands in the center of the clearing, clutching a blue binder to her chest like it's the last life vest on the *Titanic*. Next to Vlad and the two giants, she appears even tinier than usual. Her auburn hair catches the last glimmers of sunlight, throwing her pale face into even sharper contrast. She looks nervous, and very, very vulnerable. All except for the determined jut of her chin.

"I'm looking for James," Lindsay says, hugging the binder tighter and moving back a few steps when Vlad starts to approach. "Well, information about James, really. I heard you mention him earlier in the halls, and I wondered if you could tell me a little bit about him." She takes a deep breath. "Just a few things. It's important."

Vlad looks almost jovial. "Important?" He moves closer, forcing Lindsay to retreat to the edge of the trees, before he throws a playful look at Marisabel. "I fear I know very little. James is a private soul. How about the rest of you?"

Devon and Ashley shake their heads, their most communicative gesture to date. They're standing rigidly, hands behind their backs. Marisabel doesn't answer at first, just looks at him for a few long seconds.

"Vlad, don't do anything you will regret," she says softly.

"I am only trying to assist a fellow schoolmate," he says with grating innocence and then leans over so he's more on Lindsay's level. "So," he purrs. "What is your name?"

"Lindsay Allen," she says weakly, having now completed what appears to be a total body meld with her binder.

"And tell me, Lindsay Allen, do you have any distinguishing marks on your person?"

Disarmed, Lindsay's wariness evaporates. "What?"

Vlad waves a hand in the air. "Any birthmarks, moles, rashes that spell out your mother's maiden name . . . you know, marks!" He frowns down at her uncomprehending face. "How do you say it? Ah, yes, 'work with me here.'"

Lindsay pushes her shoulders back and pulls herself up to her full height. "This was a bad idea. I'm going now. Sorry to bother you. Please let James know that I am looking for him."

"I will take that as a 'no,'" Vlad says and then grabs her arm before she can move. "Not so hasty. I have a final question for you."

Lindsay orders him to let her go, her voice high, her cool composure cracking. She tugs against his grip, but Vlad just pulls her closer. Leaning down, he acts like he's about to whisper in her ear, but his next question rings out clear and strong.

"Do you think that anyone will miss you?"

Chapter Seven

There's a still moment, and then everyone's moving at once. Marisabel springs off the picnic table and runs over to Vlad, latching onto his bicep and yelling that it's time to leave. She might as well be a gnat; Vlad shrugs her off, continuing to smirk as Lindsay struggles against his grip. Devon and Ashley push in closer, putting themselves between her and the beaten-down path. Lindsay's gaze bangs about wildly, searching for an escape until Vlad jerks her close and grabs her chin, forcing her to look directly into his eyes. Her wrist goes limp.

Through the shock, the panic, and the guilt, the

thought that has been running through my mind finally takes shape. *This is bad. You have to do something. Snap out of it.* I don't think long about what to do—I can't think long. After all, stupidity got me into this, maybe stupidity will get me out. I push my way through the bushes. *Eyes. Avoid the eyes.*

"Here you are!" I say, brushing lingering leaves off my arm as I aim the biggest smile I can manage at Vlad's chest. "I've been looking all over! I thought you said to meet in the parking lot. Thank God I heard your voice."

Vlad lets go of Lindsay, more from surprise than fear. Jogging over, I loop my arm through her elbow. Her arm tightens around mine like a boa constrictor; the rest of her is still catatonic.

"We'd better get. But y'all have a nice night," I say. Apparently, fear turns me Texan. A startling personality insight that I'll jot down later if I'm not dead in a ditch. I try to pivot us both around, but Lindsay's not offering much in the way of forward motion. It's a slow, bumbling turn. Out of the corner of my eye, I see Vlad nod over our heads.

We turn right into the twin chests of Devon and Ashley. I try to move us to the side, but Lindsay's legs are tangled up with mine, causing me to step on one of their toes. I make the mistake of looking up at their faces. They don't smirk, they don't glower, and in the second before I veer my gaze away, their eyes are as dead as a flat-lining heart patient. They just . . . exist, like two towering chess pieces. The left one is still clutching the dead rabbit. It hangs there limply, like a warning.

The good news is that Lindsay is starting to show signs of life. Her eyes are glassy but there, and I can feel her fingers tapping my upper arm. She stumbles a bit to the side, of her own accord, and I do everything I can to encourage the momentum in that direction. At least until the two brick walls move to block our way.

Vlad's thighs slink into view. He is wearing black boots with tips that curl up at the ends like two little devil horns. I concentrate on the embroidered patterns on their toes, willing my head to stay down, willing my heart to stay in my chest.

"This night is shaping up to be better than I could have ever imagined," he says. "Two for one! Bingo!"

"Vlad, this is destructive behavior," Marisabel says sternly before her voice starts to wobble. "Let's just go home. Please, let's just go home."

"Be quiet!" Vlad roars. When Marisabel continues to plead for them to leave, he stalks toward her and begins to yell. "Always telling me not to kill when you should keep your mouth shut!" he roars. "If I have to hear your voice for one more second I am going to put a stake through your heart. And then you'll be dust. *Dust.*"

While he's distracted, I grab the small dome of Lindsay's shoulder and shake it. "Lindsay, I think we should make a break for it."

She swings her head toward me, and even though her eyes are worried, her face is still slack. "Legs. Problem," she says simply, just as I realize that the clearing has gone deathly silent.

A rough hand scrapes at my chin. Vlad yanks my face up to meet his gaze, his gray eyes dancing with the thrill of what he's about to do. He lowers his mouth to my ear. It smells sweet, but where I expect to feel the ghosting of breath on my cheek, there is none. I clutch Lindsay tighter.

"You are probably wondering what is happening, and why it is happening to you," Vlad says smoothly. "I suppose I can invite you into our little world now,

Sophie, considering you're about to exit yours."

"You're vampires," I manage to choke out. I swear to God, I will not leave this world to a lecture by Vlad.

For a moment he looks nonplussed. "That saves time, I suppose," he says, right before his fingers clamp down on my chin like tiny vises, imprisoning my mouth and strangling my scream before it even starts. He begins to maneuver us backward, pushing forward until we hit the scratchy trunk of a tree. I launch an awkward kick at his legs. The next thing I know his foot is grinding down on my toes, shooting a bolt of searing pain zipping up to my knee. One of my arms is trapped in Lindsay's; he pins the other to my side. I can barely see the trees anymore around his amused face.

There is no hope of escape. My breathing turns ragged, a change that makes Vlad's face light up with amusement. He gives a sympathetic *tsk*.

"It will not last for long," he assures me, his voice light and informative as though this is a theme park. "After a few minutes your vision will start to fade and then you will just be . . . no more." He presses his face forward until all I can see are his blond brows and dark eyes. "Look into them. It will be better for you in the end."

I know that I need to turn away, but I can't. It's easier to do what he says, to give in. I look into his eyes, studying the darker rings of gray as I wait to be hypnotized, to see flashing lights or feel a ripping sensation tear through my head. I feel a light breeze on my skin . . . I feel my toes throbbing from where Vlad's foot still presses down . . . I feel a cramp in my arm where Lindsay's weight sits heavy and immobile . . . but nothing else.

It takes me a few moments to realize that Vlad is no longer pinning me to tree. Instead he is looking at me with an incredulous expression that lasts three seconds before his face transforms into a snarl and he lunges for my neck. Squeezing my eyes shut, I scream into Vlad's hand. There are two slivers of glass in my neck, buried so deep that there is no hope of ever digging them out.

A shout cuts through the pain, and then I'm falling onto the ground and pulling Lindsay along with me. We collapse into a pile. Lindsay's knee jabs into the curve of my hip, and I'm staring up at the sky, full of airplane trails and the shadowy suggestion of stars just starting to pop out. I find my hand in our tangle of limbs and bring it to my neck. Hot, sticky liquid covers my fingers.

From my left come the sounds of a fight. I roll my head to the side to see if I'm in danger of being trampled, but it causes my head to spin, and I have to squeeze my eyes shut until it stops. When I open them again I see Vlad, on his back, fangs bared. And James—wonderful, wonderful James—is on top of him, fangs also bared.

Hallucinating, I'm hallucinating. I blink my eyes three or four times to get the crazy out of them. Before I can look again, I feel Lindsay sit up to my right, and then her hands beneath my back, lifting me up. My neck feels too weak to support my head, and it thuds onto her shoulder. *Bobble-head Sophie,* I think, and giggle. Her palm smacks my cheek several times before she succeeds in pushing my head back up.

"Stop giggling like an idiot and look," she whispers, amazement coloring her voice as she grabs my chin and pivots my head toward what's happening on my other side. Amazement with a heaping side dish of terror.

James and Vlad are now on their feet, glaring at each other.

"Leave them alone, Vlad."

"I fear it's too late for that," Vlad says cheerfully. "They know."

"Think. This will jeopardize your search. Two missing girls will draw a lot of attention. People will be scared, panicked."

"I do not care about people," Vlad scoffs.

"You should. They will be looking for you while you're looking for her. And then you will never find her. And then there will be no Danae."

This gives Vlad pause. Folding his arms across his chest, he tilts his head to the side and wipes at the corners of his mouth in a way that I might have called fastidious if he hadn't just been chewing on my neck.

"Perhaps you are right," he says cautiously, studying his fingers, which glisten with blood in the low evening light. He waves a hand toward where Lindsay and I huddle on the ground. "But how do you propose I clean up this . . . misunderstanding? I suppose I can wipe their minds, but that will make me even more drained, which is the reason I was going to risk eating them in the first place!" he finishes, shaking his head as if to say, "What conundrums I get myself into!"

"I'll do it," James says quickly. "I'll take care of it."

Vlad's eyebrows arch in surprise. "Really? You had given me the impression that you felt yourself above this . . . How did you say it? Ah yes, 'vampire stuff.'"

Even though I've seen the fangs, I still gasp. Or more appropriately, I suck in a large amount of air that leaves me coughing and sputtering. When I raise my eyes, James is looking at me with an emotion I can't place.

He turns back to Vlad. "I said I'll take care of it."

For a second Vlad seems appeased, like we're a set of problems he's just been told won't be on the pop quiz. But then his eyes narrow. "You like that one."

"Which one?"

"Sophie. The black-haired one."

James's expression is unreadable. "Are you kidding? She's a pain in the neck. I just want to make sure nothing gets in the way of you finding your girl," he says. "Then I stay here, and you go, just like we said."

"We also said that you would help search if I allowed you to wander off and live on your own," Vlad says, "and yet I believe this is the first day you've appeared."

"I'm here now," he insists. "Let me prove that I want to help."

Vlad purses his lips, debating the merits of letting us

go. "Very well, then," he says finally. "You may have another chance to prove yourself. But when I reintroduce myself, I expect them not to know who I am."

"Understood," James says, walking over to yank us onto our feet. We might as well be made out of Styrofoam for the amount of effort it costs him. He pushes us in front of him and tells us to march forward.

It takes forever for us to reach my Jeep, or at least it feels like it does. No one speaks for several seconds until Lindsay says, weakly, that she doesn't think she should drive. The whole time we've been standing here, she hasn't moved her eyes from James.

James turns to me. "Can you drive?" he asks, eyeing my neck, which is still bleeding. Is it my imagination or do I see a flicker of interest in his gaze? With every second I don't respond, James's face grows more concerned. "Sophie—"

"I can drive," I say.

He gives a sharp nod. "Then take Lindsay and go home, lock your doors, and stay inside. I'm going to stay here until Vlad leaves."

"But—"

"Please. He doesn't always keep his word. I want to

tell him that I've already done it, so he doesn't think about it tonight."

I know I've been dismissed, but there's something that I need to say. "Thank you."

For a second I think he looks hopeful, like he's relieved that things haven't changed that much, before his expression becomes inscrutable once again. "We'll talk later," he says before turning to face the wall of trees.

Chapter Eight

I drive like a maniac. Any cops unlucky enough to be caught in my path would be justified in thinking that I had a blood alcohol level in the "legally dead" range. But even as I race through yellow lights and tear through the suburbs, Lindsay says nothing besides a few curt directions that bring us to a white ranch with red shutters and a mailbox shaped like a rooster.

I unlock the passenger-side door, and the click echoes in the silence. She doesn't get out, just sits, staring straight ahead with her hands clenched in her lap as the front porch light throws her profile into stark relief. Her mouth twitches like she's trying to figure out where to start.

"That was a mean thing you did," she says. The car is warm, but she's shivering.

Whatever I was expecting—and it was something along the lines of "Vampires are real and they want our braiiinnns, omigod, omigod, omigod"—it wasn't this.

"I know. You have every reason to hate me," I say, undoing my seat belt and twisting to face her. "But right now there are more important things to—"

"Stop!" she yells, close to tears. "I don't want to talk about that, I want to talk about this. I know you view me as your competition, okay? I view you as mine, too. But not in a way that would ever make me sabotage you by manipulating a guy who likes me to not give you an interview. By the way, your boyfriend's a vampire, so . . . nice going there."

I swallow a snotty response about James not being my boyfriend. "Really, Lindsay, we need to talk about what we're going to do."

"He almost killed me," she blurts. "I was almost murdered by a vampire. I can't . . . I can't understand that. I don't want to understand that." She takes a ragged breath. "I thought we were friends."

It takes me a second to realize that she means her and

me. "We are friends," I say weakly.

"No," she says, hard enough to make me flinch. "I mean, I've tried to be yours. And since you didn't seem to show as much disdain for me as you do for everyone else, I thought you were trying to be mine, too." She reaches down to wrestle with the buckle of her seat belt, but it doesn't stop her tirade. "I mean, do you ever wonder why you have no friends?"

"I have friends."

"Not people you talk to sometimes," she insists. "Friends. Like, come-over-and-do-something-with-me-on-Friday friends. It's not that people don't like you, there's just a wall. A know-it-all, too-good-for-everything wall that keeps people from getting close. Although, after today, who knows if they should." She wipes at her mottled cheeks and then pushes open her door. "Anyway, thanks so much for the ride home, and give James my gratitude. Then tell him that I'm making up everything about him for the article, because I want him to stay away from me. You too," she says and then runs inside without a backward glance.

When I get home there's a small violet envelope resting at the foot of the front door. Inside I find a magazine page whose ragged edges suggest it was ripped out with quite a bit of rage. "Are You a Good Friend?" the quiz asks. Scribbled across it in what I pray is red nail polish is one word: "No."

I start to cry. You would think this would have happened sometime closer to my brush with death, but this is the tipping point. Because Violet is right—I am a horrible friend who will not only lead you to your doom in the forest, but will also unwittingly hold hands with your ex-boyfriend. The front door opens as I am wiping sloppy tears off my cheeks.

"You know that you are supposed to call if you're going to be later than—," my dad starts but then stops when he sees my face. "Are you hurt? What's wrong?"

"I'm fine," I sniffle. He's wearing the clothes that mean he's about to tinker with something in the garage: an old pair of corduroy pants and a flannel shirt that he still tucks in. It makes him look both dignified and woodsy, like a professor at a school for lumberjacks. Overcome by a wave of affection, I drop my backpack with a thud and lurch toward him for a hug. "I didn't mean to be late."

I've taken him by surprise. "It's okay. Marcie and I

are just a little on edge. Your sister came home screaming that her life was over. Marcie's up there with her
now. I think it has to do with that boy she was dating."

Caroline. I had forgotten all about her. "They broke
up," I say. "I promise you that it's for the best."

"I trust your judgment on that." Dad shoves his
hands in the pockets of his corduroys and peers at me
quizzically. "Are you sure you're okay?"

"Just a bad day."

I can't tell if he's bought it. He just studies me for a
few more seconds and then pats me on the back before
telling me that he'll be in the garage if I need to talk.

I find Marcie and Caroline in her bedroom. They
sit on her pink bedspread surrounded by a coterie of
stuffed animals, three of which are currently being
strangled in Caroline's arms. If Grover were not already
blue, he would be now. Her head is buried in a pillow
that rests in Marcie's lap. It may prevent Caroline's wails
from coming out clearly, but it doesn't dim the sorrow.
Marcie is gently stroking her hair, adding an understanding "I know" at every pause. When she sees me at
the door, she holds a finger to her lips.

Suddenly Caroline's head twists to the side. ". . . And

then he said, 'I fear you are not who I am looking for, Caroline,'" she says in a startlingly good imitation that's unfortunately ruined by the half sob, half hiccup at the end. "What does that even mean? Who knows what they're looking for at seventeen?"

"I know, dear. That's what I told you earlier," Marcie soothes, moving a strand of tangled blond hair away from her daughter's eyes. Once her vision is cleared, Caroline spots me in front of her.

"So I guess you heard," she sniffles from Marcie's lap. "Vlad broke up with me at the end of school today. Everyone heard. Even Ms. Kate." This last bit sets off a new wave of tears.

"I know. I'm sorry, Caroline." I perch on the sliver of bed not covered by something fuzzy. "You have to believe me when I say that you are better off."

At first she doesn't respond, and I'm afraid that I've said the wrong thing. I didn't think it was an "I told you so," but occasionally some know-it-all creeps in without my permission.

"Yeah," she finally says. "You were right. He's a jerk. Also . . . ," she starts, but then cranes her head to look up at Marcie. "Mom, cover your ears."

Marcie dutifully brings her hands up, obviously in a mood to humor her distraught daughter. But over her head, to me, she mouths, "Tell me if it's drugs."

"Also," Caroline continues, satisfied that Marcie's hands are soundproof, "he was not a great kisser. He bit my lip. And he really wanted me to take off my shirt."

It's nice to know that the breakup hasn't affected Caroline's desire to TMI, even when in front of parents. It used to embarrass me, but now I sort of admire it. And if Vlad's bizarre question to Lindsay in the woods is any indication, it only adds to the evidence suggesting that Vlad thinks this girl he's looking for has some sort of mark on her body. But what? A mole? A big bull's eye? A tattoo that says, "I am dying to be a vampire groupie"? Definitely number one on my "Things to Find Out" list. Well, maybe number two, after "Figure out what exactly 'mind-wiping' entails."

I start to make my exit. "Caroline, you know where I am if you want to talk," I say and give her shoulder a squeeze. She throws her arms around my neck in an enthusiastic, snotty hug that squishes my arms to my chest before pulling back abruptly.

"Why are you wearing a scarf?" she asks, curiosity

overcoming self-pity. I had wrapped an old black scarf I found in the backseat around my neck to hide the puncture wounds. Trust Caroline to sniff out a fashion faux pas in the midst of an emotional breakdown.

"I think I'm getting a cold," I say.

"Well, it doesn't match your outfit," she says, starting to tear up again. "That really goes more with a peacoat."

To make it up to her, I sit through a few more rounds of Vlad-bashing. When I'm finally able to escape to my room, I head to the floor-length mirror and de-scarf my neck. The skin is smeared with blood, and while I can still see the deep impression of two tiny holes, they seem to have stopped bleeding. That's . . . something.

After erasing as much vampire action from my neck as possible, I search for the happiest pajamas that I can find, finally settling on a pair from three Christmases ago that is dotted with smiley, spouting whales. The shirt is a little too tight across the chest and I have a feeling that an impulsive squat might spell sayonara for the bottoms, but they are comfy and worn in all the right places.

I start to slide under the covers, but the thought of

trying to sleep with, well, things lurking outside seems silly, if not dangerous. Instead, I curl up in my desk chair to keep watch, noting with surprise that it has started to rain. Raindrops distort my view of outside, fracturing the light from the nearby street lamps and blurring everything outside. The one thing I can see clearly is the window across the way. James's window.

"We'll talk," he said. Twice.

Suddenly the room feels stuffy, claustrophobic. I open the window to let in a gust of chilled air, sending whatever raindrops that were still clinging to the glass scurrying to the bottom of the pane. The silver rivers they leave in their wake slice my view of James's house down the middle, and it is a relief. Now I can't see anything.

Chapter Nine

Eventually, I crawl into bed, but I don't sleep well. My dreams resemble a flickering black-and-white horror movie. I'm in a cave swatting bats out of my hair, then fending off spiders with a can of spray paint. Finally, I end up on a windswept moor with a silver and gray wolf. He asks me to dance. I refuse. He retaliates by chewing on my toes.

My eyes snap open. It would be nice if my brain could take this seriously.

The temperature dropped in the night, and while the rain is lighter now, it's still heavy enough to drum against the attic roof. Wrapping myself in a faded afghan, I climb out of bed and shiver my way across the cold hardwood to the open window. Sliding behind my desk chair, I grasp the splintered frame and push down.

Suddenly, a hand snakes up from the darkness, and I jump back just as four fingers clamp over the sill. Stumbling over my desk chair, I crash to the floor, feet caught up in the netting of my afghan. I claw frantically at the mess around my legs as the hand becomes an arm and then a head and then a torso. A body vaults into view, filling the frame, blocking the outside light.

I have two options. Run downstairs with a rabid vampire in hot pursuit or lurch forward, close the window, and pray that the mixture of screen and glass is resistant to fists. So far the intruder isn't even scratching at the screen. For an assassin, he's taking his time, and closing the window might buy me more. Muttering "Close and lock, close and lock" like a mantra, I spring up and rush forward, hitting the window and pushing down with all my might until I hear a satisfying snick.

My attack brings more than I bargained for. Startled by my sudden appearance, the intruder loses his grip on one of the frame's sides. He swings backward like a saloon door, one hand clutching the upper eave of the window, one foot balanced on the outside cement ledge, and all other limbs dangling in space. The full glow of the streetlight floods his face, and I find myself staring into James's face—James's very annoyed, very angry face.

For one crazy, hurtling second I heave a sigh of relief; if forced to choose, he is the better option. But then again, I would also rather drown than be eaten by snakes.

Before I can figure out the next course of action, James begins to move, and move strangely. He swings his body back to and fro until he has enough momentum to bring his other foot back on the sill. Steady once again, he crouches in front of me, a particularly nimble gargoyle. So much for getting the upper hand.

"Let me in," he says, the glass muffling his voice.

He's soaking wet. His green shirt is plastered to his shoulders like a second skin, and beads of water race down his nose. I feel a twinge of sympathy, but then tell myself to snap out of it. Twinges of sympathy are better than being turned into an amnesia zombie.

"I don't care to be mind-wiped, thank you," I say through the glass. Little clouds of steam appear and vanish between each word.

"I'm not going to mind-wipe you!" he says. "I just want to explain."

My eyes take in his frown, his narrowed eyes. "Don't take this the wrong way," I say, "but you seem a little angry. Why should I believe you?"

"Because I am telling you that I won't." I must still look skeptical, because he brings his palm up to the window, pushing down so hard that I can see the small traces of his heart line. "I swear."

I check his eyes and body language for signs of deviousness, but there are none. I bite my lip, torn. *This is the moment*, I think. *This is the moment where you can make a very smart choice or a very stupid choice.*

"Sophie," he pleads again when he sees me wavering. "You've known me my entire life. You have to trust me. I'm still . . . just, please."

Memories of the last week's conversations flicker through my mind. It had all felt so normal, just like Old James and Old Sophie. Before I can think about it any more, I open the window halfway.

I am going to make the stupid choice.

"Listen," I say and then lean over to make sure that

there's no glass preventing him from hearing me clearly. "You can come in—but make any sudden movements and I swear I will run downstairs for the garlic. Marcie buys it in bulk. Already chopped, too, if that means anything."

His face breaks into a smile that would be more appropriate on the face of a lottery winner than someone I just threatened with prepackaged foodstuffs. He yanks up the screen without the slightest hesitation. If he'd wanted to bust in without asking, that barrier would have bought me a whole .42 seconds—a grim thought. His hands reach for the window next, but I bang on the glass until he lets go.

"I want a verbal commitment."

He dutifully parrots that he will under no circumstances fiddle with my mind. He caps it off with a Boy Scout salute.

"The salute was a bit much," I say, pushing the window the rest of the way up. I sweep my hand back in a welcoming gesture. "James, you may come inside."

"Aw shucks, Sophie, that's swell. I sure do hope my manners are as nice as yours one day." He ducks through the window and closes it behind him.

"I thought I had to invite you in."

"Not really, no," he corrects before stooping over to shake out his wet hair.

I dodge to the side to avoid an inadvertent shower. "I'm pretty sure that—"

"You don't." He stands up straight, surveying me as though he's suddenly seeing me in a new, geeky light. "How many vampire movies have you watched?"

More than a few, if I'm being honest. In retrospect, I should have cried vampire that first day in the auditorium, but we'll chalk that misfire up to general sanity. "Not that many," I mutter. "And there's a pretty big consensus on the invite thing, I'll have you know."

"Well, the consensus is wrong. And besides, if you thought I needed an invite to get in, why did you freak out at the window?"

It's a valid point, but not one that I feel like acknowledging. "I didn't freak out. I just thought you were the neighborhood pervert. He likes me. A lot," I say as he starts to smile. "What?"

"Did you wear the cape just for me?"

"Huh?"

He points to my shoulders. "The cape."

I look down. At some point in my terror I had seen fit to tie the afghan around my shoulders. Oh my God.

"It's just something I wear sometimes," I shrug, untying the knot at my throat in what I hope is an offhand manner. Self-conscious, I cross the room to sit on the bed cross-legged, tucking my feet beneath my knees until not even the pink of a pinkie toe is visible.

"You don't have to sit all the way over there," he says, raising an eyebrow in the way that always made me jealous back when I aspired to be an arch villain. "I don't bite."

Considering earlier events, it's a gutsy joke. "How long have you been waiting to say that?"

"Since I moved home," he says, taking a seat by the leg of my desk.

"Nice."

We lapse into silence. I lean my head back against the wall, keeping watch on him from the corner of my eye. He's brought his knees up closer to his chest, and his hands rest calmly on top of them, patient and relaxed.

"You know, you don't get a free pass here. If you want me to really trust you, you have to tell me everything. You have to answer all of my questions, no matter how stupid or invasive they are."

"Okay," he says without hesitation.

"I mean it," I say, looking at him directly. "No evasion."

"Okay."

"Fine, then," I say archly. "What did you do with the flip-flop you stole in third grade? I never found it in your yard."

He doesn't miss a beat. "I dug a hole and buried it by the swing set."

"Are you serious?"

"Yeah. With my hands," he adds. "The neighbor's dog watched me the entire time. I had to wash under my nails for weeks to get the dirt out."

"Okay. How did you become a vampire?"

He blinks a few times. "You go from zero to sixty, don't you?"

"It's the best way to get honest answers," I say. "Why? Backing out?"

"No. But I wonder if you'll answer a question for me first."

If it has anything to do with my blood type, I'm going to kick myself. "What?" I ask, suspicious.

"What bothers you more?" he asks, leaning forward. "The fact that I'm a vampire or the fact that you have me here, sitting in your bedroom, after midnight? Because I actually think it's the second one."

He flashes a toothy smile. In any other time, under any other circumstances, I would almost think that he was . . .

"Are you flirting with me?" I ask, stunned. "Now?"

I think I see a flicker of disappointment wash across his features, but it could just be a shadow. "Please," he says coolly. "I was just curious. And besides, I thought the whole vampire thing was supposed to be sexy. I just wanted to make sure you weren't going to start giggling and twirling your hair."

"I think you're safe. One, vampires lose a little something when one of them tries to snack on your neck, and two, I'm still not sure what you're doing back. So spill," I order, frowning when all that follows is a few seconds of awkward silence. "I'll get you started. Once upon a time, I met someone with really pointy teeth, and they said—"

"Okay," James cuts me off. "This isn't easy, you know? What you're going to hear isn't one of my best moments. After my parents died, it was . . . hard."

"Was it really a fire?" I ask, bracing myself for a story of how the fire was a cover-up, of midnight vampire attacks and bloody handprints smeared across white sheets. Instead he surprises me with a short laugh.

"Yep. Just one of those random tragedies everyone reads about in the newspaper and everyone forgets three days later. Except for the people it happens to."

It's hard to imagine that when I was cursing the day-to-day indignities of being a high school freshman, he was dealing with having his life suddenly ripped out from under him. Imagining James as a sudden orphan causes me to pull the afghan back up and wrap it, mummylike, around my shoulders. He's stopped talking again, but for once I don't poke or prod.

"Anyway," he continues so suddenly that I jump, "after my parents died, they had to figure out what to do with me. My grandparents had died long before I was born, and my parents didn't have any siblings. If they had left it up to me, I would have taken my chances on my own, but I was sixteen, and legally that meant I had to be placed in a foster home."

A foster home seems so . . . clinical. "Were the people nice?"

James shrugs. "I guess. They lived in an old reno-vated farmhouse with acres of fields around it. Susanna bred some form of German shepherd, and Ian spent most of his time with old tractor parts. An old country bus picked me up for school. When I went."

"When you went?"

"Yeah. I probably skipped half the time, but I passed. Barely," he snorts and then opens his eyes. "You know, when you're happy it's hard to imagine not caring about anything. But I didn't. Not myself, not my future, not anyone. Sometimes I imagined what it would have been like if we'd never moved, if we still lived next to you and your family, and if you and I still spent most of our days coming up with the perfect insults for each other. I'd stay up late at night, imagining conversations that could have happened on the way to school, in our backyards, over the phone . . . ," he says and then shoots me an embarrassed glance. "It was stupid—I had other friends, and you and I didn't even talk that much after sixth grade."

I don't know what to say. I feel like I should ad-mit something personal as well—that when he kissed my cheek on the hammock I was just pretending to be asleep. That the day his family moved away I cried. *Or,* a little voice inside whispers, *you could sit closer. That's a sure sign of emotional solidarity.* That little voice is right, and from the way James is still looking at me, I'm going to have to come up with something a little more supportive than a few jokes. Trailing a clump of covers, I scoot to the edge of the bed and then slide to the floor. Now there's not as much space separating us, but even that measly six feet has taken on the proportions of a football field. Do I scoot over and loop my arm around his shoulders, or is leaning forward with a concerned expression, Oprah-like, okay?

I'm still wrestling with myself, eyeing the floor like it's Mount Everest and wondering how the whole vampire thing fits into the equation, when James's voice pipes up. "Comfortable now?" he asks with an off-kilter smile that says he knows exactly what stupidity I've been debating.

"The bed was too soft," I say in a rush, which makes him grin even more. The good news is that he's smiling again; apparently all I need to do to make him feel better is tap into my inner social moron. "I'm so sorry, James."

He shrugs again. "Not your fault."

"But that still doesn't explain where the fangs come in. My money's on a certain girlfriend from the wrong side of the afterlife."

His expression turns cagey. "Possibly."

"You mean there are several choices?" I ask, and then resist the urge to bang on my chest. Where did that shrillness come from? Clearing my throat to evict whatever jealous-girlfriend type has come in and changed the wallpaper, I strive for something calmer. "I mean, the only logical choice is Violet."

"I had other girlfriends, you know."

"I'm not saying that the only girl who would find you attractive is one with serious codependency issues. I'm saying that I've been English buddies with Violet this past week, and she's said a few things that are finally starting to make sense. And then there's the fact that she flipped in the lunchroom when she saw us talking."

"Okay, it was Violet."

"Did you lose a bet? Check the wrong box on a survey? Because she's kind of weird."

"Funny," he says. "So I told you how Susanna and Ian's farm was in the boonies, right? There were maybe three houses within a five-mile radius. Two of those were owned by old retired couples. The other one, the closest one, was deserted. Or so everyone thought."

"*Dum dum dum*."

"Yes, *dum dum dum*. Thank you."

"No prob."

"A few weeks after I moved in, I started taking walks. Sometimes I'd even go in the middle of the night, climbing out my window and down a tree like in the movies. One night I walked farther than I ever had before—anything to keep my mind off of reality—and I came across one of those rambling old country houses, complete with a wraparound front porch. For a second, just a second, I thought it was our old house. Or this house," he says, squinting up at the ceiling. "Honestly, other than its size, it was completely different. But it was enough to make me try the front door."

"Breaking and entering. Awesome," I say, happy when it makes him smile. I prefer it to the sadness, times infinity.

"The inside wasn't nearly as rundown as I expected," he continues, "and there was an old couch against the wall. Newspapers were everywhere. Old, yellow ones. And stacked up in the far corner was what I thought was a pile of sticks," he says.

The emphasis on "I thought" makes me a little queasy. I almost don't want to ask. Almost. "Let me guess. Not sticks?"

"No," he says flatly. "Not sticks. Animal bones and fur, from a lot of animals. More than could crawl inside for warmth and then die in the exact same place. I turned and ran for the door, but then there was Violet, standing with her arms twined around the pole of the porch and smiling. You know, I think I actually said hello. She looked like a doll, especially in one of those dresses."

"Anyone can look like a doll when their waist has been cinched to the size of a milk ring," I say peevishly and then feel foolish when James gives me a confused look.

"Anyway," he says, "Violet grabbed my arm and said that she was glad to meet me."

"And then she dragged you to the shed and bit you, right?" I ask, thinking that I'm being helpful by filling in the blanks. A+++ for me. I wait for a sign of affirmation, a mouth twitch, a blink, a head wiggle, anything, but nothing comes. "Right?" I repeat.

James suddenly finds his shoelaces fascinating.

"Are you kidding me? You mean it didn't happen that night? You mean you went back?"

"After my parents died I couldn't believe how normal everything was," he says before I can ask him how he could have been so stupid. "Even though I was in a different place with different people, it still felt the same. Susanna made dinner every night at the same time my mom did. She even used some of the same magazine recipes. Every morning I would wake up to the same dumb bird chirping, and every day I would put on the same clothes. And yet all it did was remind me how different everything was, how horrible. Nothing at Violet's was the same. Not her, not the life, and not the rest of them. It felt like getting lost in a movie or book. It was an escape."

"But didn't their extreme strangeness set off any warning bells?"

He gives me a withering stare. "Give me some credit. But vampires are supposed to be outside the realm of possibility, right? And besides, I didn't see you jumping up and down in the cafeteria crying monster."

"True. But I didn't see their animal-bone collection, either."

"Fair enough," he says. "The truth is I didn't care. It felt like a dream, and I acted like it was a dream. One night Violet asked me if I wanted it all to last forever. I said yes. She bit me, she told me to bite her, and by that time I was so out of it that I did. When I woke up I thought, hey, at least nothing will ever be the same." His head thunks against the desk. "It was the stupidest thing I've ever done. You can't kick me more than I've kicked myself."

"Couldn't you have just dyed your hair purple and called it a day?" I ask weakly. When I think about the loneliness and grief that drove him to do this, I am suddenly choked up. I slide halfway across the floor to be closer, to let him know that I appreciate his honesty. When I stop, he lifts an eyebrow.

"Really? That's the best sob story I've got. What does a guy have to say to make you move all the way?"

When I don't answer, he scoots forward, closing the distance himself and leaving me to stare dry-mouthed at the inch between our knees.

"Do you know that all the blood in your body just rushed to your cheeks?" he asks. "They're glowing."

My head jerks up. Without thinking, I clap my

hands to the runaway body parts, which do feel a little bit warm.

"Whatever. It's too dark to tell that," I say with false bravado.

"Darkness doesn't matter. One of the few benefits of my new condition."

"What?"

"I can see body warmth, pools of blood. And right now, your cheeks are two giant beacons." He points at my face like I might not know which cheeks he means.

"I flush easily," I say.

"Uh-huh," he says, clearly a nonbeliever. Now seems like the perfect time for another subject change.

"So what other superpowers do you have?" I ask. "And if you say X-ray vision I am going to shoot myself."

He doesn't respond. It's obvious that the question makes him uncomfortable—he sits up straighter and shifts his weight from side to side. Apparently I am going to have to play a guessing game. "If Vlad is any indication, I would say that you have powers of persuasion."

"To an extent," he says cautiously.

"And you're stronger?"

"Yes."

"And you have heightened senses."

"Yes."

"And you sparkle in the sunlight."

His lips make the "yuh" shape, but then he does a double take. "What?"

"You, uh, sparkle?" I try again. When his bafflement fails to disappear, I begin to ramble. "I mean, now that I think about it, I've seen you in the sun and there doesn't seem to be any glitter action. But aren't you not supposed to go in the sun?" Someone really needs to step in and universalize vampire lore, pronto.

He continues to look at me as though I like to eat grass in my spare time. "Sunlight doesn't kill us, but it makes us weaker. So does using any of our gifts," he says, and the sarcasm is thick on the last word. "The more we use them the more we need to . . ."

"Need to what?" I prod.

"The more we need to drink," he says.

My stomach lurches. While I knew that vampirism was a blood-sucking operation, this is James. *James.* He likes red licorice and banana-and-peanut-butter sandwiches. I know this because he used to steal them out of my lunch box all the time and replace them with pieces of paper that said, "James: 1, Sophie: 0."

I turn to study him in the moonlight. He has gone back to studying his shoes, but I can tell that he is watching me from the corner of his eyes. My mind is tossing up images of him bending over the ivory columns of exposed necks and snatching up rabbits in the woods. In these images he is dressed in a cape with red lining and a tailed tuxedo, not the T-shirt and jeans he's wearing now.

Unconsciously, my fingers creep up to my neck. The puncture wounds have scabbed over into two bumps that are hard and curved like tiny turtle shells. Perhaps I should be more worried than I am.

"Yes," James says darkly. "I do drink blood. But never yours. Never anyone alive's really. Too dangerous. And . . . you know. Wrong."

His voice startles me—I hadn't thought that I said anything out loud. I look at him, confused.

"Er, right. We can sort of read thoughts when we're close to someone. Sometimes. Occasionally. We have to be touching you if we want to go very deep. But it goes hand in hand with the mind-wiping thing that we should talk about."

I know that I should be like, "Yes! Mind wiping! Please explain at length and in detail!" but right now I just feel like seeing if I can stuff myself beneath my bed for the rest of eternity. I frantically try to think back to the times we've been "close" in the last week. There was that first night in his backyard, and then today in the lunchroom, and then—

"Now," James fills in helpfully.

I scoot sideways faster than anyone has ever scooted before, and I don't stop until my back is against my bedroom door and there's at least twelve feet between us.

"Oh, come on," he says, "I haven't picked up on anything embarrassing. Although it's nice to know that someone thinks my arms are pretty." His mouth starts to twitch. "Well, mine and Danny Baumann's."

Dear God. Danny Baumann was something that I had meant to take to my grave, unless that fantasy played out where we met at a twentieth high school reunion and he was blown away by my poise and reporting experience, and I got to spend a lifetime staring at him before we were buried side by side. Which would still mean taking him to my grave, actually. So yeah.

"This is not funny," I say when I can finally speak. "This is an invasion of privacy. Stop it."

"I would if I could," he says. "It just happens. They say that you learn to control it as you get older—the other vampires can—but so far it's been a year and it's still going strong." He rubs his eyes, suddenly weary. "I'm glad this came up, because we need to figure out what's going to happen on Monday. Vlad will be expecting you to know nothing about what happened today in the woods. If you show the slightest ounce of mistrust, he will become suspicious, and I can't predict what he'll do next. If you haven't noticed," he says wryly, "he's kind of a loose cannon."

"So what am I supposed to do? Not think?"

"No. But if the way you followed four hungry vampires into the woods is any indication, you weren't doing much of that this afternoon anyway."

I hold up a finger. "Okay. *One*, I didn't know they were vampires—I just thought they were part of some sort of weird cult thing. And *two*," I add, because number one doesn't sound all that smart in retrospect, "insults are not going to help me keep my neck intact. Seriously, what am I supposed to do?"

"There are things that make it harder for us to pick up anything."

"Like what?"

"I've noticed that if people are concentrating really hard on something, I don't hear anything. It's the stray thoughts that come through, the departures from regularly scheduled programming." He stops, a new emotion flickering across his face. "Are you really going to keep hiding in the corner?"

"Can you hear me over here?"

"Not really."

"Then yes," I say, and he frowns a little and looks away. I may not be able to read minds, but he's obviously hurt, and that makes me feel guilty. Especially considering that the reason he's here tonight, telling me all of this, is because he had to stop me from becoming Vlad's very special Pringle.

Knowing I'm going to regret this later, I scoot back across the room until there are only a few inches between our knees.

"Okay, let's practice. Try to tell what I'm thinking,"

I say, but he's already dropped his gaze to squint down at my legs.

"What are those? Dancing raisins?"

"Whales. And I would kind of like to focus on the tips and tricks to vampire mind defense right now, not my pajama decisions."

"Fair enough," he says and then leans forward, close enough that I can make out the green of his eyes. I'm suddenly distracted by his bottom lip, which really is very nicely shaped. And there's a freckle punctuating the corner of his mouth that I can't recall from our early years.

"That's because I doubt you ever looked at my mouth this closely when we were eight," he says.

I rear back. "I wasn't ready!"

"Sorry. It's not a one-two-three-go kind of situation."

I point behind him. "Argh. Just . . . go to that side of the room."

"What?"

"You say you have to be close to hear anything, and since I can see Vlad coming, I should at least have two

—161—

or three seconds to start concentrating. So go over by the bookcase and then walk toward me." When he doesn't move, I add, "Any time now."

Reluctantly, he stands up and moves to the far wall, and I search for a topic. I could choose a subject like the weather or why I hate the word "pungent," but that's not going to prove that I can hide my thoughts when it really counts.

After I hop to my feet, he starts his re-approach. I close my eyes and try to concentrate on the things that I would never ever want to say aloud.

James, the fact that your new hobby is drinking blood does not disturb me nearly as much as it should. Also, you have grown up to be quite cute.

When I open my eyes, his chin is in front of me. I look up to find him staring down at me with patient attention and something else that I can't quite define.

"It worked," he says after a few moments. "Nothing but fuzz."

"Really?"

"Yep. Complete blank. What were you thinking about?"

"Er, nothing important," I say, staring up at him.

When did he get so tall?

"Sophomore year," he says and then winces. The brief courage that came from my previous success starts to crumble.

"How am I supposed to do this?" I ask.

"Avoid Vlad. Period."

"But I have English with him! I mean, he sits in the front and I sit in the back, but—"

"It should still be fine," he says, sounding about as reassuring as a doctor who's just dropped his keys in his patient's open heart cavity. "Like I said before, Vlad's old enough that he won't be picking things up unless he's actively trying. Just try not to let him get too close."

Realizing how close I am to James, I retreat to take a seat on the end of my bed. "What about Violet? She's in my English class too."

"Violet doesn't use her powers very often. It's draining, and she thinks blood drinking isn't very ladylike. Besides, she has enough problems in her own head to worry about anyone else's."

"Harsh words for your girlfriend."

"Ex-girlfriend," he corrects quickly. "If that."

"Nice."

James blinks in a way that would be cute if he were not being a dirtbag. "I don't understand why you're angry."

"Maybe I just think you should be a little nicer to the girl who shared eternal life with you."

He runs his hands through his hair, which I am quickly learning is his I-am-exasperated-with-your-craziness tell. "Eternal life that I don't want," he stresses. "A girl that I don't want. If we're being completely honest, I *want*—"

I cut him off. "You should have thought of that before you let her give you an undead hickey. And while we're at it, what's so bad about eternal life? I mean, maybe it's time to focus on the positives."

"Besides sun headaches and the blood drinking and the insane company?" he says, and for the first time since we began, James is getting angry, honestly angry.

"And the superstrength," I counter, "and the mind reading and the coolness factor and the—"

"I don't want to talk about this anymore!" he interrupts, walking over to look out the window. "I don't even know how we got here. Let's talk about something else."

He's right. Time to change the subject. "Okay," I say.

"What is Vlad doing here?"

James studies me for a few moments. "Vlad is looking for a girl," he says finally.

"I got that much," I say with hard-won patience. "What does this girl do? Fly?"

"No."

"Does he *vant* to suck her blood?"

James shrugs. "He hasn't really kept us in the loop."

Up until now, James has been nothing but an open book, keeping his gaze on me far more than my fluttery stomach can take. But now he's deliberately turned away from me. As he pretends to peer out over his backyard, it strikes me that I recognize this pose from when we were kids; this is James keeping a secret.

"What don't you want to tell me?" I ask.

Instead of answering, he walks across the room to the bulletin board that hangs over my dresser. Leaning forward, he points at the picture wedged in its corner. "Isn't this that karate class they asked you to resign from? Are you the small, scowling one?"

This source is obviously tapped. "It's late, and I am exhausted," I say, and it's not a lie. A weight has settled between my eyes, and the pillow on my bed is growing larger and more appealing. Like a giant fluffy marsh-mallow filled with Marshmallow Fluff.

"You're kicking me out?" James asks, surprised.

"You seem to be done talking."

A wave of irritation dims his features. "I didn't know that I was just here for information."

"You're not! It's just that I'm tired and I was attacked by vampires in the woods today and their leader seems to want me dead when he's not too busy being the most popular person in the world, and I would just like to go back to sleep and forget about it for a little bit," I finish, realizing that I'm not handling this well at all.

James watches me for a few moments. "Vlad's not the most popular person in the world," he says.

"What?"

"In the vampire world he's not popular at all. In fact, he's an outcast. Persona non grata. If there were vampire restaurants, they would have signs that say, 'No Stakes or Vlad.'"

If James had said that Vlad liked to wrap himself in cellophane and sing show tunes for fun, I couldn't be more surprised. Considering his penchant for sticking his nose up in the air and acting better than everyone else, I assumed he was at the top of whatever food chain would take him.

"But why?" I ask.

James takes a seat in the desk chair, leans back, and looks at me with eyes that are too artificially wide to be innocent. "Do you still want me to leave?"

Well played, James, well played. For a brief second I wonder why he is so resistant to going home, although way back when, Marcie said that if he was over here more often they might as well adopt him.

"You can stay," I say.

"Good," he says, stretching and settling in. "The vampire world is built on hierarchy. Take the stupidity of high school, multiply it by eighteen, add a side of twisted, and you'll end up with something close to what living in vampire society is like. There are hundreds of families, and every single one can tell you who ranks above and below them."

"Vampire families? Like brother and sister?" I ask, thinking of Marisabel. Maybe they *were* siblings, kind of.

"Sort of. When you are made into a vampire you are reborn with the name of your maker, and you're pretty much stuck with it. You can marry out of it, but that hardly ever happens—apparently most vampires would set themselves on fire rather than marry down."

"Fifty dollars that Vlad's name isn't really 'Smithson.'"

"Vlad doesn't have a name. He was made by an Unnamed. They're considered parasites in the vampire community, vampires that were made off the grid."

"So . . . then you're all Unnamed."

"Pretty much. All of us that Vlad made."

"Okay. But what does that actually mean? You don't get chosen first for dodgeball?"

"More like we have no rights at all. At best we're ignored, and at worst we're killed. That's why most Unnamed lay low; they're the ones hiding in empty houses and creeping out only at night."

In other words, exactly what James was doing before I lured him back to the exciting hallways of Thomas Jefferson. I look to James with a smile, expecting to find some sort of wry recognition, but he doesn't seem to have made the connection.

"Vlad doesn't seem like the laying-low type."

"He didn't for a long time—apparently when he

was first made, he loitered a little too closely to the legitimate families and a lot of them wanted him dead. But then he cooked up this Danae scheme and has been working on that ever since."

I lean forward, excited now that we're getting to something that I might already have an inkling about. "The Danae," I say. "I know that Neville is a part of it, but what is it?"

"How do you know that Neville is a part of it?"

"He has a tattoo with a 'D.' I've been investigating."

James doesn't look entirely thrilled by that revelation. "I don't know all that much about it," he says, "other than that it's a sort of vampire secret society with members all over the world. There are official vampire courts, but the Danae is what really pulls the strings. Kind of like a high-class Mafia."

"But then that means that Neville can't be Unnamed. Why is he slumming it with Vlad?"

"He claims that the Danae is interested in seeing where Vlad's search might lead. Vlad, of course, is thrilled. He thinks that if he finds this girl, they'll make him a member."

"That's weird."

"Yeah, that's kind of par for the course with Vlad."

"No, I mean about Neville being a representative of the Danae. Because in our interview, he seemed pretty bitter about them. He said he wished he could remove the tattoo," I say, but then shake my head. We're getting off track. All I really need to know is who this girl is and why finding her will be enough to break through the social barrier. But when I ask James why they would care about finding her, he hesitates again, and I wonder what it is that makes him so close-lipped on this one subject.

"I think I'm going to turn in," I say, faking a yawn.

James smiles. "I can see your belly button," he says, and I immediately put my arms down, embarrassed at my blatant attempt at manipulation. We sit in an awkward silence, until he relents.

"I really don't know that much about her," he says. "Vlad's only told us what he wants us to know. I know that she has some sort of star birthmark."

"You're kidding me. A star?" I ask. This sounds more like a My Little Pony than a person.

But James nods his head and confirms that yes, it's a star. "And I know that she's a sort of legend in the vampire community," he continues. "I know that there are certain beliefs about her blood."

"Beliefs like what?"

He hesitates again. "Some say that it can make a vampire's powers immune to the sunlight, some say that it's an aphrodisiac. And some say that it can reverse vampirism entirely. And that's it. That's all I know."

I wonder why he was so reluctant to tell me, but I'm glad that he did. "Thanks," I say. "We don't have much to work with, but if Vlad's working with the same amount of cluelessness I think we'll be okay."

"Be okay for what?"

"For beating Vlad to the punch. For finding the girl, warning her about whatever he's going to do with her." I stand up, my legs tingling after all this time on the floor. After nudging James's legs to the side with the tip of a toe, I grab my sophomore yearbook from the bottom drawer of my desk. "Vlad has rejected Caroline, so we only have three hundred more high school girls to go. You know, maybe Vlad knows something he's not sharing about finding her among the popular girls. He did home in on Caroline very quickly," I say, and then I realize that I've been chattering on without asking for advice from the person with insight into the vampire in question. "What do you think?"

James is silent. I turn to find him staring at me with a look that contains such a mix of guilt and shame that I can't help but ask him what's wrong.

"What if we let Vlad find her?" he suggests softly.

"I don't understand."

He doesn't respond, just continues to look at me, and suddenly I get it. "You think her blood might turn you back," I say in disbelief.

"It's just one girl," he says, but I detect a note of uncertainty that suggests he's been trying to talk himself into this way of thinking for a long time. "We don't even know what they'll do with her."

"I think we can assume that it's not give her a free shopping spree to the mall! I would say that anything Vlad is wrapped up in is probably hazardous to her health. And you know that," I say, "or you wouldn't be sitting on the sidelines. You don't want to be a part of finding her, but you're fine with reaping the benefits if it does happen."

And then James is standing, only I don't see him stand. One second he is looking up at me from my chair and the next he is across the room, staring at me angrily.

"Since when do you even care about your classmates, Sophie?" he says. "Today I saw you sell out the only friend you seem to have. And for what? A stupid journalism project?"

"Hey," I say. "I feel really bad about that. And in a non-psycho universe, it wouldn't have led to her ending up in the woods with a pack of hungry vampires."

"But it did."

"Fine. I'll haul myself up on the stage and let people throw stones at me on Monday." I lower my voice, hoping to go down a path that's more persuasive than accusatory. "But you know there's danger and you're letting someone stay in its path. In fact, you're hoping that the danger catches them."

"So what do you want me to do? Just stay like this?"

I wait for the echoes of his question to die away. "You chose it," I say, wincing at how harsh it sounds.

"It was a mistake! And, okay, I watched a lot of Psy-chic Network back when I couldn't sleep after my parents died, but maybe there's a reason that Vlad thinks he's going to find her here. Maybe it's a chance to start over. Maybe—"

"Are you listening to yourself?" I ask, and then try to be more diplomatic. "I'm sorry that you are upset, but your mistake isn't something someone else should have to pay for."

"You can stop," he bites out. "I get it."

The curt reply gives me pause. After a few moments of tense silence, I say, "So you'll help?"

"Help you get in Vlad's way? No."

"Then I guess you should go," I tell him, trying to make my voice firm where my resolve is not.

This time he doesn't protest. He looks out the window, and at this moment, I would give anything to have his mind-reading powers. But since I don't, I cross the room, open my bedroom door, and peer down the short hallway to the stairs.

"You'll want to be extra quiet by my parents' room—Marcie's a light sleeper," I say. "But once you reach

Caroline's, you're good. She could sleep through a monster truck rally," I whisper, but when I turn back to check that he's heard, the room is empty and the window is open. James is gone.

Chapter Ten

Saturday morning breakfast is a dismal affair; Caroline is still sniffling over Vlad and complaining that her pancakes are bubbly, I hardly slept for thinking about my conversation with James, and my father is upset that he can't find this morning's paper.

"I don't know who took it," Marcie said.

"Vampires," I mutter as I smoosh a piece of pancake deeper into the syrup. From here on out, that's my go-to theory for everything. Marcie gives me a strange look before announcing that she has good news.

"You found it?" my father asks.

"No, Fred," she says patiently, "I did not find it while

sitting stationary in my chair. I was talking about how we have new neighbors!"

I drop my fork. "What? No we don't."

"Yes, we do," she insists.

"Who are they?" my father asks, having resigned himself to eating his breakfast sans paper.

"Well, I don't know that part yet," Marcie admits. "No one answers when I knock. But I left a cake and a card on the porch last night, and this morning when I was jogging I noticed that it was gone."

I can't believe James was duped by a cake, especially since he can't even eat it. But I guess I shouldn't be surprised—there are a lot of things I can't believe about James as of late. Still, that doesn't mean I should sic Marcie on him and let her get caught up in this too.

"That could mean anything. Maybe raccoons took it," I suggest and then want to do a forehead smack. Discovering vampires has really thrown a wrench in my concept of reality if my first theory is cake-stealing raccoons.

"The dish was gone."

"Or thieves?" I try again. "Dad's paper is missing too," I say, grateful for my father's commiserating nod.

Marcie doesn't say anything else, but she's still emanating a faint glow that I recognize all too well as investigative pride. It's only a matter of time before she lays another booby-casserole.

After breakfast I try to call Lindsay's cell, but there's no answer. I try again after lunch, and three more times after eating dinner. Finally, on Sunday morning I call her house. Her younger brother picks up. He sounds about nine.

"Can I speak with Lindsay?" I ask, and then listen to his thunderous footsteps as he runs to find her. He returns a few seconds later, breathless.

"She says to tell you that she doesn't want to talk to you. Not now, not ever. That is a quote."

Even though it's what I expected, I'm still disappointed. "But she's okay?" I ask. "No one's visited the house?"

"Robert came over."

"But no one else?" I prod.

"Um . . . no?" he says, starting to sound a little nervous. "I have to go now. I'm not really supposed to answer the phone."

"Wait! Can you tell her I'm—"

He hangs up. Defeated, I return to my desk, where I've been staring at a blank page for the last three hours. It's difficult to write perky, upbeat articles about the new students when you keep wanting to end sentences about their hobbies with "P.S. He's a vampire." Even though the profiles are light-years away from what they should be, I finally give up and print them out, thinking how funny it is that a week ago I would have been up until three A.M. debating whether to use "of" or "for." But now I need to make sure that what almost happened in the woods on Friday never has a chance to happen again.

Pulling out my yearbook, I set to circling possibilities. Considering how quickly Vlad targeted Caroline, I decide to start with girls who are similar to her—in other words, popular upperclassmen who have lived here their entire lives. When I've got a list of about twenty, I plot how best to find out if they have any starry birthmarks. Most of them seem to be involved in either cheerleading or athletics, which is promising, but lurking next to the locker rooms without a reason will not win me any awards for subtlety. I need a cover.

Idly, I flip through the team photos in the hopes that it

might inspire me. A tiny "© Mark Echolls" can be found beneath the majority of them, and Mark himself even pops up in a few, his bespectacled face shining. I suspect this is less from endorphins and more because he's surrounded by fourteen tall, vibrant-looking girls. A senior now, Mark has been covering girls' sports since I started. Mr. Amado tried to take him off of it once, and he almost cried.

But this is a matter of life and death—if I can convince Mr. Amado to let us switch up the assignments, writing up the sports articles would be a perfect reason to be in the gym. Not to mention that it would show a lot of organizational initiative and "thinking big," something that puts Mr. Amado over the moon. He still raves about how last year's editor in chief took it upon herself to restructure the way we route articles for copyediting. This could be my way of staying in the game. Two goals, one stone. Bingo.

I am on a roll. Now all I need to figure out is exactly what the Danae will want to do with this girl once they find her. Much as I hate to admit it, I think I've burned the few vampire bridges that I had. Violet's unlikely to talk to me ever again, and James . . .

My eyes wander to his window, which is dark as usual.

What does he do over there all day, anyway? Knit with the blind? I yank the shade down so hard that it bangs against the window. I need to focus. Why is it when you need a few prophetic dreams or a creepy librarian with a book called *Vampyre*, they're nowhere to be found? Instead I've got a tattoo, a name, and sixteen years of conflicting pop culture, which is no help at all . . . or is it? James seems to be a walking grab bag of popular vampire mythology. Since I don't have any better options, I brainstorm what else pop culture has taught me about vampires.

- Vampires could really use a sharp push out of the nineteenth century.
- Half-breed vampires often find themselves compelled to fight crime.
- Someone should study the correlation between broodiness and vampirism.
- Vampires love cliques, they just call them covens.
- No one ever expects a vampire baby.

As I write the last one, something niggles at the back of my mind. My sophomore-year English class was taught by a woman with horrible time management skills, which meant we spent approximately twelve weeks of the first semester on Greek mythology and two weeks on the entire works of Shakespeare. I Google "Danae" and am rewarded with confirmation that in Greek mythology, Danae was the mother of Perseus, one bona fide miracle baby. It's not a lot, but at least it's one working theory. And hey—Vlad may have the strength, the knowledge, and the high levels of insanity, but I have Wikipedia.

The next morning I oversleep, ruining any chances I might have had of hitting Mr. Amado with my proposition before the bell. By the time I make it to Mr. Baer's pre-calculus class, he's already so lost in Mathmagic Land that he barely turns to take my permission slip. Afraid that he might mistake my proximity as a desire to answer a problem, I scuttle to my seat in the back just in time to continue a worksheet conga line. After selecting one for myself, I hold it over my shoulder for the last guy to take. Nothing. I shake them. Still nothing. Intending to give the delinquent paper-taker behind me a lecture, I turn around only to come face-to-face with James's smug smile.

"Nice of you to show up," he mouths.

I drop the stack of papers on his desk, pleased to hear a soft curse and the rustle of frantic gathering behind me. After a few moments, he taps my shoulder.

"What are you even doing in here?" I ask over my shoulder, disturbed by how happy I was to see him in the split second before I remembered his end goal. "This is a junior class. 'Special' or not, you're a senior."

The squeak of his chair warns me that he's moving closer, but I still don't expect his low voice whispering in my ear. "The power of persuasion occasionally has its perks," he says. "I have your whole schedule. So what do you think we'll be doing in art class?"

More fun with pinecones, probably, which serves him right. "So this is your plan?" I ask, twisting around. "Stalk me until I find her and then pounce?"

James looks annoyed. "I'm here because I told Vlad I would be," he says, leaning forward. "Remember?"

A flash of guilt clouds the anger. I do remember—no matter how annoying he's being, he did stop Vlad from killing us in the woods.

"And have you ever thought that I might want to keep an eye on you as you try to smash Vlad's hopes and dreams?" he continues. "You know, for protection?"

"That was a one-time thing," I insist.

"Sure it was."

The skepticism in his voice makes my blood begin to boil. "Okay, Saint James, are you still planning on making an after-dinner drink out of whoever we find?" I ask, and when he doesn't answer, add a prim, "That's what I thought," before turning to fake attention in the equations Mr. Baer is scribbling on the board. The chair behind me squeaks again.

"Have it your way," he whispers in my ear, "but just so you know, don't expect to go anywhere without me following until this is settled."

Oh, really. I raise my hand, and keep it raised until I catch Mr. Baer's attention in one of his checks to see if we're listening. He looks surprised.

"Miss . . . McGee?" he tries.

"Can I please go to the nurse?" I ask sweetly. "I'm not feeling well. I thought I could make it, but I think I might vomit if I have to sit here for one more second."

Mr. Baer is overcome by a wave of teacherly indecision; since we've only had a week of class, I'm an unknown quantity. After a long pause, he finds the pad of pink passes among the stacks on his desk, scribbles something down, and puts it on my desk. "Do page eighty-three for Wednesday and feel better," he says and then turns back to the board.

I scoop up my books just as James raises his hand and speaks without waiting to be called on. "Mr. Baer, I'm not feeling well either," he says.

"Then put your head between your knees and wait for the feeling to go away," Mr. Baer says without turning around, obviously hip to the error of giving out two hall passes.

"But Mr. Baer," James tries again in a more coaxing voice. "If you just look at me—"

"No. You can go when Miss McGee gets back."

With an exultant look at James, I walk out, head held high and heart full of the delight that comes from seeing mister almighty vampire humbled by hallway rules. That delight stays with me until I realize that the last thing I want to do is go to see the nurse. The library is off-limits without a special pass, and sitting in the hallway will leave me exposed to any wandering teacher.

I set off for the band hallway, deciding to check on the Lindsay situation. If she's playing clarinet at eight in the morning, I'll know that she's at least in the recovery stage. Just as I'm turning the last corner, however, Ms. Kate's squat form waddles into view. I duck into the nearest bathroom; it smells of pink soap and cheap paper towels, but thankfully seems to be empty.

I hop up onto the side radiator; might as well get some work done. I've just started paging through my yearbook when a choked sob swells up from the last stall, followed by the sound of furious scratching. If it didn't mean falling into the clutches of Ms. Kate, my first instinct would be to flee. Caught, I try to ignore the escalating sounds of a meltdown, but when I hear the violent *thunk*s of something striking porcelain, I can't help it any longer. Padding down the aisle, I knock gently on the stall's mottled green door.

"Are you okay? Do you need anything?" I ask. "A tissue, a wet paper towel . . ." I trail off, looking around the restroom for anything else that might be useful. A used piece of gum? The butt of a cigarette? Half of a sticker that says "Kitten Diva," whatever that means?

"Just leave me alone," a muffled voice orders between

sobs. After a few moments the scraping sound resumes.

"Are you sure?" I ask. "It sounds like you're trying to flush yourself down the toilet."

The door flies open, barely giving me enough time to avoid a sharp whack to the nose. Marisabel is crouching on the checkered tile, clutching a pair of scissors like they are the Holy Grail.

I can imagine the expressions that flicker across my face; there's the "Crap, she is a vampire," followed by "Crap, I am not supposed to know she is a vampire," followed by "Crap, I think she just realized that I still know she is a vampire." Even if she couldn't mind read, I'd be totally screwed. Marisabel raises a hand, and I flinch instinctively, expecting it to go for the tasty parts of my heart. Instead, she waves it dismissively.

"Oh, stop," she says, and then for the benefit of my baffled look, adds, "I don't care if you know, and I'm not going to tell Vlad. I hope his idiotic plan fails." She turns back to the stall wall and resumes her work, a sprinkling of green paint chips falling around her feet. She's done a decent job of scoring the graffiti away, but I can still see a few "Vlad + Whatever Girl with Bad Taste Was Here Last" rambling across the wall. Attacking one beneath the toilet paper roll, she rakes the scissors across the door so furiously that she bangs her elbow against the toilet seat.

"How do they even manage to write down here?" she huffs.

"Girls can get very bendy when they are in love," I say, and know immediately that it was the wrong thing when Marisabel stops scraping, distraught.

"You think they're in love with him? I'm in love," she cries before resuming her destruction of property with even greater fervor. "Have they been with him for fifty years?" she asks, now shouting to make up for all the scraping noises she's making. "No! Have they hunted down rotten little squirrels when he asked, even though he knows that they have a fear of rodents? No! Did they change their name from 'Mary' to 'Marisabel' because he thought that it would be more 'vampire'? No!" she yells one last time, stabbing the scissors into the wall so deeply that they hang there, quivering. After a few moments, she smoothes her hair and tugs them from the wall. "Forget that you saw that," she says far too calmly.

Time to take my chances with Ms. Kate. "Well, you seem to be doing better," I say, "so I'm going to—"

"Wait!" she yells. "Do you think that we're good to-gether?"

"Who? You and Vlad?"

"No, you and me," she says, straight-faced, but then rolls her eyes. "Yes, me and Vlad."

Vampires should not be allowed to make jokes. "I really don't think that I'm qualified to say."

Marisabel's eyes narrow. "Try."

"I think that you may have grown apart over the years."

Marisabel nods gravely. For the first time since I met her, she's wearing pants, a pair of vintage jeans that are artfully worn at the knees. In spite of everything I know, she looks innocent, the girl-next-door who chose the wrong door to get next to. Biting her lip, she turns her head to stare once again at her work of calculated destruction and then traces the sharp peak of an en-graved "V."

"Vlad was not always like this," she says wistfully. "When we first met, he was so charming."

I find it difficult to believe that Vlad has ever been charming, but Marisabel looks at me expectantly, and I realize that I am being held hostage until I give up some good girl talk.

"Well," I offer, "people can change a lot in . . . what? Fifty years?"

"Give or take a few," she replies. "The first year was nice. He was willing to risk a trip to Greece then. We couldn't sit on any beaches, but I've never found anywhere else where the night air is so warm and delicious. We made a vampire there. We made him together." Marisabel frowns. "But then Vlad got mad and set him on fire."

I really hope this bonding session doesn't end with an invitation to look at scrapbooks. "Sounds . . . romantic," I say, trying not to heave.

"It was! But then he started sneaking away every few months for 'research purposes.' I thought finding the girl was just a hobby, but then it became an obsession. I don't understand why he couldn't just be happy with what he had. When he came back, he was always in a terrible mood, muttering about dead ends and unhelpful records. And then there were the headaches. I've told him not to use his powers so often, especially when we have limited food resources."

I've been holding my breath throughout this entire speech; I hadn't even thought of Marisabel as a source of information. Hopping up on the side radiator, I try to strike a pose that will help my casual probing look more casual; it involves a lot of leaning and resting things on my knees.

"It's not fair that he's brought you here to look for another girl," I say. "You're his girlfriend."

She blinks at me for a few seconds before lighting up in delight to finally have someone's sympathy. "I know! I think that I've been very understanding."

"Totally," I agree. "What's so great about her anyway? Is she, like, some miracle child?"

"Supposedly," she says with disdain, while I struggle to keep my delight in check at having called it. "She's said to be the great-great-great-great-great-granddaughter of some dumb baby of some musty vampire family named Mervaux."

"Let me guess. A half-vampire baby?" I ask, leaving off the ". . . who fights crime."

"No!" Marisabel says. "A plain old human baby. That's what makes the whole thing so weird. Who cares about a human baby? People have those all the time."

She pauses. "Well, I mean, not vampires. They never have any babies, which is good because child vampires are *freaky*." Suddenly, her face turns severe. "You're not going to tell anyone this, right?"

"Oh, no way," I say quickly, shaking my head. I want to ask more questions about the connection between this child of the Mervaux vampire family and the Danae, but Marisabel's burst of sharing starts to fizzle.

"I mean, I try so hard to be enough," she sniffs. "But he's never happy. I'm starting to think that even if he finds her, that's only the beginning. I would just like for this to be over. If Vlad could just see that this wasn't going to work out, if he could just see that it's not going to be so easy, then maybe he would give up." She sniffs again. "Maybe you could keep getting in his way."

I can hardly believe my luck—here's the perfect source of information, and it's offering to crawl into my lap. But there's something fragile in Marisabel's voice that keeps me from pouncing.

"Is Vlad really worth this?" I ask. "He's kind of mean to you. Do you—"

I'm interrupted by the click of heels on tile. There's no way that staccato terror belongs to a student. My eyes roam over the utter ruin of the bathroom stall; the last thing I need right now is a charge of petty vandalism. Holding a finger to my lips and motioning for Marisabel to climb up on the toilet, I push the door shut just as Ms. Kate rounds the corner. Clutching my stomach, I do my best to imitate a victim of cafeteria food poisoning.

"I thought I heard something in here," Ms. Kate snaps as she approaches me. "Hall pass?" When I hand it over, she barely even looks at it; years of practice have made her able to distinguish types of hall passes through the power of touch alone. "This is for the nurse," she says. "You are in the bathroom. What is wrong with this picture?"

Apologizing, I tip forward like I'm about to hurl on her ugly black pumps. "I thought I was going to be sick." I cast a queasy look at the door behind me. "Don't go in there."

I don't know if she believes me, but her expression of slight disgust tells me that she's thankfully not willing to investigate. "Let's go to the nurse, then," she says, walking me out the door and through the halls. She makes no move to leave me alone, not even when we hit the labyrinthine hallway that leads to a cluster of guidance counselors, speech therapy rooms, and the dreaded nurse's office. If you're truly sick, you can't expect to receive much more than generic aspirin and an embarrassing pamphlet about your growing body.

We find Nurse Ellis alone and shaking her head at a copy of *Us Weekly*. After Ms. Kate stomps off to catch more students unawares, Nurse Ellis spins toward me on her stool, a trusty stethoscope looped around her neck. Her light-brown hair is dusted with gray, and she has a round face and equally round body.

"Not feeling well, Sophie?" she asks, genuinely concerned. "You do look flushed."

Thank God for pale skin and wimpy blood vessels. "I feel nauseous and light-headed," I croak.

"Well, why don't you lie down on one of the cots and give it some time? If you still feel bad in a little while, we'll see if we can reach your parents."

A fabulous idea. I lie down on the nearest cot and draw the hanging curtain around me. This should help me avoid Vlad, as well as keep me out of James's way for a while. Researching with him on my tail is going to take a lot more cunning than being the first person to

—194—

ask for a hall pass. Who knows the next time when I'll have a moment alone?

I sit up. I'm alone now, and who better acquainted with the student body's bodies than the school nurse? The metallic curtain rasps as I push it back.

"You don't happen to know of any girls who have a strange and unusual birthmark, do you? Like a star?" As soon as I say it, I realize what a weirdo question it is. Oh well—no guts, no glory. Although one could also argue that "No guts, no extreme social embarrassment" is just as accurate a statement. "Like on their backs or their legs or their shoulders, maybe?" I add.

To her credit, Nurse Ellis says nothing, just squints at me for a pregnant moment before wheeling herself over to a wall that's close to buckling from the weight of multicolored pamphlets. She plucks out a dark yellow one and hands it to me. "Is What I'm Feeling Normal?" the bold headline asks. Boy and girl stick figures hold up their hands in "Why me?" gestures, their heads surrounded by a cloud of question marks.

"Read this, Sophie. Then let me know if you have any questions," she says, passing it over and giving me a gentle pat on the hand before closing the curtain.

I flop back on the cot. This is off to a great start.

When Nurse Ellis asks me how I'm feeling an hour later, smiling as though we now share a great secret, I tell her that I'm ready to go back to class. Chemistry is in full swing by the time I hand my pass over to Mr. George, and surprisingly, there's no James. This should be a relief. Why am I now consumed with curiosity over where he's run off to? Maybe he was bluffing.

Hopping up on my stool, I open my chemistry book and prepare to do more research under the cover of balancing equations. Because of an unfortunate incident involving mixed chemicals and Greg Ives's knee, I have no lab partner. I'm busy spreading out my things when a figure walks past me to Mr. George's desk. I watch James's back as he introduces himself to the teacher, who pulls out his seating chart.

"Okay, then, Mr. Hallowell. Why don't you have a seat by . . . ," he starts, but then frowns at the paper in front of him, scans the room, and then frowns again. "Well, it looks like you'll have to sit by Miss McGee."

Unbelievable. When James turns around, I prepare to withstand a cocky grin, but his energy level seems to have taken a nosedive since last period. His face looks drawn and tired, his skin stretched and tight. Math class is no fun, but I've never seen it take this much out of a person.

"Having trouble keeping up?" I whisper when he slides onto the stool beside me.

"I had something to take care of," he says tightly. "Since we're not sharing anymore, I won't tell you what it is."

I'm about to retort that I'm not interested anyway and warn him to guard his knees, but then I see that his fingers are shaking as they open the cover of his textbook.

"James, what's wrong?" I ask, my annoyance taking a backseat to sudden worry.

"Nothing."

In my experience "nothing" doesn't make you seem like you're about to keel over at your desk. But James ignores my worried looks, studying the periodic table like he's Marie Curie.

"I'll see you after lunch," he says as soon as the bell rings and then leaves before I can respond.

Chapter Eleven

James doesn't come back after lunch, and he's still MIA when the final bell rings. On my way to my locker, I poke my head into the journalism room only to find that Mr. Amado is missing too, although his perpetually wrinkled jacket and messenger bag are still hanging from a cabinet hook. I wait for a few moments, but when he doesn't show up, I take a casual peek at his planner. Staff meeting: 3:30. Nuts.

Since I have time to kill—and since, so far, Vlad has left me alone—I decide that French club can be approached with caution. Still, knowing his habit of roaming the halls, I tape a few pieces of paper over the narrow window as soon as I close the door.

"Hello, Sophie," says a high, dulcet voice.

Oh crap. Violet. Violet the fluent French speaker and newest member of our miniscule language club. I'm starting to lose track of all the people I need to avoid. When I work up the courage to turn around, she's smiling at me serenely, her hands folded primly in front of her, always the lady, even when plotting my demise. Regina Michaels and Calvin Abrams flank her on either side. Luckily, they seem oblivious to any tension as they argue about the sex of various fruits. I've come to learn that arguing about French is how they flirt. The *imparfait* debate is third base.

"Are we going to do drugs?" Calvin asks nervously when he notices my makeshift window coverings. "Because I am president of the 'Just Say No' Club, and we had to sign something saying we would never—"

"Don't worry about it, Calvin. I left my stash at home," I say, trying to play it cool but still keeping my eye on Violet. At this point, I'm not sure how much I am supposed to know around her. She wasn't there for the forest debacle, but Vlad has surely talked . . . unless he doesn't want them to know about the "misunderstanding." Her cat-with-canary face isn't helping me decide.

"*Je suis désolé,*" Regina pipes up, "*mais je ne comprends pas l'anglais.*"

I'm sorry, but I do not understand English. Technically, the rule is that we don't speak any English once the meeting has begun. I made that rule up. I hate myself.

"*J'ai dit,*" I begin, repeating my earlier joke to Calvin, "*N'inquiète pas, Monsieur Calvin. J'ai laissé mon 'stash' à la maison.*"

"'Stash' is '*un cache,*'" Violet corrects, and then pats the seat beside her. Deciding that the current threat to my safety is at least limiting her attacks to my foreign language skills, I slip into the seat.

We chat for thirty minutes about simple things: winter socks, our favorite type of pie, and Calvin's fear of ladybugs and getting stuck in a ticket turnstile. He and Regina soon launch into an argument about the difference between a *croque-monsieur* and a *croque-madame.* Violet takes the opportunity to wiggle her desk closer to mine, a noisy, thumping endeavor that should be as intimidating as being rushed by a blind, three-legged dog. Should be. It makes me nervous enough to check the exits again before she leans over and whispers in my ear.

"*N'inquiète pas,* Sophie. *J'ai trouvé un nouveau petit copain. Donc, nous sommes encore amies, non?*" she says and smiles warmly, if a little too widely.

Don't worry, Sophie. I found a new boyfriend. So we are friends again, right?

Well, that was fast. The rush of my relief is quickly replaced by a new worry: If history has taught us anything, it's that falling into Violet's lovesick clutches means that there will soon be another teenage vampire running around my high school.

"Who?" I ask, dropping any pretense at French.

She holds a finger to the tiny bow of her lips. "*C'est une secrete,*" she says with a coy raise of her eyebrows. It's a secret.

Before I can start digging for more information, there's a rap at the door, and Mr. Hanfield, Spanish teacher and study hall minion, sticks his bald head in to tell us that we need to clear out.

"Who taped this up here?" he asks as he rips it down. "You know we have to have a clear view into all class-rooms at all times."

I'm fairly sure he just made up this rule, but I don't

argue. We agree to meet again next week and part ways. Or at least I try to part ways; while Calvin and Regina argue in the opposite direction, Violet glues herself to my side, chattering on about an article on getting over a bad breakup that she read ("Supremely helpful, even if I couldn't partake of the sugar-free ice cream.") and how she thinks Calvin is a little strange. Her still unnamed new boy is strange, she admits, but not that strange. At least he's not afraid of inanimate objects.

"And I do believe he really likes me," she says as we round the last corner before the main lobby. "I mean, men are always difficult to fathom. One moment they want to run away and elope, and the next they leave you sitting alone on a park bench in the middle of the night, ruined and with no place to go."

I look at Violet, wondering if this was pre- or post-vampire. She is studying her shoes, a small frown playing about her lips. In that second, I want to say something comforting, but I don't know whether or not that will invite too many questions about what I do and do not know. So instead I just pull her to the side so she doesn't walk into a cement column.

"I did not see that at all," she says, and I'm happy to

hear some of the old perkiness. "To continue what we were speaking about before, I gave James what he wanted too soon. I know that now," she says. "But it does not matter; the periodical says 'Sisters before Misters' and I have decided to adhere to that."

Not only do I want to find her magazine source, kill it, and skip around on its grave, I want her to understand that James is not my mister in any sense of the word.

"Violet, James is not—," I begin before the sight of what's waiting for me at the end of the hallway stops me in my tracks. "You've got to be kidding me."

There is a vampire roadblock at the end of the hallway and everyone's invited. Vlad, Devon, Ashley, Marisabel, Neville . . . and James. James is waiting for me. With them.

I duck into the nearest open door, which happens to be Mrs. Elton's government class. She coats her walls with American flags and badly printed photos of the current president. I'm so dazzled by the red, white, and blue that I don't realize Violet has trotted after me until it is too late. *That's great, Sophie, bring a vampire with you to your hiding place from the vampires.*

"What is this about?" Violet asks, tugging her jacket down schoolmarmishly. "I understand why I don't want to see James, but you should try not to be so standoffish. It will give him the wrong idea." She smiles at me, and I realize that she really doesn't know anything about what happened on Friday—Vlad's keeping his setbacks close to his chest. But before I can answer, her gaze shifts to something beyond my shoulder. "Oh, hello," she says. "Are you crouching here like a deranged person as well?"

Caroline is slouched in the back corner, and from the looks of things, she's been camped out for a while. Her feet are bare, having kicked the strappy sandals she tottered around on all day to the side. She rarely puts her hair up—she thinks it's lazy—but now she's scraped it into a mushrooming bun.

"He won't go away," she says, sliding down in her chair until all I can see is the fluff of her bun. "And the evil janitors locked the side doors. I mean, hello. Fire hazard."

"Who won't go away?"

Straightening back up, she gives me a look suggesting that I could win this year's Miss Idiotic pageant by a landslide vote. "Vlad. I have been sitting here since three waiting for him to leave. Why? Why does he want to humiliate me? Isn't breaking up with me enough?" She bangs her fists on the desk. "He's a satanist!"

She probably means "sadist," although for once, option number two isn't all that wide of the mark. Still, I doubt that Caroline's his target. I'm guessing that Vlad wants to make sure I've forgotten his fangy little secret. But considering my audience, I scan my mind for some excuse as to why Vlad would be loitering for an hour and a half. He's hypnotized by shiny wrestling trophies? He is conducting a sit-in to protest the ban on pointy shoes? Violet moves to console Caroline before I can even try.

"It's horrible, isn't it?" she soothes. "I'm going through a broken engagement myself at the moment. If you would like, I have a magazine article that might help."

Caroline perks up. "Really?"

"Yes. Sophie doesn't seem to put much faith in what they have to say, but I think they are a wonder."

"Sophie doesn't put much faith in anything but her own loud voice."

"Yes, she can be very resistant to new ideas, I think."

It's time to nip this conversation in the bud. "I hate to break up your bonding session, but I would like to leave the building at some point. And Vlad's still here."

"But why are you hiding from Vlad?" Caroline asks. Oops.

"Sisterly solidarity?" I try.

Caroline blinks at me a few times and then launches in for a hug, nearly knocking the small desk over in her enthusiasm. "Oh, that's so sweet. Thank you."

I hug her back, feeling nice and fuzzy and like a good sister for once. There's no reason I can't be avoiding Vlad for sisterly solidarity *and* the overwhelming desire to live, is there? When I am finally released from her body-lotioned death grip, the three of us peek around the corner to find Vlad and Neville in the middle of yet another debate.

"But *High School Musical*?" Vlad says. "It's not even something civilized."

Neville crosses his arms tightly over his chest. "You said that we should join in school activities."

"Join in activities so we can find the girl. Not so you can twist and twirl about on the stage for your own amusement!"

Beside me, Violet emits a tiny snort. "Vlad can be so overbearing at times," she whispers in my ear. "And he lies; he told me that this place would be filled with eligible young gentlemen."

"Really?" I whisper.

"He told us all sorts of things to lure us along."

"Lying poophead scumbag," Caroline says. "Anyway, how do we get out when their stupid butts are blocking the door?"

"Why, we will have to walk our stupid butts out the door!" Violet cries, clearly getting into this. After we shush her, she tries again more quietly. "What I meant to say was we will need to act like their presence does not bother us. For example, I will act like I do not even notice the presence of James. You do the same with Vlad. Believe me, it has worked for hundreds of years." She looks at me. "You do whatever you think sisters of the brokenhearted do."

This sister of the brokenhearted is trying to remember exactly what James told her three nights ago and marshaling all the puny acting talent she possesses. Now's the time for my first-grade experience as Silent Woodland Animal #3 in *Snow White* to really pay off.

Try not to let him get close to you. Concentrate if he does.

I take a deep breath. "Ready?"

Violet and Caroline nod furiously, but our first attempt is stalled by Caroline's hand on my shoulder.

"Wait. Is that James Hallowell?" she asks.

"Yep. He's living next door again," I say, still stinging from his betrayal. But instead of making me feel better, revealing James's secret only makes me feel petty. "Don't tell anyone."

"Why?" she asks. "Oh man, Amanda said that Danny said he was back, but I thought that she had just finally lost it. He got cute," she says, and I don't like the undercurrent of "oooh, gimme" in her voice.

"Just . . . please, Caroline?"

She shrugs. "Sure, whatever."

How reassuring. "Are you ready?"

"Yes," Caroline says. "Wait! I mean no. My shoes. This is not something I want to do barefoot."

We wait for Caroline to shoe up for battle, and then walk out the door, marching toward the vampires. James snaps to attention as we approach. Vlad and Neville are still knee-deep in their argument, with Neville explaining the plot of *High School Musical* and Vlad countering that he may not be exceedingly familiar with this world, but he is certain that basketball players do not sing. Hope balloons in my chest; maybe they won't even notice me. We are swerving around the edges of their huddle when Vlad's voice rings out.

"If it isn't the girl I want to see," he says, his hand snaking out to block my way.

"Excuse me?" I say, trying to act confused as I back away. I try to remember James's lessons on how to keep one's mind impenetrable, but it's harder said than done. I think of how much I hate him, how much I want him out of this school, this town, this universe. But how do you tell if it's working? Other than the fact that he hasn't yelled "Gotcha!"

Vlad steps forward, eating up my hard-won buffer of space. He starts to reach for my chin, and a chill of panic rushes over my body. But before he can touch me, Caroline pushes Vlad away with an unladylike grunt.

"What's wrong with you?" she asks as I take the opportunity to step away. "You're acting like you've never met."

"We have not," Vlad says, obviously annoyed. He scowls at me over his head.

She turns around, looking for a denial, but I force myself to nod and agree. She frowns for a few seconds, giving me a look that says she thought I was on her side. Finally, she says, "You're both crazy," and marches toward the door.

We listen to her heels as they click across the lobby's floor, and I try to gauge everyone's suspicion level. Neville is still pouting, while Vlad watches Caroline's back with a moody scowl. Marisabel stands beside him, trying so hard to look innocent that she might as well stick her head up in the air and whistle, and Violet continues to study the five food groups display so James will see that she has moved on to better things, apparently fruits and vegetables. Against my better instincts, I sneak a glance in his direction and am met with a small smile that does nothing to mask the worry in his eyes.

"Wait a moment," Vlad says, and I whip my head around to find him watching me. I feel the fluttery, zooming sensation in my heart that means I'm starting to panic. And when I start to panic, my mind goes blank. The more I try to train my thoughts into one orderly progression, the more they want to scream "Vampire, vampire, vampire!" James steps forward, worry on his face, and it heightens my panic. If he can tell, anyone can tell.

As if on cue, Vlad's countenance darkens. I prepare for the worst. This is it. This is the end. But Vlad doesn't reach for my throat—instead he pulls away, disappointed. It takes a few seconds to realize that it's not because James has betrayed him; no, it's because he has no excuse to kill me. I've passed. Somehow, I've passed.

"Maybe I'll see you around," I say, giddy with good luck, and head toward the door, half expecting to be tackled from behind. Soon enough, however, the *High School Musical* argument starts up again. Talking to Mr. Amado can wait until tomorrow. Right now I need to get out of here and go where I can be sure my thoughts are completely my own.

I'm almost to the door when James catches up with me. A part of me wants to yell at him, but his relief at not being found out is plain, and for a moment, that's something we share. If I'm being honest, the temptation to put everything on hold and celebrate is overwhelming, especially when I note that he seems to have recovered from whatever was ailing him.

"Are you feeling better?" I ask, just as a figure appears at the other side of the lobby. It's Lindsay, the girl I almost let become the prime entrée of a vampire buffet. Now she's heading toward us with a determined stride, her hands hidden by the stack of papers clutched to her chest. Plea for forgiveness number one is on my tongue when she bypasses me for James.

"Thanks again for finding me today," she tells him with no hint of ill will. "The articles are due to our journalism teacher tomorrow, so my head was about to, you know, spin around and pop off."

"No problem," he murmurs.

"It's so great that you're going to join our class," she continues. "Maybe we can work on something together."

"Sure," he says, but his eyes are on me.

Lindsay follows his gaze, and I brace myself for another well-deserved telling off. But all she does is apologize for ignoring me and ask if I've given any more thought to joining the collection drive for Greenpeace. "I think we could really use you," she says. "Final sign-ups for the planning committee were on Friday, but, well, this whole weekend is kind of a blur." She frowns. "I think I need to stop pulling all-nighters."

It's like our almost death never happened. I look at

James for an explanation and find one in his guilty expression. So that's why he was late to chemistry, and that's why he looked so tired. He may not have mindwiped me, but he had no problem doing it to someone else.

Lindsay picks up on the tension immediately. "Okay, then. I'm, uh, just going to go. Check in with you later for Greenpeace," she says, and then bolts out the front door. I try to follow but James steps in front of me.

"I had to," he says. "I tried to explain some things to her, but she freaked out and started screaming. She's safer this way, I swear. The fuzziness wears off after a few days."

"Where were you after lunch?" I ask, even though I already know the answer.

His jaw tightens. "I had to find Vlad," he says stiffly. "It took more out of me than I expected."

"There's not going to be an extra space in the front row tomorrow, is there?" I say. It's a bad joke, mainly because I'm half serious.

James's face wrinkles in disgust. "No. Vlad has a cooler from—"

"The fair," I say quickly. "I know."

"I don't want to know how you know that. Sophie, I'm serious, this is not a stupid journalism assignment. You need to stay away from him. You're lucky he was distracted. I could hear you, and I was farther away than Vlad. You may think that you're a fortress of snark and bad-assery, but you're not."

The fact that I didn't entirely succeed in wearing my antivampire hat is not exactly comforting, but I can't let that deter me. "Not until I make sure the girl is safe," I say. "I won't just leave people in danger."

James's face hardens, and I realize that I've just destroyed any chance of a truce. He steps to the side to let me pass. When I exit into the sunlight, he doesn't follow, leaving me to wonder exactly how many reminders I need before I realize that he's not on my side.

Chapter Twelve

Mr. Amado collects our Welcome Back articles the next day. When it comes time for me to hand mine over, I experience a moment of panic. Last night I caved and looked over them again, after which I tried to do some final-hour touch-ups, but they are still hovering more toward the "suck" end of the spectrum than the "stellar."

"Thank you, Sophie?" Mr. Amado says calmly, tugging a few times when my fingers continue to clutch the end. "I'm taking them now."

Left with little other option, I let go, and he moves on to the rest of the students. I notice that Lindsay doesn't hesitate at all when it's her turn; she offers her handful of pages proudly and with a bright smile that Mr. Amado returns. Mind-wiping, and Other Keys to Better Journalism: An Exposé. Maybe I should have asked James to go ahead and wipe me as well.

I risk a peek at the back corner of the room, where James has stashed himself in the most isolated desk and is now propping his cheek up with his hand as he watches the proceedings with a bored eye. This has been his position of choice in all of my classes, with the exception of English where he finagled a seat directly between me and Vlad and sat up so straight in his seat that I couldn't even see the tippy-top of Vlad's head. We haven't exchanged a single word since yesterday's fight in the foyer, although once when he caught me looking at him, I thought I saw the ghost of a smile before he schooled his face back into impassivity.

Mr. Amado has finished his rounds. I force my attention back to the front of the room just as he sets the stack of articles on his desk and then sits on its corner. "This is great, guys," he says. "On Thursday we'll start using the computers to lay everything out—and remember, if you need to brush up on your InDesign skills, I'm holding refresher workshops after class for the rest of the week." He claps, which I've learned is his way of drumrolling. "But right now I wanted to check in and see how you are all holding up after the first assignment and brainstorm ideas for the next few issues. Remember, this is a forum and I am just the steward here to help you."

"What's a steward?" Neal asks.

Mr. Amado's mustache twitches. I also noticed during the assignment roundup that Neal turned in a handful of comics and not an article about the missing blood. That makes me happy, but it means that Mr. Amado's Neal Frustration Level is high.

"A guide, Neal," he says. "A guide."

"I want to keep covering girls' sports," Mark Echolls says before anyone else can stake claim to his territory.

"I anticipated that, Mark," Mr. Amado says. "I don't see any reason why—" He stops when he notices that I've raised my hand. "Sophie?"

I was really hoping to suggest this in a one-on-one meeting, but it looks like I'm going to have to do it now since Mr. Amado turned into a Super Sophie Evader over the weekend. "I've been thinking that maybe we should shake things up this year," I say. "I mean, Mark, you're excellent at girls' sports, but you've been doing it forever. And I've been doing the investigative stuff forever, and Emma has been doing the horoscopes forever. The paper might be fresher if we all brought a new perspective to the articles."

I stop, realizing that most of my classmates are glaring at me. Well, except for Lindsay, who is doing her best to look encouraging, and James, who's watching this with more interest than anything else that's happened today.

"Also, it will make our clip files more diverse for when we're applying for colleges and university newspapers," I finish in a rush. "We'll have so much more experience."

"That seems like a fair point," Mr. Amado says. He's trying to act casual and facilitatorish, but I can tell that he likes the idea. "What do the rest of you think?"

"But I spent all summer reading Linda Goodman's *Love Signs*," Emma says, flipping her black, curly hair over her shoulder. "That's not going to help me if I'm stuck watching the school play three thousand times."

"And I've always covered girls' sports," Mark says. "They know me."

There are some murmurings from the rest of the class. Mr. Amado is looking at me with a newfound admiration, and that gives me the needed boost to press forward. "But don't you guys want to try something new?"

"No," Mark says emphatically, pushing his glasses up his nose.

I should have waited until I caught Mr. Amado alone. He's not against getting dictatorial with individuals, but he won't support something that the class is clearly against. And if I don't have the girls' sports cover, then I have no idea how to even start looking—

"I think it's a great idea," Lindsay offers. "I mean, I cover almost all of the volunteer drives, and it's wonderful and everything, but maybe I'm missing something because I've gotten so used to it. I don't see why it would hurt us to try it for at least one or two issues."

She smiles at me, and I'm overcome by a wave of gratitude, but also guilt, considering that she was robbed of the right to be angry. It feels like I've gotten away with something that I shouldn't have.

"That's one vote for yes," Mr. Amado says, "and two votes for no." He folds his plaid arms across his chest and leans backward. "Anyone else for yes?" he asks hopefully.

The bulk of the new sophomore staff members raise their hands along with me and Lindsay, clearly wanting to get on Mr. Amado's good side right from the get-go, not to mention either one of the editor in chief hopefuls.

"That's twelve yeses," Mr. Amado says, and then blinks a little because the no's have already raised their hands. "Okay. And that's eleven no's. Did anyone not vote?" he asks and then frowns. "Neal?"

Neal looks up from his binder and rubs his cheek, leaving a smudge of dark blue ink on his chin. "What are we talking about?"

"Whether we want to switch up assignments for the next issue."

"I want to keep doing the comics. So . . . no?"

Mr. Amado sighs. "Of course. Twelve and twelve. Who's our tie-breaker?" He scans the room until he finds James, who's been doing nothing but idly rolling his pen back and forth throughout the whole thing. "What do you say, James?"

James is obviously frustrated to have been singled out. *Please say yes*, I think, even though I'm fairly sure that he's too far away to hear me. I wonder if he realizes my ulterior motives for this switch. Even if he doesn't, he might vote no just because we're on the outs. I'm still holding my breath when he looks at the ceiling.

"Yes," he says finally.

"Wonderful!" Mr. Amado says. "Why don't you guys think over what you want to handle and come talk to me when you're ready to pitch article ideas."

I'm at his desk before he's even halfway in his seat. When I tell him that I want to cover girls' sports he does a double take. "Are you sure?" he asks.

"It will be a challenge," I say, doing my best to put a Future-Journalist-of-America spin on it, "and I really want to try my hand at something new. Cross-country, soccer, and tennis all have their first official matches next week."

"We usually do a full spread for the sports pages. Can you write enough to fill that or do you need a buddy?"

"I got it," I say.

"Then it sounds good to me. Great idea, Sophie. Really," he says, and for that moment, it feels like it might just be easy to fix everything after all.

One week later, when I'm about to be hit in the nose by a flying soccer ball, I realize that feeling was premature. "Watch out!" someone yells, and even though I duck soon enough to avoid being beaned, I drop my pen beneath the bleachers in the process. Seeing that the game is paused due to some infraction (note: find out what sort of penalties there are in soccer), I jump off the side and crawl beneath the risers, kicking aside stray cups and candy bar wrappers until I finally find it plopped in the center of a cheesy leftover nacho tray. By the time I've successfully de-cheesed it and made it back to my spot, the entire Thomas Jefferson girls' soccer team is hugging one another and jumping up and down. I have a sneaking suspicion I've missed something important.

Sure enough, one of Caroline's friends breaks away from the pack and jogs over, her blond ponytail swinging.

"Did you see it?" she asks, half out of breath.

"See what?"

"Um, my penalty kick. My game-winning penalty kick."

"Oh, right. You kicked the ball and it went in that net," I say, pointing to the goal at the far right end of the field.

"No," she says, pointing in the other direction, "it went in *that* goal. Where's Mark? He always covers our games."

Mark is probably in an underground lair sticking pins in a Sophie voodoo doll, but I lie and say that he really wanted to cover the fall play this year. "Apparently he's a big *High School Musical* fan," I add, feeling the jab of another imaginary pin.

"Fine, whatever," she says. "Just make sure that you list my name as 'Marta' and not 'Martha.' He always gets that wrong."

"Noted," I say, expecting her to run back to her teammates, but she continues to stand there. Thinking I'm supposed to offer some encouragement, I add, "Really great game by the way. You kicked the ball really far. Like, I didn't think it could go that far, but then it did."

"Thanks," she says dryly. "Aren't you going to interview me?"

"Oh, right. I was going to interview you all in the locker room."

"Like when we're getting dressed?"

"Yeah. I thought it would make for a better article that way," I say. "You know, smell the sweat; feel the camaraderie. That sort of thing."

She looks at me like I just said I wanted us all to hold hands and then play spin the bottle.

"Come on," I say, trying for peppy obliviousness as I stand up and nudge her toward the locker room. "We can get started on the way."

I ask Marta questions for as long as it takes to confirm that she's not bearing any star birthmark, and then move on to the rest of the team as they trickle in to wrestle out of sports bras and wiggle into skinny jeans. After I exhaust my soccer questions, I recycle the icebreakers from the new-student profile. Finally, one of the sophomores slams her locker shut with a clang.

"I mean, my favorite color's burnt orange, but seriously—what does any of this have to do with the game?"

The rest of the girls murmur in agreement and start

to brush past me, some of them picking up their remaining clothes and walking out in their soccer uniforms. When the room is empty, I close my eyes and fall back against the wall. On the upside, I have another seven girls to cross off my list, which makes about thirty when you add in all the other locker rooms I've been lurking in. On the downside, at this rate I will get a name for myself as the creepy reporter who insists on interviewing subjects while they are half-naked.

I wait a few moments before pushing through the swinging door. Unfortunately, my delay tactics were for naught; a gaggle of them are huddled in the center of the gym around a bright blond head that I know all too well.

"Vlad, I thought you said you were going to come to our game," pouts one of the team members that I've just crossed off my list.

He smiles. I've been doing my best to avoid him these past two weeks, but even I know that's occurred less and less regularly since his kissy lips have failed to locate the girl among the cheerleaders. He's been losing patience with teachers, and yesterday I even overheard him snap at Ms. Walpole for asking how his paper on *Frankenstein* is going ("It's not, you harpy"). But now that he has an audience, he's all sweetness and light. I watch as he clasps a hand to his heart.

"I know, and please accept my deepest apologies for missing it," he says. "I hope that the upcoming party my friends and I will be throwing is enough to make up for my absence."

"Party?" Marta says.

"Yes," Vlad says. "And there is even a theme."

She claps her hands. "Theme parties are my favorite. What is it? Twenties? Pimps and Hos?"

Vlad just raises his eyebrows mysteriously and puts a finger to his lips. "The invitation will say more. In fact," he says, making an elaborate show of looking at his watch, "they should be in your lockers now."

The girls look at one another and then head for the door—apparently I'm the only one who wants to vomit at the prospect of a Vlad-catered party. I can only imagine what the theme will be . . . "Show Off Your Birthmark Night"? As if I didn't have enough to deal with already, Vlad has to learn how to multitask.

After verifying that the coast is clear, he pulls the

small black journal from his back pocket. He's been scribbling in it more than ever—in English, in the cafeteria, in the middle of the hallway—and I want to know what. I haven't had the chance to try and squeeze more information out of the Sophie-friendly vampires. Marisabel has either been absent or too close to Vlad, and Violet seems to have taken a vow of silence; every time I try to speak to her in English, she just presses her lips together and whispers, *"C'est une secrete."*

Suddenly, Vlad looks up, and before I can think of a suitable hiding spot, he's heading my way. Since that day in the lobby, he's looked at me several times with a suspicious glint in his eye. When he's about twenty feet away, I panic and let my feet walk in whatever random direction they would like to go . . . which happens to be halfway up the bleacher stairs. My flight instinct needs a better sense of direction.

Realizing that I'm trapped, I turn around and try to pretend that's what I was intending on doing all along. I take a seat, but keep to the edge just in case I have to move quickly.

"What are you doing here?" Vlad barks up at me

from the bottom step.

I hold up my notebook and do my best to feign a natural indignation at being harassed by what is supposed to be a near stranger. "Um, reporting on the soccer game. I was just going to jot down some notes."

"You were here yesterday outside the locker room as well. After the other meet concluded, the one where they run around in the forest for no reason."

"Yeah, I cover cross-country, too," I say, trying to keep my voice as even as possible. "What's the big deal?"

Vlad continues to stare at me, lips pressed so thin that they are nothing more than a slash. The high lighting is hitting his cheekbones in a way that emphasizes the chalky quality of his skin. He's not looking as debonair as usual—I wonder if he's stretched himself too thin. But my observations are cut short when his face turns resolute and he takes the first two steps in one stride. My mind scrambles for something to concentrate on when a voice calls out from across the gym.

"Hold it right there, young man," Mr. Hanfield says from the doorway. "You are not supposed to be up there when no game is in session. Bleachers are not toys."

Vlad's tenuous hold on his temper snaps. "How is standing on it treating it like a toy? And I am not a 'young man.'"

Talking back only makes the small teacher puff up in indignation. "Come down right this instant," he says, scuttling over to look up at us sternly.

"Unlikely." Vlad stomps a few times, hard enough that the entire section rattles. "*That* is treating it like a toy."

Mr. Hanfield pulls a small white pad out of his front pocket. "We'll see how cocky you are when you have detention. Stay right there," he orders and then turns to me. "What about you, young lady?"

"I've got no problem getting down," I tell him, resisting the urge to pat him on his sweatered shoulder as I head down the stairs. When I reach the door, I risk a look back just in case Vlad has already mumbo-jumboed his way out of detention, but he's just scowling as Mr. Hanfield continues to lecture. Another close call—time to declare quits for the day and go home, try to write an article about a game I still don't quite understand, and then take a nice bubble bath. All I need to do is pick up my backpack and . . .

As soon as I turn the corner I stop dead in my tracks. James is leaning up against the wall of lockers, and Amanda is leaning toward him. She's in full cheerleading regalia, but she's hiked her skirt up a few inches to show more tanned leg. I start to feel a little nauseated; I tell myself that it's just because I'm sickened that James is helping Vlad, never mind that Amanda is the only girl I've seen him talking to for the past week (and, if the rumor of an impromptu make-out session with Vlad in the janitor's closet is to be believed, already off the list). We still haven't spoken.

"Remember when we went to homecoming in eighth grade?" Amanda asks and then giggles annoyingly. Determined to prove how much this does not affect me, I walk toward my locker and start to twist in the combination.

"Yeah, it was fun," I hear him say. "Danny got that limo and we kept throwing Coke cans out of it."

Amanda giggles again. "That's not what I remember."

The door of my locker clangs as I slam it open. Oops. Out of the corner of my eye, I see James straighten up enough that Amanda has to step back or lose her balance. He says my name.

"Don't mind me," I say as I reach for my bag. I'm so intent on not looking directly at him that at first I don't realize that there's actually something in my locker that deserves attention. An envelope is wedged in the slats, and the giant black seal on its back is staring at me like an ominous eye. *Dear God*, I think as I wiggle it out and tear it open, *do not let this be another one of Violet's quizzes.*

The good news is that it's not a chance to reevaluate my flirting potential; the bad news is that now I know Vlad's theme.

Bring your bathing outfits and throw caution to the wind! You are cordially invited to our Fall "Luau" this Friday, October 1st.

Who:
Vlad, Marisabel, Violet, Neville, Devon, and Ashley

Where:
235 Preston Dr. (Map included)

When:
9:00 P.M.

Mandatory bathing suits? In October? Vlad is evil.

A small piece of paper is folded inside. "Hope you can make it!" says Marisabel's loopy handwriting, and beneath that she's drawn several hearts and written "Wink," which I assume is the fifty-year-old vampire version of an emoticon. At least this solves the problem of how to get into the party.

After I wedge it into my backpack, Amanda asks, "Are you going to that?"

I say yes at the same time that James says no. Amanda looks back and forth between us a few times before her eyes narrow.

"I mean, no one cool is going to be there. I wasn't even invited." She turns to James. "We should go to the movies or something instead."

The wide-open hallway suddenly feels as spacious as

a sardine tin. "Have fun," I say, shutting my locker and leaving before I can hear his answer.

I ignore the bathing suit situation as long as I can. The last time I went swimming I was eleven, and it was only after being promised a juice box, animal crackers, and my turn with the inflatable raft shaped like a dolphin. I am no longer that stupid. Or that fond of floating toys.

Still, knowing Vlad's motive for throwing the party, I doubt I'll be able to get in without showing skin, not even if I say "pretty please with A-positive on top." At 7:54 on the night of Friday, October 1st, I drag myself to Caroline's door and knock with questionable enthusiasm. When it opens, Caroline has a phone cradled in the crook of her neck and a flat iron hard at work on her bangs. She waves me in with her free hand—that, or she's trying to dry her nails. I choose to view it as an invitation.

"No, we're not going to crash it," she tells her phone buddy with a note of finality. "Like I want to hang out in his dirty, musty house ever again." She graciously allows the person on the other end a few opinions. "Yeah, okay, I'll see that. Meet you at the theater in thirty?

Fab." After beeping off, she tosses the phone on her bed, where it bounces a few times before coming to a plush resting place between Grover and a nameless stuffed penguin. After fluffing her bangs and unplugging the flat iron, she finally speaks.

"What do you want?" she asks, arranging herself on the bed so as not to muss her strapless navy sundress and sandals that tie up the calf. She plays with the chunky beaded necklace around her neck, choosing to study it instead of me. Caroline has still not forgiven me for my "Vlad-related amnesiosity."

"Do you have a bathing suit I could borrow?" I ask.

Her eyes narrow. "You're going to Vlad's party," she says, more statement than question.

"Yes," I say, keeping things simple. I might actually have an easier time convincing Caroline that Vlad's a vampire than explaining why I hate parties that have no purpose other than to drink things and mingle.

She studies me for a few seconds, her dilemma clear: She can stay mad at me or play clothes fairy. Lucky for me, the latter wins.

"It's going to be lame, but okay," she says, hopping off the bed and crossing to her dresser. She flings open the second drawer. "What kind? One piece, two piece—"

"Red piece, blue piece?" I try.

Caroline is not amused, and for once her exasperation is probably justified.

After wading around in the drawer for a few seconds, she comes out holding two red triangles held together by a piece of yarn. In other words, something that looks more like a preschool craft project than a bathing suit.

"No way," I say. "Next."

She rolls her eyes but puts it to the side, digging around until she surfaces with two more options. One is yellow with big pink flowers blooming on the nipples, and the other has "Flirt" written in purple block letters across the butt. You've got to be kidding me.

"I'll take the red one, I guess," I say, holding out my hand. "You have no shame, by the way."

"I'll take that as a compliment," she chirps and tosses it at me. "No, try it on," she orders when I make to leave. "We're not the same size. You might have to be happy with the flower-power boobs."

Reluctantly, I step behind the door and do a quick Clark Kent. After tying the top around my neck, I step out to show Caroline. She makes a face.

"It would be nicer if you weren't clutching your jeans and T-shirt over your chest like a big weirdo. Drop them," she orders. I unclench my fingers, letting my clothing shield fall to the ground. "That actually looks really nice on you, Sophie. Who knew T-shirts could hide that much boobaliciousness?" All of a sudden she squints. "It would look better with a tan and fewer freckles, but, well, you know . . ."

"Yes. I know." I pick up my wrinkled black T-shirt and drag it over my head before thanking her for the bikini.

She waves a hand in front of her face. It's a throw-away gesture, but I can sense she's starting to think about the injustice of my invitation, her non-invitation, and a world gone topsy-turvy. She chatters to make up for the tension as she goes to wrestle a purse from the mound of bags that line her closet floor.

"I have to meet Amanda at the movie theater," she says.

"Is James going?" I ask because I have absolutely nothing resembling willpower at all and should probably be quarantined for further study. But Caroline either doesn't hear me or chooses not to answer.

"She wants to see that one about the zombies who eat New York or something," she continues, her voice still muffled. "Whatever. The main guy is hot. I just hope no one munches on his abs." She tugs on the strap of a gray suede slouch bag and pulls it free with one swift yank before turning to me with a serious glint in her eye. "Oh, and remember; you have to tell me everything that happens tonight. Everything," she repeats, and then gives me a bright, genuine smile before heading out the door.

Vlad's place is part of an older subdivision, complete with sprawling grandfather trees and retired couples who are even older. When I drive through the twisting streets, the majority of the houses' windows are already dark. Every so often I spot the flickering pulse of a television or a lone bedroom light, but for the most part, Shady Grove has closed up shop. Just as I'm turning the last corner onto Preston Drive, a raccoon darts out in front of my car, eyes glowing like iridescent marbles. I slam on the brakes, and it runs for the cover of a nearby parked car. It wasn't even a close call, but my heart stutters. *Thank you, nature, for putting me more on edge.*

When I am finally able to control my breathing, I realize that the parked car is one in a very long line of parked cars despite the fact that it's nine on the nose. Obviously, this crowd threw any thoughts of being fashionably late out the window.

I park my car and trudge toward the sprawling two story house just as more cars pull up behind me, spewing their giggling occupants into the street, most of whom are already wearing their bathing suits. Personally, I plan on keeping my shirt on until someone ties me down and rips it from my body.

After I pass the final street lamp, the only light left is what pours out from the lower floor of Vlad's house. I see floor-to-ceiling windows, gray, rickety shutters, and a wraparound porch that is illuminated by a single jaundiced light. Moths flutter around it in a vibrating nimbus, and every once in a while one kamikazes into the huddled mass of bodies crowding the doorway. Going by turnout alone, I'd say Vlad's party is a success.

I join the group crowding the porch. A girl in a simple one-piece suit to my left is crying, "But this is the only bathing suit I have!" while her pixyish friend clumsily pats her on the back and stares longingly at the party beyond. Her suit is a size too large, but at least it's a two-piece. She bites her lip before turning back to her distraught friend. "Why don't you go buy one at Wal-Mart and then meet me back here?" she says. "Or we can, like, cut yours."

I'm jostled to the front of the pack before I can hear her decision. Looking up, I find myself staring into the brown eyes of Devon—or perhaps Ashley—now on guard duty. It's the first time that I've seen one without the other, and it's an unsettling feeling. D'Ashley's eyes rake over my body, narrowing when they hit my offending piece of clothing. He points at my shirt and then jerks a thumb to the side.

I grasp the hem, wondering why I'm the only one who's showing any resistance to the forced disrobing. Overtaken by a sudden fit of stubbornness, I pause halfway and tug my T-shirt back down. I wait for D'Ashley's next move. After a few seconds of cartoonish confusion, he makes a motion suggesting that my time is up and I should move out of the way to let in the less difficult guests. When I make no sign of complying, he grabs my shoulder and starts to push me from the porch. Suddenly a hand clamps down on my shoulder.

"Hey, Sophie," James says, sidling up beside me. He looks disgustingly attractive in dark blue jeans and a smoky gray T-shirt. I wasn't expecting him to be here, so my reply is a mixture between "Hello," "Huh?" and "Excuse me?" I sound like a thing that just gurgled its way out of the swamp. He's nice enough to pretend that I have spoken English.

"Ready to go in?" he asks, and then turns to D'Ashley. "She's with me."

There is no way I am taking anything off now, not with James standing less than two feet away from me. I grab the dangling ends of my bikini top and waggle them at the hulking bodyguard. "I have my suit on. See?"

D'Ashley starts to shake his head, but a burst of laughter draws his attention to a point behind me. A new gang of students, about twenty in all, are stumbling up the hill. Fear flashes across the large boy's face; I don't think he was prepared for bouncer duty, and the students are becoming restless.

"Are you going to let us in or what?" James says, making a point to look at his watch and shake his arm like it's burning a hole under his sleeve. "Looks like you've got a lot of people left to check. Vlad won't be happy if it's ten o'clock and half of his guests are still waiting at the door."

The threat of Vlad's displeasure does the trick. D'Ashley gives a terse wave.

We slip in, pushing through a crush of people cluttering up the foyer. At first I check backs and stomachs for any marks, but the bodies are packed so tightly that it starts to feel claustrophobic. I struggle my way to the bottom step of the ornate staircase that leads to the dark second floor. It smells musty, like fall leaves after a rainstorm. Still, this is better than drowning in a swimsuit calendar.

"Thanks for that," I say when James steps up the stairs beside me, and then, because I can't resist, "I thought you were going to the movies with Amanda."

"Nah," James says, and I have to distract myself to hide what I am sure is a glow of pleasure. I look away to do a quick scan of the room. Girls outnumber the boys three to one, and the small number of males present wear their friend status like lodestones around their necks. Most of them hide in corners, staring into their plastic red cups like they might offer up what to do next.

As for the girls, a few of them have grass hula skirts—whether vampire provided or not, I don't know—but as expected, I am the only person not showing any real skin.

"If you want to remove your protective shell," James says, "you won't hear any complaints from me."

"That's okay. I'm here as more of an observer."

"I figured you weren't here for the company."

I study his face in the shadows cast by the sharp angles of the stairway. Except for that one time during chemistry, I've never seen him looking less than healthy and refreshed. Now he's leaning back against the railing and studying me with a smile. I've missed talking to him, I realize. I've missed it a lot.

Feeling exposed, I glance to the top of the long stairs. The other half of D'Ashley is standing there like a golem, his arms crossed over his chest as he stares down at us.

"What's he doing there?"

Reluctantly, James follows my gaze. "Vlad doesn't want people going upstairs."

"Why?"

"He's got this thing about people touching his stuff."

"That's all?"

"Pretty much," James says. "There aren't any giant wall diagrams that say, 'This is My Evil Plan,' if that's what you're thinking."

That is what I was thinking.

"Let's go up," I say, suddenly inspired. "He might let me through if I'm with you. We could find out more about who he's looking for and what the Danae wants with her."

He looks away. "I knew this was a mistake," he mutters.

Frustration takes over. "Then why do you keep helping me? First with the journalism project, and now with the party. You have to know why I'm here."

He opens his mouth but then seems to be at a loss for words. "I don't know," he finally says. "Vlad told us we had to come, and I saw you standing there and maybe I just thought that the party would be more interesting with you in it," he says before the sincerity is ruined with a twitch of his lips. "I mean, there was that party at Morgan Michaels's house in sixth grade where you drank all that orange soda and then left when everyone started playing kissing games."

"I didn't leave," I say, even though I'm pretty sure I did.

"It was right when we started. I remember." Something warm has crept into his eyes. There's a brief second where my body feels carbonated, but then I think I hear the burst of Vlad's laughter above the din, and it reminds me that no matter how much we skip down memory lane, the cold truth is that we are still at odds. I can't keep doing this; it's distracting, and it only makes me want things that are impossible.

"I have to go," I say and head down the stairs. He calls out behind me, but I've already squeezed between a girl in a nautical-themed suit and a senior wearing a kiwi wrap over her black string bikini. I dart through a doorway on the right, where raucous shrieks mark the hub of the party.

The room's high ceilings and large windows make it a coveted living room, or at least it was once. Between the shuffling feet of party guests, I catch glimpses of the dark, couch-shaped patches where furniture must have once protected the burgundy carpet from decades of sun. The cream wallpaper is stained along the top border, and in many places it curls at the edges. A tattered Victorian couch sits in the corner, covered in gray velvet and missing a few buttons, and folding refreshment tables are set up at the far end of the room. The Hawaiian theme isn't going to win any decorating contests; the room looks more like Dracula's dungeon than a balmy island getaway. A limp sign, with ALOHA written in crooked yellow letters, wilts over the punch bowl, and a few dejected leis hang off the ornate chandelier that hovers above the sea of bobbing heads. Ambiance is obviously a low priority when you have young girls to kidnap.

I make my way to the refreshment table, trying to figure out my game plan as I go. Avoiding Vlad's notice is priority number one, although I still need to keep an eye on him in case he targets anyone in particular. And then there's the little black book. Now that I've infiltrated his home base, there might be a chance to get my hands on it.

I pick up a flimsy paper plate and survey the meager offerings. Not surprisingly, vampire catering leaves something to be desired. Generic cheese puffs lie scattered around a bowl of congealing ranch dip that still holds the shape of the can it came from. The carrots should be a safer option, but instead of being cut into stick form, someone has sliced them into tiny coin-sized discs. How appetizing. I pick up a carrot medallion and start to nibble, swiping a cup from the leaning tower to my right and heading toward the punch. It looks orange, sugary, and unnatural—normal enough. I'm tentatively ladling some into my glass when someone comes up beside me.

"Yo, Soph, what's up?" Neal Garrett says, resplendent in neon green swim trunks. He grabs a cheese puff and pokes it into the ranch dip. "Cool party, huh?"

"What are you doing here?"

"I came with my girlfriend," he says proudly. After checking to make sure no one's listening, he leans down to whisper, "We're playing hide-and-seek. She's kind of bad at it, though, so I thought I'd take a breather and let her think that it's taking me a long time." He pauses. "What are you doing here? You never struck me as the party type."

"It's a long story."

"I've got time," Neal says. "I'm counting to ninety-one thousand."

I open my mouth to tell him that it's not important

when I spot Violet charging toward us angrily. She's not wearing anything so revealing as a bathing suit, but she's gotten into the spirit of the evening by wrapping a flowered sheet around her body like a toga. It makes her stumble a little as she bears down on us. Neal yells her name, his voice a mixture of surprise and pleasure.

"What are you doing?" he says. "You're supposed to be hiding!"

"I was sitting in that dusty old cupboard forever," she pouts.

"The cupboard in the study? But you hid there the last time! And the time before that."

Violet shrugs; I'm not surprised that her favorite part of hide-and-seek is being found.

"Is the cupboard upstairs?" I interrupt.

"Sophie!" she cries, delighted. "I thought you would not come." When she notices that my eyes have slid to where she has looped an arm through Neal's elbow, she giggles. "Oops," she says. "We have been keeping it a secret, but you can be the first to know. Neal and I are courting."

"Congratulations," I say, my stomach sinking. A serious talk about not turning one's boyfriends into vampires is on the horizon, but right now I need to focus on Vlad. "Can I, uh, play hide-and-seek with you?"

Violet lights up. "Of course!" She orders Neal to start counting again. "And this time I *won't* be in the cupboard," she says, and then grabs my hand and pulls me through the crowd.

When we reach the top of the stairs, D'Ashley stands, an efficient sentry. Violet slips beneath his arm without hesitation, but when I try to do the same, I feel the heavy weight of his hand on my shoulder.

"Oh, do let her in, Ashley. Neal is probably at fifty by now!" she yells and follows it up with a kick to the shin. Clearly disgruntled, he lets me pass, and I am plunged into the darkness of the hallway.

✳
Chapter Thirteen

Violet's eyes adjust to the gloom far quicker than mine, or at least I assume so because she's running down the hallway while I'm still clutching at the wall. "I am going to hide in the cupboard," she says excitedly before dashing into what must be the aforementioned study.

Dust pervades the air, and I try not to cough as I grasp the handle of the door closest to me. Apart from a few scattered drop sheets that lie wadded in the corners, the first room is empty. The second turns up more dust bunnies, and the third is filled with a collection of tattered couches and armchairs that were most likely granted a last-minute reprieve from the garbage truck.

They are arranged in a cheery circle, almost as if the vampires spent their evenings in discussion. An old TV is pushed to one side, and beneath it are stacks of DVDs. Unable to resist, I sort through them to find that Vlad has amassed every high school comedy imaginable, from John Hughes to *10 Things I Hate About You* and beyond. This is what he was using as research to infiltrate our high school? That almost frightens me as much as anything else.

It strikes me that I haven't come across any beds, and I don't find any in the fourth and fifth rooms either, although clothing hangs in the closets: velvet for Violet, knee-length skirts for Marisabel, and a row of white shirts for Neville. I realize that I never asked James if he sleeps. I hope so; the image of him sitting alone in his old bedroom, awake, all night every night, makes my throat constrict. No wonder he didn't want to go home that night, I think, and I feel a rush of overdue guilt.

Now there's only one room left, and I begin to lose faith that my brilliant hide-and-seek spying technique will turn up useful information. When the last door swings open to reveal one lonely rocking chair, my heart sinks. I do a loop around the room anyway, hoping that the thump of music downstairs is loud enough to cover the creak of floorboards. The chair is positioned to face the window, and the high vantage point of the house means that the sitter has a vaulted view of the neighborhood down below, with its slanted roofs and twinkling house lights. It's as majestic a view as you're likely to find in suburbia.

I wander to the far wall and slide open the closet door, pushing when it sticks. There is clothing here, as well, but while the other closets were a jumble of styles and owners, this is organized to the level of neatness normally associated with former military men, serial killers, and Marcie. To the right are shirts and jackets, all covered in plastic and arranged by color. I recognize the black jacket that Vlad wore on the first day of school, and look down to find the pair of pointed boots from that afternoon in the woods gleaming up at me in the dark. An unbidden shiver shoots through my body, and it takes a moment to regain my composure.

His jeans hang on the left side, and while they aren't covered in plastic, they each have an individual hanger, back pockets facing outward. This proves that old maxim that people who hang their jeans up are to be feared, even if I just made that maxim up.

I start to push the door closed, thinking that I would have learned more hiding in the cupboard with Violet, when a bulge in the back pocket of the outermost pair catches my eye. At first I don't believe what I'm seeing. But no—Vlad's journal is still there, stuffed in the back pocket of his jeans. He left his plans for vampire domination in his other pants.

I pull it out so forcefully that the jeans fall off the hanger. I rearrange them, heart pounding, and then open the pages with trembling fingers. Vlad's cramped, flowery handwriting covers every bit of paper, with lines squeezed into the margins or running up the spine and dead-ending in the corners. I go to the rocker and let the small bit of light from outside pour down over the yellowed pages.

The first few pages are just a list of names and dates, beginning with "Anton and Evangelique Mervaux (d. 1815, burned)" and ending with "Christiana Jones (d. 1999—killed)." Beneath that Vlad has written question marks of all sizes, some scored so deeply that he's torn through the page. If what Marisabel told me was right, this must be the list of the girl's descendants that he's been piecing together through the years—but if he knows where it ends, why is he here?

Next comes a series of journal entries, the first of which dates from 1966. They are terse reports of research, mentions of lost children, dreams of what life will be like once he is Danae and can get revenge on all the vampires who have snubbed him, and complaints about being Unnamed. There are years of time in between entries, *years*, and a small part of me can't help but admire Vlad's tenacity; the longest I ever pursued a story was one month.

I stop at an entry of unusual length.

March 13, 2000
New Orleans

Third appeal to join the Society of the Divine One denied, even with fake identity. Broke into their archives. The last descendent was (obviously) female, recorded death in Canada. No further research done. Obviously a society of incompetence to which I would not want

*to belong anyway. Three-year gap from
Christiana's last sighting in Michigan
unexplored. Previous flights had been
limited to months. <u>Why three years?</u>*

The next few entries outline his theory. Christiana stayed in Michigan because she had fallen in love and become pregnant. What's more, he thought that she had given birth to a child, the next descendent of this family tree that everyone thought had died out a long time ago. But soon after arriving here, she adopted an alias that he has still not been able to discover, although her child would have to be anywhere from fifteen to seventeen.

November 23, 2009
New York Upstate Wilderness

*Truly, everything is coming together.
Met a vampire named Neville, who bears
the mark of the Danae and who seems
very interested in my work. This is my
link to them; this is the sign I have been
waiting for.*

The following entries all detail his preparations to bring the group here, which included glamouring people out of their money and possessions and being blood-drive bandits. My heart skips a little when James's name first appears.

April 11, 2010
New York Upstate Wilderness

Violet's new conquest, James, has actually turned out to be useful for reasons other than to stop her incessant sulking. He is not only familiar with the location of the girl, he may have attended school with her during his early years. At first he seemed reluctant to return, but was convinced by yet another example of particularly clever thinking on my part. "Well used are those cruelties that are carried out in a single stroke."
—Machiavelli

I frown, wondering exactly what "particularly clever thinking" and that quote are supposed to mean—it can't be anything good. Maybe I should show it to him in yet another attempt to lure him over to my side, or *at least* give him a heads-up—I shake my head, realizing this is just another example of Distraction via James. *No.* Girl. Danae. Moving on.

We've reached Vlad's first day at Thomas Jeff.

August 30, 2010
Town of Michigan

Infiltration of Thomas Jefferson school successful. The child is here. I can taste her. . . .

Why is this woman still talking? If she thinks that I am going to stop wearing my pointed boots, she is sadly mistaken.

I let out a loud snort and then turn the page quickly, feeling guilty at being amused by Vlad's ramblings.

Thankfully, the following entries putter out into endless rants about how the other vampires aren't helping and he doesn't even know where James is. I move past a number of blank pages to the next section, which is a listing of girls he's rejected. Caroline sits proudly at the top, followed by approximately thirty other girls that I'll cross-reference with my own list later. When I turn the next page, I swear that my eyes start to tingle. This. This is what I've been looking for.

Vlad has made a rough sketch of Neville's tattoo, large enough that the star's four main points touch the edges of the page. By each tip he's written a name—last names from the look of it, unless there's some poor soul wandering around with the name "Vandervelde." I squint and look closer. Instead of a "D" in the center, Vlad's written "Mervaux," the big, bad, human-baby-having vamp family itself, and I would guess that these others are vampire families as well.

Excited, I move on to what appears to be a timeline. Some dates are far apart and others are crammed together, and they're all in different colors of ink, like this is something that he's been adding to for a long time.

1798: Human child born to the Mervaux and named Mercedes (star mark on right shoulder). Vampire families are split between those who think it is a miracle and those who think that she is an abomination, including the ruling family of the time (Desmarais—now extinct)

1799: In fear, Mervaux call for help. Nine families answer—Vandervelde, Doyle, Greco, Rose, Wolf, Magnusson, Kaya, Quinn, Pavlov. Danae treaty signed.

1806: Desmarais falls. Nine families take power under new name of Danae.

1820 (?): Mercedes gives birth to child (vampire father?), also human, also female. Named Melisande (star mark, lower abdomen).

1845: Under pressure, Danae abdicates in favor of elected leaders and is forced to disband as a condition. Do so publicly, but not in private. Tattoo is designed so that members will know one another.

1847: Melisande gives birth to daughter (definite vampire father), child still human. Named Michelle (star lines on palm).

1869: Michelle disappears. Reason unknown.

1902: I am born.

1965: Victor Petrov circulates influential work, The Lost Daughter, underground, in which he argues that the human line of Mervaux vampires continues. Later recants and says, "It was just a novel," but then disappears.

I turn back to the beginning of the journal—Vlad's first entry is dated in 1966. Victor's "novel" obviously converted Vlad enough that he's spent the last half a century searching for her. I read over the timeline again, doing my best to make sense of the rush of dates and bite-sized history. The Danae isn't just looking for the girl because of her supposed powers; they're looking for her because she and her line are their crown jewel. Or at least she was until she vanished.

When I flip to the next page, I find more cramped writing and the header "Collected Myths and Legends." Before I can start to read, however, the door creaks behind me. I whirl around to find Neal standing in the entranceway, staring at me with surprise. Guess what? His neon swim trunks glow in the dark.

"Found you!" he says before his face wrinkles in confusion. "Why are you standing in the middle of the room? You're worse than Violet." His eyes fall to the book in my hand. "What's that?"

"Nothing," I say, annoyed at the interruption until I realize that I'm lucky it's just Neal. Vlad might be hunting for this, which means that I should save a more thorough read for later. I attempt to shove it in my pocket, but girl pants are not as accommodating as boy pants. Left with little other option, I lift my T-shirt and wiggle it into the space between my back and the waistband of my jeans; at least if Vlad tries to take it back it will be covered in girl cooties. Holding up my hands, I say, "You got me!" just as Violet's blond head appears behind his shoulder. She tickles his sides, and he jumps.

"Too long *again*," she says, but she is smiling. "Let's go downstairs. I am tired of the cupboard."

I let them walk in front of me, head still pounding with new information until the way Violet loops her arm through Neal's and he bends down to whisper something in her ear makes me think this might not be a problem that can be moved to the back burner. *This is not good*, I think as her giggle bounces up the stairway. *This is not good at all.*

When we get to the bottom of the stairs I grab Violet's free arm. "I need to talk to Violet for a second," I tell Neal. "Go have another ranchy cheese puff. I hear they're magically delicious."

"But—"

"We'll find you," I say and pull Violet into the next room: the kitchen.

A thick layer of dust coats the new appliances. The sink's faucet is a dull green, and the only light still working is the one hanging over the oven. Cobwebs cling to every corner, including the slatted pantry door. The most neglected room in the house, it's been left mostly empty by the other partygoers.

Mostly. A girl I recognize from the soccer team and her friend stumble in, gossiping about how so-and-so just threw herself at Vlad for the third time, energetically enough that her top slipped down and exposed her man entrancers to the world. "And he just studied them for a few seconds," she says, "then pulled up her top and said, 'Thank you, that was an immense help.' Sometimes he's so weird."

Her friend nods enthusiastically and then points to her throat. "I'm thirsty," she mouths and goes to the fridge, which I assume is filled with items that are more frightening than mystery mold.

"There's punch in the living room," I tell her, blocking the handle. "It's rude to poke around in people's refrigerators." As I jerk my head to point out the right direction, I do a quick skin sweep. She has a small birthmark on her hip, although it would be the most circular star ever made. I ask for her name anyway. I'll admit that it comes out a little boot-camp.

"Uh, Grace," she says, eyeing me like I might order her to drop and give me twenty at any second. "And we'll leave the fridge alone, okay? You don't have to freak out," she says and drags her friend toward the living room. "Who's that?" I hear her ask before they disappear into the hallway. "Oh you know, *that* girl."

Fantastic.

"There's nothing in there, you know," Violet says from behind me. I twirl around to find that she's hopped onto the counter, dust be damned. She swings her crossed ankles back and forth, not minding when they bang against the lower cabinet. "You really should give us some credit," she continues. "We may be a little behind the times, but we are not naive enough to leave blood lying around for just anyone to find."

"I don't know what you're talking about," I say, trying to look fluffy-bunny innocent despite her doubtful look.

"Marisabel told me about your conversation in the ladies' room. I never had the courage to tell her myself, but I agree that they should call it off. *Seventeen* would deem it a verbally abusive relationship."

"Who else knows?"

"Just us!" Violet says, but I still feel a little sick to my stomach. Violet must see my unease, because she adds, "I would not worry about it if I were you. Well, unless you're in front of Vlad. Then I might worry about it."

That's quite the disclaimer. "Why?"

"He has been snapping at all of us lately. Neville came home yesterday with the announcement that he won the lead in the school play, and Vlad nearly staked him on the spot. I really wish he would find the girl he wants so we can all forget this nonsense and start to concentrate on what really matters. Like Neal!" She claps excitedly. "Oh, Sophie, he is fantastic! I hardly even think of James anymore."

"You mean you want to stay here?" I ask with obvious disbelief. "Even if Vlad finds the girl?"

She either misses my tone or chooses to ignore it. "Of course. This is much more fun than that dusty old farmhouse! Why? You don't want James to stay?"

If that isn't the million-dollar question. It's not something I want to contemplate, so I try to change the subject. "Violet, about Neal—"

"I am aware that he is a little strange," she interrupts,

"but I firmly believe I can get him to stop carrying that rodent around in his pocket."

"It's not that," I say, choosing my words carefully. "In the past, you may have been a little hasty with your . . . gentlemen friends."

"What do you mean?" she asks, starting to frown as her swinging feet go still. Ominously still.

"I mean, well . . . you like Neal a lot, right?" I ask, plunging ahead despite my better judgment.

"Oodles."

"Then perhaps you should try something different this time," I say.

"And what do you mean by that?"

I check to make sure that the coast is clear before I delve into the Monster Mash portion of this conversation. When I've confirmed that it's just us here in this kitchen—a kitchen that is feeling more and more claustrophobic by the second, I might add—I say, "I know that in the past you have turned your boyfriends into vampires, and I am wondering if maybe you should try not to do that with Neal."

She gives a dainty sniff. "You don't have to say it like it's a dirty word."

"What? Neal?"

"No," she corrects. "Vampire! There are quite a few people who might like to be one of us. I think they are called Erica," she adds, naming our school's resident Goth. "And besides, I cannot make him unless he agrees."

"Really?"

"Well, that is the common practice. But sometimes I do cheat a little and ask vague questions. Like 'If you were accidentally stabbed in the stomach several times, would you want to live?' And if they say yes, then I can reasonably assume that they would like to be a vampire, because we are the only beings who would survive that. See?"

Her logic leaves me speechless. She takes the silence as my assent.

"Lovely, it is settled. I am going to find Neal now." She hops off the counter, but her tone still makes it sound like a threat. Before I can tell her to wait, she knocks into my shoulder as she brushes by me, hard enough to knock me into the refrigerator door. This is swiftly spiraling out of control.

"What would *Seventeen* say?" I call out, desperate to regain some leverage.

She stops. "What do you mean?"

"I read an article once about how you shouldn't try to, er, change your boyfriends?" I try. At this point I am just treading water, but Violet seems to be considering it.

"I may have read this article," she says finally. "There was a story about a girl named Amy whose boyfriend was some sort of athletics person but she wanted him to like jazz."

"And?"

"And ultimately it tore them apart. It was very tragic."

"See?"

"Perhaps," Violet says, trying to be arch and coy, but I can tell that for now, at least, I've managed to save Holland with my thumb.

"Promise me that you won't turn Neal," I say.

"But what if—"

"If you don't," I say, "I'm going to have to warn him. And I really don't want to have that conversation. I'm getting enough of a name for myself as it is."

Her face falls as she bites her lip. "I like him, Sophie."

"Then promise," I insist.

There is a brief pause, and I fear that I have pressed my luck too far. But then Violet flounces over to stand by my side, pulling up her toga when it threatens to slide off her shoulders.

"Very well!" she says, perky once again. "What do I have to sign?"

"No contract necessary. Just your word," I say. I would do a blood pact if I didn't think it would be an invitation to snack.

"You have my word," she parrots gravely, and then leaps toward me for a hug. "Oh, I am so glad we are friends now!" she exclaims and then pushes me back to stare into my eyes. "Please endeavor not to steal Neal."

"No worries there, I promise you."

"This is going to be so fun! Do you want to come over for tea tomorrow? I mean, I cannot have any, but I'll make some for you!"

"Let's take it one day at a ti—," I begin, but stop when Violet's fingers dig into my shoulders.

"Go to the pantry," she says, urgent all of a sudden.

"Huh? Why?"

"Vlad is on his way over here," she hisses, "and he suspects that you know more than you should." Her eyes widen as she takes in my outfit. "You are also improperly attired for his party."

She pushes me toward the slatted doors and opens them with a free hand. The odor emanating from the pantry is foul.

"But—"

"In," she insists. "I will come retrieve you when it is safe. You may thank me later," she whispers, and then, with one swift shove, closes me in the pantry. The inside is just as rank as you'd imagine a small, unused, and unwashed room to be. The empty shelves stack all the way up to the ceiling, and in the weak light that squeezes through the slats, they look vaguely skeletal. A mildewed mop stands forlornly in the corner behind me like a vengeful ghost from a Japanese thriller. This better save me from certain death; otherwise I'm stuffing Violet in the oven as payback.

I peer through the gaps just in time to see James enter the kitchen from the other door and tap Violet on the shoulder. She yelps. It takes two seconds for her flustered expression to turn flirtatious as she looks down at the floral tent she's wearing and asks him if he likes it.

"It's lovely," he says. "Have you seen Sophie?"

"Yes!"

"Good. Where?"

"Have you met my boyfriend?" Violet asks, apropos of nothing. "I am speaking of my new boyfriend, of course. He should be by the refreshment table. Eating cheese doilies."

"I'd love to meet him—later. Right now I'm looking for Sophie," he says, stretching out my name until it sounds like two distinct words. "Where is she?"

Holding a finger to her lips, she points to the pantry.

"Why is she in the pantry?" James asks before his expression melts into horror. "Violet, what did you do?"

"Nothing! I am trying to help her. Quick! Vlad is coming."

James's eyes widen, and he jogs toward the door. Before I can fashion a NO BOYS ALLOWED sign, he's opened it, closed it, and is standing in front of me. His body blocks most of the light, so I can't see the expression on his face, but I can feel him looking at me, even though he doesn't say anything. I try to think of a joke to cut the tension, but the only things that come are of the knock-knock variety. ("Knock knock." "Who's there?" "A steadily shrinking pantry!" "A steadily shrinking pantry who?" "Get out, please.")

The silence ticks on; all I can hear are the sounds of my own breathing and the thrum of tropical music leaking through the walls. The thin bars of light squeezing through the slats make him look like a trendy tiger. Finally, I can't take it anymore.

"This is an abnormally small pantry. I'm going to write a letter," I say, leaving off the part about his shoulders seeming abnormally large. I'm thinking that I'm going to write a letter about that too when James suddenly blurts that he wants to apologize.

"Really?" I ask, surprised.

"Yeah. I think it's brave what you're doing. And I've tried to stop hoping that there's some way to change this, I have. Because I hate the way that it makes you look at me, like I'm some kind of criminal."

"That's not what I think," I say, and it's true. I open my mouth to tell him this, but the particles of dust stirred up by his entrance tickle my nose. I cover my mouth and sneeze as quietly as possible. It still sounds like a chipmunk that's recently had a sex change operation.

"That's not exactly the pledge of understanding that I was hoping for," James says, "but I'll take it."

The dark is making his voice lower, warmer, and more rumbly. His shoulder is level with my ears. I don't know if it's a trick of the light or what, but at the moment it looks very comfortable. *Distraction,* I try to remind myself, but my brain doesn't care. It would be so easy to just sort of rest my head on it for a few to see if it's as comfortable as it looks. . . .

"You can if you want," James says.

I will be so glad when James is finally done with vampire puberty. "You have to stop doing that."

"I can't help it. Your thoughts are very strong," he says. "It's another reason I would like to not be . . . this . . . anymore. Mind reading is fun until you find out that your chemistry teacher dreamed he was a transvestite the night before."

"Mr. George?" I ask, suddenly beset by an image that is both hilarious and terrifying.

"Mr. George," James confirms. "The thoughts of yours I catch are at least amusing."

Is it wrong to be flattered by that? Because I am. Until I am struck by a very important distinction.

"Amusing ha-ha or amusing he-he?" I ask.

"I have no idea what the difference is."

I give him a withering look that is unfortunately wasted in the dark. "Amusing ha-ha is funny. Amusing he-he implies snickering. Obviously."

"Got it," he says, and then makes me wait for the answer. "Amusing ha-ha."

Okay, I am flattered. It nudges me to suggest something that has been rattling around in the back of my mind for these past few weeks. "What if, when I find her, we talk to her. Explain things to her. Then if she wants to help you, if she chooses to help you . . ." I trail off, but the meaning is clear. "We could work together."

"Together," James says as he steps closer, only the way he says it makes it sound about thirty times sexier.

"Together," I repeat, starting to ramble in an effort to cover up the fact that my heart is pounding so loud that I imagine my other organs might complain. "It wouldn't be that different from asking someone to donate blood. I mean, I'm not all that sure about the particulars. Like do you have to actually drink it from her neck?" I ask. "Or maybe we don't have to tell her. Can we say it's for needy children and then, I don't know, put it in a thermos? I'm not sure about that from an ethical standpoint, but we should discuss." I stop when I realize that he's gone still, most likely out of disgust. "It was the thermos bit that took it over the edge, wasn't it?" There's still no answer. "James?"

I barely have time to register his head swooping down in the dark, and then he's kissing me and even though this is a distraction, I want this. His lips are firm but cool, and I grab the side shelving to keep my balance. At first I'm too stunned to do anything normal like close my eyes, and I'm thankful that he has his closed so he doesn't see me staring at his cheekbones like some sort of goggle-eyed amphibian. I lower my lids and concentrate on kissing him back, offering up a fervent prayer that my repeated viewings of the last five minutes of *Grease* in the fifth grade will finally pay off. Because he's definitely improved since the hammock.

He smiles against my lips, and I realize that he must have heard that, but for once I don't care. His hands slide to my waist, and I lean forward to wrap my arms around his neck. He tugs me forward against his chest, his palms brushing against my sides as his hands slide upward. I'm standing up on tiptoes to move closer when suddenly he pulls back. Even in the dark I can tell that he's puzzled.

"Are you wearing a battery pack?" he asks.

His fingers have found the hard edge of Vlad's book. Evidence of my snooping will bring a swift end to the kissing truce, and I was just getting the hang of it.

"Oh, well, funny story . . . ," I start to say as his fingers continue to explore upward. When they reach the bare skin of my back, I jump. "Your hands are cold!"

That was the wrong thing to say. James backs away.

"Not bad cold," I say hastily. "Cold like eggs! Like eggs when you take them out of the refrigerator."

He makes a sound that's half laugh, half choke.

"And eggs are, um, full of protein." *Shut up, Sophie. Shut up.*

James doesn't agree or disagree with my nutritional claims. Instead he peers out into the kitchen. "I should go," he says, and I can tell that I've ruined the moment. "There's no sign of Vlad. You should go too."

I suddenly feel a little guilty for hiding in a closet kissing people when Vlad is out there stalking the girls I supposedly came here to protect. "I'm not finished at the party yet," I say, just when a familiar voice echoes from the room beyond.

"What is it, Marisabel?" Vlad says, annoyed. "There are girls with skin to check. And have you seen my journal? I was sure that it would be upstairs."

James looks at me, his eyes narrowing. "Sophie—"

"It's fine," I hiss, rushing to the door to peer through the slats. Vlad is leaning against the oven while Marisabel faces him. Violet has cleared out, and from the way Vlad is scowling, I would say that was a smart move. His right hand flexes with impatience. When Marisabel doesn't respond, he clangs it down on the front burner.

"What is it?" he snaps again.

"Just hold on a second, would you?" Marisabel says, and then closes her eyes as she massages her temples. "This is hard for me."

"Thinking? I know."

Marisabel's eyes snap open. "That."

"That what?"

"That attitude, that tone, is why I'm doing this. You don't give me the respect I deserve," she says heatedly, and if noiselessness weren't vital to my well-being, I would clap.

Vlad, however, doesn't applaud; he rolls his eyes.

"Really, Marisabel. Do we have to do this now?"

"Don't act like we've done this before. I've kept my mouth shut for sixty years. I've done everything for you. I hand-wrote one hundred invitations to this stupid party just so you could find your precious girl, and I didn't even get a thank-you."

He sniffs in disbelief, but it only makes her speak more loudly.

"I hunt for you when you're lazy," she continues, "and I clean for you when you're disgusting. And I'm done. We're done, Vlad."

The pronouncement hangs in the air. I can tell that Marisabel's waiting eagerly for his reaction. One of the only joys in ending a bad relationship, I imagine, is seeing if you can make him cry. But if that's what she wants, she doesn't get it. Vlad does look shocked—after sixty years of getting away with snide comments, this speech must come as a surprise. He doesn't, however, get down on his knees and beg.

"I think it's for the best," he says calmly. If he looks anything, it's relieved.

Marisabel's confidence wilts. "I don't understand," she says, her voice thick with emotion. "Don't you care?"

"It was going to end soon anyway."

"What do you mean?"

"I think that it is better this way," Vlad non-answers. "To make a clean break."

Marisabel turns and stares intently at a far corner of the room, biting her bottom lip as though struggling not to cry while Vlad looks like he could whistle.

"Something's not right here," James murmurs from beside me, and I jump at the reminder of how close he's standing.

"What do you mean?"

"I've never seen Vlad give up something this easily," he says.

"Why did he drag her all the way out here, then? I mean, if he doesn't care . . ."

"I don't know."

I open my mouth to ask another question, but end up sucking in a lungful of dust, sparking a coughing fit. Alarmed, James claps his hands over my mouth, but it's too late. Vlad's head snaps toward the pantry, and before I can blink, the door flies open.

Fingers clench around my bicep, and I'm dragged out into the dim light, disoriented and still hacking. Vlad's hands press down on my shoulders. I try to tear them off, but it only causes him to dig his fingers deeper into the tender flesh of my neck.

"You!" Vlad snaps, angrier now than when he was being broken up with. "Always you! Asking questions, meddling . . . I could go on," he says coldly and drags me up until my toes strain to stay on the ground. "Who invited her?" he growls, and then looks to where Marisabel is hovering. "Did you invite her?"

"Maybe I did," she says with a shaky bravado as her hand curls around the handle of the refrigerator like a vine. "But who cares? I don't have to listen to you anymore."

"I will deal with you later," Vlad says, not bothering to hide the undercurrent of menace. We have drawn a crowd. Violet stands, saucer-eyed, at the front of the pack, and Neville's disapproving head towers over the rest of my hushed classmates. For a second Vlad looks shamed. I see him try to shake himself back into the role of benevolent host. His grip on me sags as he adopts a tight smile. "This is a private matter," he says, and a handful of people actually turn around and start to head back to the living room. Relieved, Vlad reminds them cheerily to try the cheese puffs. But then James's voice calls out from behind us, and curiosity draws them back.

"I don't know about that, Vlad. Seems like something's going on. Why don't you just let her go and we can talk about this?" he suggests, nodding to the audience before stepping forward with a hand out, as though he can gently nudge the irate vampire away from me.

Vlad explodes, removing one hand from my neck to shove him back into the counter.

"You stay out of this!" he hisses as I scramble to keep at least one foot on the ground. "You are as bad as she is! Always lurking about—it's like you forget what you're here for!" When James says nothing, he turns back to me. "Tell me why you were in that pantry."

"I was . . . talking with James," I say weakly. Technically it's not a lie.

"Wrong," Vlad says. "Try again."

I can't think of a good excuse. "I was talking with James," I repeat.

"Lies!" he snaps, and drops me so fast that I fall to my knees and heave toward the tiled floor. I fully expect a swift kick to the stomach or a karate chop to the back. I don't expect to feel the back hem of my T-shirt being dragged over my shoulders and torn away while Vlad yells, "And the invitation clearly dictated bathing suits only!"

The shirt catches around my neck and ears, and for a second I am smothered in cotton. When it is finally free and I am allowed to fall back forward, the rush of air feels like the breeze before the storm. I should look at Vlad's face, prepare myself for the coming violence, but any willpower I might have possessed has abandoned ship. I wait for him to strike. *If I contract every muscle in my body it will make my skin into a fortress!* I think wildly, but the truth is that I will be lucky to escape this without something breaking. Still, he can't kill me in front of all these people. He'll kick me out for spying, but he doesn't know how much I know. Right? Right. No need to panic.

And then I realize that the warm, flat weight on my back is Vlad's book, tucked into the waistband of my jeans.

"Vlad," James says, his voice urgent, panicked, but Vlad cuts him off.

"So," Vlad says from above me, "a thief and a spy. Read anything interesting?"

I feel the cool scrabble of fingers on my back as he slides the journal out, not bothering to keep his nails from scraping my spine. The pain is just the shock I need to scramble to my feet and charge toward the door.

"Let me through!" I yell when I hit the wall of chests and elbows that clutter up the main hallway, and to its credit, the front line tries to part. But the crowd is too deep, there's nowhere for them to go. Whirling around, I see that James is blocking Vlad, arms outstretched. But Vlad is not trying to move forward, and the expression overtaking his face is not one that I've seen before. It's not angry, it's not even jaded or cynical. Instead, Vlad is blinking in amazement.

"Turn around," he says suddenly.

"What?" I ask, confused. If Vlad thinks that I am going to do the hokey-pokey before he kills me, he is sadly mistaken.

"Turn around!" Vlad roars. "Show me your back."

"No!" I yell out of habit, and regret it immediately. Perhaps I should do what the angry vampire says. My eyes search out James's, hoping for some hint of encouragement, but he looks just as confused as I feel. I swing my questioning gaze to Violet, who stands at the front of the crowd.

"Well, there are quite a few freckles on your back," Violet says as though breaking bad news, "but I think Vlad is overreacting. It does not look so horrible."

Vlad turns to address the clutch of students still huddling by the door. "I sincerely thank you all for coming. Do show yourselves out, and feel free to take a carrot for the road." When they make no move to go, he crowds them back through the door. "Really, if you do not move your foot I will have to kick you," he tells some unfortunate student. "Thank you."

He thinks it's me. He thinks it's me because I have freckles on my back. This entire time I've been assuming that Vlad's plan had some basis in reality merely because he had followed it so diligently, but now I see that he is crazy on top of crazy on top of crazy. The realization cuts through the fog of shock and confusion that has been keeping me immobile. I make a break for the side hallway only to skid to a stop when a large form swims out of the darkness.

"Ah, Devon, you are here. Tell Ashley to make sure all of our guests have vacated the premises and then guard the front door," Vlad orders before turning around and starting to walk toward me with a smile that's wide enough to show his incisors. "Now, let me see your back."

"They're freckles," I say and then turn around. "Not a birthmark. Freckles."

Jabbing a finger against the base of my spine, he starts to count. "One, two, three," he says, growing more excited with every number. "Four, five, six, seven, eight. I admit, it is not what I expected, but it is a star. It was said to appear differently every time."

James steps between us and points at what I assume are different freckles. "Nine, ten, eleven, twelve. I could make anything. I could make the Big Dipper."

"It is true," Violet says solemnly. "I see a heart. And a pineapple."

Vlad levels her with a dark glance and then reaches out to grab my arm. James knocks it away.

"Don't touch her," he says, all traces of diplomacy gone as he steps between us once again.

"This is getting tiresome," Vlad says. "Do you think

you can keep her for yourself? Because you did not provide much help. But I will make a deal—move away and I will—" He stops abruptly, his eyes trailing over James's shoulder, to where I am doing my best to blend in with the counter. "Why does she not appear more confused?" he asks and then looks back at him with a chilling anger. "You told me she had forgotten."

"Guess I lied," James says, and though it comes out laconic, I feel his muscles tense in preparation for Vlad's next move. The other vampires are sharing nervous looks; Neville, especially, seems like he is about to be sick. But even his expression changes to shock when Vlad starts to laugh.

"I suppose it is only fair," he says when it's faded to an intermittent chuckle.

"How is it fair?" James snaps.

"I lied to you," Vlad says. "That nonsense about her blood being able to restore your humanity? I made it up so that you would come here and help search."

"No. I don't believe you," James says, but I remember his note.

Vlad chuckles again. "Ask Neville if you do not believe me. No one knows more about the girl than the Danae."

If possible, Neville's face has gone whiter. "I have never heard that particular myth, no," he says. "But I should say something—"

"See!" Vlad says to James. "There is no reason to guard her anymore. Step aside."

But James just backs closer to me, close enough that I could reach out and grip his back. *I'm sorry,* I think, hoping that for once he will hear it. I can't see his face. I wish I could see his face.

Vlad's eyebrows dart up. "You are making a dangerous choice," he says. "Even if you survive this, which is highly doubtful, you will have to—Violet, please get out of the way, I am trying to threaten him."

Violet is standing by James's elbow, tugging up the arm of her sagging costume with purpose. "I do not think that it is Sophie. And even if it were, I think I have changed my mind about helping."

"Me too," Marisabel says defiantly, pushing away from the refrigerator to flank James's other side. "I think it would be for the best if *you* left."

Vlad's lips curl in disbelief before he lets out a bark of laughter. "Neville, help me."

But Neville doesn't move; he begins to ramble. "I

think you have been under a lot of pressure. I know I myself am crippled by the number of take-home essays that dragon who teaches German has been assigning. Perhaps you should rest awhile, and then if you still think that she exists, we will—"

"If she exists?" he roars. "*If* she exists? You are Danae! She is the reason *you* exist! Your entire organization began as a pact between families to protect *her.*"

"About that, yes, well, you see, I didn't really think that it would come to this, but I suppose . . ." He pushes his shoulders back, gathering courage. "I have a confession to make. I am not in the Danae."

"Not Danae?" Vlad asks. "But you know everything about them. Your knowledge surpasses mine, even after decades of research." Striding across the room, he grabs Neville's arm and pushes up his sleeve. "You have the mark!"

"Let me rephrase," he says, extracting his hand. "I *was* in the Danae, but I was expelled for reasons that I would rather not go into."

"I knew it!" Marisabel says. "I told you he was fishy, I told you!"

"I am indeed fishy," Neville says sadly. "But you

have to understand—being expelled from the Danae is a death sentence. I barely escaped execution. And I thought, what better place to hide than with a family of Unnamed?"

He is cut off by Vlad's hands wrapping around his throat and slamming him into a cupboard. "You will take me to them," he orders with murderous softness, "and you will tell them that I have found her, like we planned. I do not care if they kill you."

"Even if I take you to them," Neville rasps, "they will not care!"

"What?"

"They do not believe the child exists," he says. "I am sorry. I should not have encouraged your wild goose chase, but I thought I would be even safer in a human high school. No one expects to find vampires in high school," he says, attempting an apologetic smile.

Vlad throws him back against the cupboard hard enough that it cracks. He points at me, his finger trembling. "*She* exists," he seethes.

Neville shakes his head. "They performed extensive research in the nineteenth century; the Mervaux line is dead. It's true that every so often people show up claiming otherwise, but we—they—laugh them off as kooks. And that's when they want to be reminded at all."

"Kooks?" Vlad echoes.

"Yes. Like that man who wrote that book? What was it? *The Lost Daughter*? Or one of those humans who believe in Largefoot." He chuckles nervously. "I mean, you have to admit, it all sounds a bit unbelievable, all these long-lost human vampire children running around with star birthmarks. And besides," Neville continues, "the Danae would never let in an Unnamed. They only select their members from the original nine families."

For a moment there is complete silence. Then Vlad rips the microwave off the wall and hurls it at Neville, who barely has time to duck before Vlad advances, roaring death threats about how he will twist Neville's head from his neck using his bare hands. James nudges me toward the kitchen's side exit.

"He's distracted," James says, taking my hand and pulling me through the dark hallway. When we reach the end, he peeks around the corner. "Devon and Ashley are still at the front, but there's a back door through that room. Try to avoid them on your way to the car."

His face is turned away, all I can see is the tic of his jaw working. "But—"

"Sophie, it's too dangerous for you to be here."

"I can't just leave!"

"Yes, you can."

"But what if—" There's a loud crack as Vlad tears the pantry door off its hinges. After smashing it against the floor and picking up one of the fragments, he chases Neville into the living room. Violet and Marisabel follow, yelling at him to drop it. Three years of karate or not, vampire fights are probably out of my league.

"They are," James says and then looks at me with a new intensity. "I'm asking you to go. Please. We're working together now, right? I can't do this if I'm worried about you."

With a sinking feeling, I realize that I have no other choice. When I say okay, I'm met with James's overwhelming relief. Before I can regret it, I grab his cheeks and kiss him on the mouth, hard. "It's the adrenaline," I blurt, and then leave him to fight alone.

Chapter Fourteen

That adrenaline, which got me down the hill and into my car, abandons me as soon as I reach my house. Vlad's plan is in shambles—I should be ecstatic. Instead I'm sitting with my head on the steering wheel, wondering how to combat the worry that is threatening to choke me. No matter what James said, I shouldn't have left. I could have at least sat on the sidelines and thrown cheese doodles at Vlad or offered an appropriately timed "Watch out!"

Caroline's VW Bug pulls up behind me, and she slams the door closed, not minding the late hour. She hums as she rifles through her bag, throwing out gum wrappers whenever she finds them—and here my dad has pinned the rampant littering on the paperboy. She stops mid-hum when she reaches my rearview mirror.

"Omigod," she says, bending forward to talk to me through the window. "Marta texted me and said that Vlad had some sort of meltdown at the party and kicked everyone out. You have to tell me what happened."

"I really don't want to talk about it," I say, forcing myself to get out of the car. What didn't happen would be the more accurate question. Caroline's heels make eager clicks as she follows me up the porch stairs.

"But she said that you and he got in a fight and—" She stops when she catches sight of my face. "What's wrong? If Vlad was a jerk, I will totally mace him on Monday. Or was it James? I don't know him as well, but whatever, I'll mace him too."

"No macing necessary."

She puts her hand on my wrist. "I mean it, Sophie. You're worrying me. You never look this sad. You're usually just kind of . . . intense."

"Gee thanks," I say as we push into the dark foyer, but I am stunned to realize that at the moment I would give anything to sit down on the couch with Caroline and confess everything while strangling one of her stuffed animals. But I can't, so I just tell her not to worry and that I just want to go to bed and sleep forever.

"Well, okay," she says, hopping onto the first step. "But anyone who wants to wake you up tomorrow has to go through me. I mean, after I'm up, which probably won't be until, like, eleven. But after eleven? No way is anyone knocking on your door."

"Much appreciated," I say, and then smile at her back as she disappears up the stairs. I have no intention of going to sleep. I walk into the living room, grab a blanket out of the trunk that serves as a coffee table, and head for the uncomfortable chair by the window that nobody likes to sit in, but which has a direct view to James's front yard. But before I sit down I catch a glimpse of myself in the long mirror above the entertainment cabinet.

My black hair is falling out of the bun I twisted it into at the beginning of the evening. I look paler than normal, I note, and the fact that residual stress is making it hard to unclench my jaw isn't doing any favors for what I've always thought is a chin that leans toward the pointy side. Somehow in all the drama, I forgot that all I'm wearing is a red bikini top. Curious, I contort myself as much as possible to study the freckles on my back, which have always been too many to count. It's true that some of them are darker than others, but I certainly don't see any kind of a star. To be fair, I don't see a pineapple, either.

Feeling stupid for even looking, I curl up in the chair as best as I can and watch James's driveway. I don't know when my eyes betray me and I fall asleep, but I wake up to groggy light pouring through the window and a Post-it note stuck to my head.

Told you I wouldn't let anyone wake you—didn't know you'd be sleeping in THE CHAIR, still wearing MY BIKINI. Seriously, something's up. Anyway, Dad went in to work and Mom and I went to the mall so I could take back that pink dress I bought when I was dating Vlad. 'Nuff said. —Caroline

The mention of Vlad brings the events of last night rushing back. My eyes fly to James's dark house, but considering his no-lights-ever policy, that means nothing. Tossing the blanket aside, I stagger to the front door on legs that are cramped and half-asleep, telling myself that of course he'll be there. Because I don't want to face what it might mean if he is not.

The doorbell rings when my fingertips are only inches from the knob. Relieved, I yank it open without thinking. "About time. I was starting to get—"

The words die on my tongue. Vlad is standing on my porch, the black T-shirt I wore last night dangling from one finger.

"I have come to return your blouse," he says congenially, but wedges a black boot in the door when I try to slam it closed. With practiced ease, he grips the knob and pushes it forward forcefully enough that I stumble backward. After he walks inside, he surveys the foyer with curiosity. I should run, bolt through the kitchen and tear outside, but then to . . . where?

"You can keep it," I croak, gripping the wall in a futile attempt to feel secure. "Get out of my house."

He ignores me, tilting his head to the side and examining the shirt with what I can only call brave affection. "Perhaps I should start calling you Cinderella," he jokes. "Although next time I might prefer a glass slipper instead of such a . . . well . . . a well-loved blouse."

It strikes me that Vlad alive, quipping in my house means . . . "Where are the other vampires?"

Vlad says nothing, just continues to do his best impression of an evil coat rack. I realize that I will get no answers unless I play along. Darting forward as quickly as possible, I rip the shirt from his hands and wiggle into it. The thin barrier of cotton does nothing to make me feel safer.

Vlad pulls out his little black book. "I hope that you will take this as a gesture of goodwill, *dorogaya*."

"I don't want your feelings journal, thanks."

"Then why did you rifle through my belongings? You have followed me around since the very beginning, interfering, asking questions about my history and my vehicle preference."

"That was back when I thought you weren't just someone who's spent too much time with the books in the back of the library."

Anger, dark and ugly, washes over his face, and I think that I've gone too far. There is no reason now for him not to kill me and get a blood boost as a consolation prize on the way out of town. I am going to run; at least I won't die without a fight. I dash for the living room, planning to head for the back door, but he's in front of me before I can even make it to the couch. When I look up, he's peering down at me with a brittle smile.

"Wonderful idea, Sophochka," he says from between gritted teeth. "Sit and I will explain the reason for my visit," he says and unfurls a hand toward the sofa.

"How did you find me?" I ask, cautiously sitting.

He gives me a withering look. "I did endure your sister for a very lengthy week. But even if that were not the case, Violet always chattered on about how she would call on her good friend Sophie, but she had used her last card." He pulls a ragged square of paper from his pocket and flicks it across the coffee table. "I found this in her possessions."

I open it to find the address I scrawled down for her that first day in English class. What must have happened to give Vlad the opportunity to prowl through Violet's belongings? My fingers tremble. I never should have left.

"Where are the other vampires?" I ask again, but

Vlad has already sauntered over to the far wall that Marcie has transformed into a shrine of family photographs. It runs chronologically from left to right, from pudgy snowsuits to Caroline and me trying to be ironic while standing next to Minnie Mouse and failing because we both still secretly loved her.

"Where is your mother?" he asks as he examines our early years.

"The mall."

He gives a strained chuckle. "Your real mother. Because here you are with cake on your face at what I hope is an early birth celebration," he says, pointing at a red-framed photo, "and there Caroline is at hers, but you do not appear in the same photographs until . . . here." He points at the photo of all of us standing in front of this house; I was five and Caroline was six, and we had all just moved in together.

"That's none of your business," I say. The truth was that my mother left when I was two, and no matter what tricks I pulled, my father wouldn't talk about it. As I got older, I realized that someone who didn't bother to stick around to take care of her two-year-old wasn't worth the fascination. Child psychologists may call me a liar, but I honestly don't think about her much, other than to curse the genetics that turn me into a lobster after one hour in the sun while everyone else gets to look like a sexy peanut. And now I can add giving a conspiracy-theorist vampire more fuel for his theory.

"You still think that it's me," I say. "After everything Neville told you, you think that it's me because I have a stepmother and you can play connect the dots on my back."

He turns to look at me. "I have other reasons."

"Mental illness?"

His nostrils flare. "Neville's betrayal was a blow, to be sure, but perhaps they kicked him out because he is not to be trusted. And then there is my recent realization," he says, and then pauses as though waiting for a drumroll. I refuse to give it to him.

"Where are my friends?" I ask again.

"They are gone!" Vlad explodes. "They have left! I told them if I ever saw them again I would burn them all alive myself."

I don't move. He is not boasting of killing them, and knowing Vlad, he would if he could. But James wouldn't have just left without saying good-bye; he couldn't. When I continue not to say anything, Vlad throws his journal at me hard enough that it *thwaps* against the couch cushion. After a few moments he clears his throat and pretends that handing it to me was his intention all along.

"Please, Sophochka, turn to the marked page and read the underlined section aloud."

I pick up the journal with trembling fingers and begin to read the beginning of the section I didn't make it to the night before. "And the child of the Mervaux was mortal, immune to the vampire. There were those who thought that it—"

"You can stop," he says and then leans forward to tear it back out of my hands. "Do you see?"

"See what?"

"I cannot influence you," he says. "I always assumed that 'immune' meant only that the child was mortal in birth, but now I see the evidence was there all along. I can sense your thoughts flickering, but I cannot grasp them."

I'm relieved that this is his big revelation. Frankly, exceptions to their powers ranks right up there with miracle babies on the list of things that vampires should stop being so surprised about.

"Sorry to burst your bubble, but James taught me how to prevent you from butting in."

For a second, his triumphant expression wavers, but then he doggedly shakes his head. "No. That first night, in the woods, I tried to use my sway over you and it did not work. You wiggled when I bit you."

It's on the tip of my tongue to tell him that James hears more than enough of my thoughts, but I stop, partly because thoughts of James will make me lose my focus and partly because I make the mistake of meeting Vlad's eyes. They are steel gray and glittering with single-minded purpose. He's pursued this for almost half a decade; no matter what I say, he will twist it around to fit his theory. Even if I do manage to convince him that I'm not the one he wants, he will start his search again, and I'll be back to lurking in locker rooms trying to predict his next target. Or dead.

"Maybe it is me," I lie, "but like Neville said, you have to be one of the original nine families."

"Neville underestimates me if he thinks that I was not aware of that," Vlad snaps, and then just as suddenly, stands and walks to the bookcase. "Do you know how old I am?" he asks, slipping out one of my father's historical tomes and idly paging through it. "One hundred and eight. I grew up in—"

"Romania," I say.

"Why does everyone always assume that?" he asks, genuinely perturbed as he shoves the book back onto the shelf. "I am Russian. I have been speaking glorious Russian endearments to you." He closes his eyes and touches the bridge of his nose, what I'm coming to understand is the vampire equivalent of taking a calming breath. When he opens them, he asks, "Do you want to know why I became a vampire?"

Latent egomaniacal tendencies is my guess, but I just shake my head.

"My family had fallen, along with the czar, during the revolution. Everything, everything we were, was stripped in an instant and we were forced to throw ourselves on the mercy of relatives who we would not even have let in our door a year earlier," he sneers. "But then . . . then came this creature who offered a chance to be above all that. Power, strength, eternity, all in one bite. Little did I know that in the society of the vampires she was nothing more than a parasite. I started my eternal life even lower than my mortal one," he says, turning to face me with his eyes lit up with more pure emotion than I have ever seen him show. "But you . . . you are my way back. I have dedicated every day of the past forty-four years to restoring you to them. To restoring me. I will not give up now."

Suddenly, he is kneeling in front of me, gripping my fingers and holding on tight when I try to pull away.

"I have come to admire many things about you, Sophochka," he says. "Your unique sense of what should be worn and when. Your eccentric wit. Your relentless curiosity, and your . . ." He blinks as though he's come up blank. ". . . your pluck. Is that the right word? I do not know the contemporary phrase. Nevertheless, I would be honored if you would become my vampire wife."

For a second I can only gape, and then I am yelling, all thoughts of diplomacy disappearing in a vortex of shock.

"Are you insane?" I scream, scrambling over the back of the couch in my effort to get away from him. My leg catches on the way over, and I fall, banging my knee against the hardwood floor. The next thing I know he is beside me, extending a gentlemanly hand and chiding me for crawling around on the floor during such an important moment.

"But why?" I ask when I can finally form words again.

He does everything but roll his eyes to show his impatience. "You are Mervaux. And since you are of greater rank, once we marry I will be Mervaux as well." He pauses. "Also because of the previous attributes I mentioned. Well, what is your answer?"

"No," I say. "No. Never. *Nyet*."

My vehemence throws him off for a second, but not much longer. "You are being coy. You should be grateful that I came here to pull you out of obscurity. Not many at your high school even know who you are."

"I like it that way."

He chuckles until he sees that I am serious. "No one likes it that way. Come now, you must agree, or it will not be valid," he insists. "I will wait here and ask your father for your hand. Will he be long?"

The thought of Vlad having any contact with my parents, of edging any further into my world, makes my heart seize in terror. He is playing nice now, but who knows how long it will be before his patience thins. I need to get him out of my house; I need space to plan.

Doing my best not to wobble, I get to my feet. "I need time," I stall.

"Time? What would you possibly need to consider? I am offering you an eternity of prestige."

"You tried to kill me."

"I was not aware of who you were," he says as though I am being childish, but when he sees that this is not enough to make me swoon, adds, "I understand your surprise and hesitation, *dorogaya*, I do. I have been remiss in not courting you with more . . . delicacy. I will tell you what—I will make a few circuits around the neighborhood, and when I return you may give me your agreement."

"A month," I say, and then immediately wish that I had said a century. Or an eon. Or a googol-eon.

Vlad shakes his head. "This has taken far longer than I expected already. I had assumed that your vampire lineage would raise you above your human peers, which is why I began with your sister. Little did I know you would be a l—" He stops, reevaluating his word choice. "A diamond in the rough. No, I will give you a day to understand that I am not someone to fear."

My tenuous grip on sanity starts to crumble. A day is not enough time. I'm so wrapped up in my thoughts that it takes a moment before I register the sound of Marcie's minivan bouncing into the driveway and her shout at Caroline to come back and help her carry in all the diet soda that she made her buy. This is it. Everything's going to collide and there's no way to stop it from spiraling out of control. I look up, expecting to find him watching me with a triumphant look, but instead he's watching the door with an unadulterated terror that almost mirrors my own.

"I need your answer now," he snaps. "Your sister has been sending me letters, endless letters asking me to tell her what went wrong in our relationship."

"A week," I say quickly. "Give me a week."

He hesitates. Footsteps reverberate up the wooden porch steps.

"A week," I insist.

"Agreed," he says. "Now, quick, point me to the back entrance. She cannot find me here. I have told her we are different people a thousand times."

"A week without you coming to see me," I clarify as we hear the jingle of keys in the lock.

"Fine!" he yells. "Where is the exit?"

I point to the room behind me. And then with a whoosh and the sound of a chair toppling in the dining room, he's finally out of my house.

When Caroline bangs into the foyer, she's clutching a twelve-pack of diet root beer. "Why is there a silver Hummer parked on the street?" she says excitedly, ripping the iPod buds out of her ears. "Seriously, what is wrong with you? You're standing in the middle of the room like you're cataclysmic or something."

"I just woke up," I say, but it sounds hollow even to me.

"Right, okay, whatever," Caroline says, looking around the room. "Is Vlad here?"

The eagerness in her voice is only a hard-edged reminder of what I am dealing with, how hard it will be to keep everyone safe. "Why would Vlad be here?" I say as casually as I can.

"I thought maybe he had gotten my note and—"

"He's not here, Caroline."

"Oh," she says, her hope visibly deflating. "Anyway, warning—Mom was out jogging this morning, and she swears that she saw a boy who looked like James Hallowell going next door. I tried to tell her she was crazy, but I'm pretty sure she suspects. If I were you, I'd pretend you don't know anything."

Joy bursts through the catatonia, and I grab Caroline by the shoulders. "James? James is next door?"

"Good. Act exactly like that!" she calls out behind me as I run out the back door and across the yard.

Chapter Fifteen

I bang on James's back door, and then, when that fails to make it open, kick it at the same time. It's no longer a knock, it's a cacophony, and I keep it up until the door finally swings inward.

"What—," James begins, but he stops when I hug him like someone they just let out of the asylum for hugging maniacs, but only because they were facing overcrowding.

"You're alive," I say into his neck.

"I think you're strangling me."

"You don't breathe."

"Good point." After a moment's hesitation, he wraps

his arms around my back and slips his thumbs into the belt loops at my waist. It feels familiar and intimate and I like it. I allow myself a few moments to bask in this joy before I have to face the new situation with Vlad.

James pulls back and frowns. "What situation with—," he starts to ask, but I punch him on the shoulder.

"Why didn't you let me know that you were fine?"

"I tried!"

"When?"

"I threw rocks at your window as soon as we made it back."

"We?" I ask just as I spot Violet in the room behind, dwarfed by an oversized T-shirt and gray sweatpants that are rolled up at the cuffs to expose their fuzzy underbelly. Her hair is still pulled back, but a few loose tendrils curl around her ears. A floral sheet is draped over the end of the banister.

"Marisabel's here too," James says quickly.

"And that makes this . . . better?"

His eyes widen. "No! I mean, Marisabel and Neville." He runs a hand through his hair. "I probably should have said him first."

"You didn't tell me you were having a slumber party," I say, but Violet bounces over before he can respond.

"Oh no, it is nothing as fun as that," she says. "Vlad kicked us out and ruined the dress I made."

"Vlad tried to kill us, Violet," he says.

"Well, yes, that too. Come on—we are discussing our next step in the salon," she says, grabbing my hand and dragging me behind her.

James has added a few things to the living room since I first peeked through the window that first day of school, most of which I've seen gracing the neighborhood curbs this past month: an orange-and-brown plaid couch that could only have come from the seventies, a small television that still has a VHS slot, and an uneven coffee table that's only standing because there's a thick copy of *The Wall Street Journal* beneath one leg. What do you know—a vampire really did steal my dad's paper.

I take a seat beside a despondent-looking Marisabel. She's alternating between staring into space and idly trying to pick out the tangles at her shoulders.

"What were we talking about?" James says, suddenly sounding very weary.

"I would like the largest room," Marisabel says.

"Violet claims that she should have it because there are purple curtains, but I saw it first."

"You did not," Violet says. "And I still do not see why you do not want the bedroom with the green paper, because it matches your eyes."

They both look at James, who is rubbing his own eyes in frustration. "I told you both that I don't care who has the master bedroom; you're not going to be sleeping in it anyway. And this is just temporary until you find out where to go."

Marisabel's face crumples. "But I don't have any-where to go!"

Violet shoots him a dirty look before moving to pat Marisabel's knee. "You can be very insensitive at times," she tells James. "Do you know about this aspect of yourself?"

Before James can defend himself, Neville stands. He's been sitting against the wall looking guilty, but now his face looks determined. "James may be insensitive, but he is right. Now is not the time for discussing bedroom arrangements. We barely managed to escape with our lives last night, and I for one do not believe that the danger has passed. He might very well be coming for us, and we need to be ready; we need to be prepared; we need to be at full streng. . . " He trails off when he sees that I've raised my hand. "Yes? Sophie?"

"I don't think you're Vlad's number-one concern," I begin, but then catch sight of Marisabel's face. Ever since we stopped talking about bedrooms, she's done nothing but sniffle. The fact that Vlad has proposed to someone else a day after they ended a sixty-year relationship and tried to kill her might be the final stake to the heart. While Violet continues to pat her consolingly, I look at James and Neville. "Can we talk somewhere else?"

"We can go to my room," James says, his face worried. "Just to be safe."

As we wind past the dining room on our way upstairs, I notice that the wild floral wallpaper hasn't changed—the last time I stood in that room was when we said *adios* to the Hallowells over chips and dip. Marcie made a heartfelt toast while I stood in a corner and tried to blend into the jungle of mauve flowers, hoping no one—especially James—noticed how miserable it was making me. But everything else is different. The hallways are eggshell blue instead of the old hunter green, and the stairs beneath my feet have been varnished to a different woody hue.

"Even my baseball wallpaper is gone," James says when we've reached his room. I study the place where I spent hours trying to beat him at all of his video games. Back then the floor was always littered with sports cards and electronic wires, but now there's nothing but dust. It used to be crammed with bookshelves, but now the only piece of furniture is a full-size bed covered with a navy blue spread. Unlike everything else in the house, it looks new.

"Sophie, what happened?" James asks.

As I take a seat on the bed next to Neville, I search for words that will make it sound less insane, but then realize that they don't exist. So I calmly explain the facts about the particularly demented way that Vlad has decided to proceed. The reactions are as expected.

"Ha-ha," James says flatly. "No, seriously."

"*Seriously*," I say. "He shoved his way into my house this morning to backhandedly propose."

"But why—"

"He thinks it will make him Mervaux," I say and then look to where Neville has put his head in his hands. "Will it?"

"If you were who he thought you were, I suppose," Neville says. "Oh, I should never have encouraged his delusions."

I'm thinking that that may actually be the understatement of the year, when James clears his throat.

"Uh . . . did you tell him no?" he asks.

I give him the death look to end all death looks. "Yes, James, I told him no, but for some reason he wouldn't accept 'Thanks, but no thanks.' I finally got him to agree to give me a week to think things over, but who knows if he'll stick to that." I turn to Neville. "What exactly happens at a vampire marriage?"

"The usual. You exchange blood before witnesses who will testify to the courts that it was done properly."

Right. Totally the usual.

"But he can't marry you unless you are a vampire," Neville says. "Human-vampire marriages are forbidden."

This gives me a tiny smidgeon of hope. "Violet said that you cannot make someone a vampire unless they agree."

"Ha! No one enforces that. Take me, for example. There I am, fresh from a wonderful performance as

Oberon and feeling generous, so I agree to let the fan who has been sitting in the front row for the past ten shows back for a chat and an autograph. And what does she do? The crazy lady *bites* me. The next thing I know I'm staring up at her and she's saying that she has given me a very special gift and that now I am something called Vandervelde and she will make sure that I am offered a spot in the Danae because she has very powerful connec——"

He stops when he sees my face, which I'm sure is leeched of all color now that he's snipped the small thread of hope I was clinging to. He does his best to train his expression into something encouraging.

"But no, he is not supposed to, and I imagine he will not want to risk the Danae's displeasure. They do like enforcing rules even if they themselves do not follow them," he says before adding more brightly, "Worst-case scenario, he does make you a vampire, but you will still have to agree to marry him. Forced marriages have been held as unlawful in the vampire community for at least three decades."

"You mean centuries," James corrects.

"No, decades," Neville says cheerfully and then gives me a thumbs-up.

Yet another compelling reason for my Why I Should Not Become a Vampire list. The giddiness that came from finding out that everyone was still alive is starting to fade, slowly replaced by a simmering panic. A week is not much time. I need a plan. I need a plan and a big laser gun that takes out any vampires who want to marry me.

"We'll protect you," James says firmly, and while I admit that for a moment my heart melts like a microwaved Reese's Peanut Butter Cup, hiding behind vampire bunkers is only going to get me so far.

"There are five of us, and three of him if you include Ashley and Devon," I say. "There has to be a way that we can get him out of our lives for good."

At first no one says anything, and I wonder how I can be the only one who thinks Vlad has worn out his welcome on this planet.

"Before we can plan anything," Neville says, "we need to deal with—" The gong of the doorbell interrupts him, and the room falls silent; it's probably too much to hope that someone in this crowd ordered a pizza. One second Neville is sitting beside me, and the next he is at one of the small windows, leaning as far forward as it will allow. "I cannot tell from here," he says, "but I find it hard to imagine that he would ring the doorbell before coming to kill us."

I'm about to say that I wouldn't be so sure, but footsteps are already thundering up the stairs. James and Neville flank the door on either side, alert and ready to strike. Whoever is on the other side knocks lightly.

"Are you in there?" Violet chirps. "There is a woman at the door with a very large container. She is asking if Sophie is here, and would like to speak to James as well."

James looks at me questioningly.

"Um, yeah. Marcie knows you're living here," I say and then hold up my hands when he seems perturbed. "Sorry, but I kind of thought Vlad took precedence on the list of things to worry about."

Before he can answer, Violet knocks again. "Hello? I have told her I would return with a decision on whether or not she is to be admitted."

I'm sure that went over well. "We probably have a better chance of getting Vlad to leave town than getting Marcie to leave the door," I tell them.

"Okay," James says. "We'll be down in a second."

When we open the door, Marcie is doing her best to sweep fallen leaves off the porch with the side of her foot while holding a large foil tray of what I would guess is her famous baked ziti. As soon as she sees James she places it on the ledge and gives him a hug, rambling the whole time about how she knows he is a teenager now but she is going to do it anyway.

"I was so sorry to hear about your parents," she says when she pulls away. "Are you all right? Do you need anything? Sophie should have told me that you were back."

"I'm doing okay," James says, a little dazzled. "Thank you for the cake. And the card."

"Oh, you were always so polite," she says, and then looks at me for the first time. "Unlike some children I know."

So this is how she will wreak her vengeance; she will embarrass me to death. There's no great excuse for why I wouldn't have mentioned this to her, so I play the dumb teenager card. "Sorry," I say. "I forgot."

Marcie says nothing, just picks up the tray of ziti. "Can I put this in the kitchen?" she asks James, trying to peer around him.

"I'll do it," I say, eager to escape. After grasping the tray by its edges, I do my best to telegraph a message to James. If she steps foot in the house, we'll be lucky if she thinks James is a vampire rather than a serial killer.

When I get to the kitchen, I flip the wall switch. Yellow light floods the room, exposing a grimy tile floor and a row of empty shelves to my left, their contact paper curling up at the edges. I set the ziti down next to a familiar maroon cake pan—Marcie's previous offering—just as the refrigerator rattles to life. I stare at the metal handle, suddenly gripped by a perverse curiosity. After a few futile seconds, I give in, and then wish that I hadn't. One dark red pouch sits by the meat tray, looking lonely and viscous.

"Marcie went back next door," James says from behind me, and I whirl around to find him leaning against the entryway, watching me calmly. I slam the door shut, embarrassed to be caught rudely poking around in his refrigerator, but he just asks me if I want a drink. "I have water. Well, water and . . . I have water." While I'm still struggling to overcome my shame, he moves to the cabinet and grabs a novelty mug that says, "Don't Let the Bastards Get You Down." After filling it, he hands it to me. "This was left here, by the way. It's not a personal motto."

I take a sip. The water has a metallic edge, and I'm pretty sure that's dust I'm tasting on the rim, but I am nervous enough that I drink it anyway. "So how were you able to get rid of Marcie?"

"She spotted Neville and Marisabel on the stairs, and I told her we were busy working on a group project for school," he says. "I don't think she really bought it, but I still have enough sympathy points that she wasn't going to challenge me. But you might not want to ever go home."

I can only imagine. I look around for a place to sit down, but there are no chairs, only a precarious-looking folding table set up in one corner. Crossing my fingers that it doesn't collapse beneath me, I jump up and joke that maybe I could stay here.

He takes a seat beside me. "Why not?" he says. "Everyone else is. Just don't say that you want the bedroom with the purple curtains."

"I would definitely want the one with the bed," I say and then realize how that sounds. I wonder if I will ever be able to flirt intentionally, as opposed to just accidentally.

"Really?" he says, a little too innocently.

I can do this—I can say something flirtatious and mean to. "Or maybe not. You were always horrible at sharing your things," I tease, but then realize that was just an insult said with an eyebrow wiggle.

James leans in close enough that our arms touch and he smiles, slow and deliberate. "I've gotten better."

I think all of my internal organs just evaporated. "Why do you have a bed if you don't sleep?" I blurt. "It looks new."

"Yeah, that's not where I thought this conversation was going at all," he says before settling back against the wall. "I ordered it. I mean, I sit on it. And sometimes if I close my eyes and lie still for a long time I can . . . blank out for a little bit. It feels like sleeping." He rubs his eyes. "I guess I should get used to it."

In the midst of all the fighting, and preparing, and fielding my stepmother, we haven't had a chance to think about Vlad's big party revelation. "Do you want to talk about it?" I ask.

"What's there to talk about?" he asks bitterly. "I was stupid enough to believe Vlad, and then I was stupid enough to follow Vlad. It serves me right."

"But that doesn't mean—"

"It's fine, Sophie," he says in a way that suggests it's not fine at all.

Unsure of what to say, I look around the room. The previous owner left a decorative plate over the window. Pumpkins dance around the rim, and the central figure is an apron-wearing turkey. Someone went a little crazy at a Yankee Peddler Party.

"I should take that down," he says. "It's weird. And sometimes I think it's staring at me." Realizing that he's answered an unspoken thought again, he shoots me an apologetic look. "Sorry. Your opinion on the plate was very strong."

It's a little eerie how much I've started to take the mind-dropping in stride. "There are worse things, you know."

"Than inheriting turkey apron plates?"

"No! Worse things than being a . . . well, you know."

He doesn't answer at first, and I assume I've tried to push too far again. But then he says, "Like what?"

I hate it when people ask for examples. "Well, you could be *dead* dead, for one thing. And don't even say that would be better," I order before he has a chance to say anything stupid.

"I wasn't."

"Good. And you could be one of those vampires who looks like Batboy and has to sleep in the dirt of his homeland."

His lips twitch into the tiniest smile. "Tell me more, vampire expert."

I choose to ignore the subtle mockery in his voice as long as this makes him feel better. "You could get all bumpy when you want to, er, drink." I watch him, nervous that he can sense my lingering uneasiness with his new diet, and then point to my forehead. "Like a Klingon. Or an allergy victim."

"You sure do know a lot about vampires," he says, leaning close enough that our shoulders touch again.

"I know a normal amount," I say, embarrassed and more than a little distracted. "I can find you twenty people who know more. Most of them have book deals." I suddenly remember something else. "Oh! Oh! You could've lost your soul."

"Lost my soul?"

"Yeah. And while it doesn't completely rule out romance, it makes it trickier."

"We wouldn't want that."

"Nope," I agree before realizing that the atmosphere has suddenly turned . . . crackly? I don't know. What I do know is that his eyes are warm as he leans forward; this is either a kiss or a very slow head-butt. And as much as I would like to make out right now on this card table, I don't think that I can add another Serious Life Development to the pile. Not with everything else swirling around me.

"Vlad wants to marry me!" I blurt when he is only inches away.

He pulls back, obviously uncertain how to react. "Congratulations?" he tries.

"No, I mean, I want to figure out this Vlad thing before I can think of . . . anything else," I say.

"Oh," he says. "Okay."

"Right."

"Yes, right."

There's a moment of awkward silence. "So . . . any great ideas? I think that we should tell him there's a one-day boot sale in an abandoned warehouse and then pour molten lava on him from way high up in the rafters."

James just looks at me with an expression that I am

choosing to interpret as admiration. "You are an interesting person, Sophie McGee," he says. "A strange, interesting person."

Says the teenage vampire who only buys furniture he doesn't actually need. "What's your idea then? Preferably something that can be done by Monday."

"Why Monday?"

"School."

"You're kidding me."

"There's a soccer game that I have to cover."

"So find someone else to do it."

"Yeah, because pawning off articles is going to look really good when Mr. Amado is about to pick editor in chief. Anyway, since he thinks he's already found me, maybe he won't even go."

"Do you really want to risk it?"

Truth be told, the thought of meeting Vlad again post-proposal makes my skin crawl more now than when I thought he just wanted to kill me. I don't want to risk it. Considering that so far the only thing that's slowed him down at all is Caroline, my house might be the safest place yet. But still.

"We can come up with something. All we need to do

is . . ." I trail off, realizing that maybe it's presumptuous to think that the other vampires will want to help me. But when I say so, James just shakes his head.

"It's not that. Neville wants to fix this, and I'm pretty sure Marisabel would be first in line to help take Vlad down. Violet will probably just fight in whatever direction you point her."

"Then—"

"We're out of blood," he says. "Last night took a lot out of us, and I barely had enough just to make sure that everyone healed. We can't even think about going up against Vlad until we're at full strength."

"Oh," I say. "What do you guys normally, uh, do about that?"

"We've never done much of anything," he says. "Vlad handled all of that stuff. He liked to hit up blood drives—there are usually a lot of volunteers and people are a little more lax with their records. But first we have to find one, and then we have to get there. Just stay at home for the next couple of days," he says. "And then we can all come up with a plan."

"I hate hiding."

"You're not hiding," James says, "you're playing the

long game. Think of it like a giant game of chess, only one with vampires instead of bishops."

"Fine," I say, reluctantly agreeing to lay low but leaving out the most important thing: I've always been horrible at chess.

Chapter Sixteen

I call Mark Echolls on Sunday to ask if he can cover the soccer game on Monday because I'm going to be out for "personal reasons," aka crazy vampires. The crushing silence that follows my request does not bode well.

"Look, Mark," I say, "I know that you're mad——"

"Do you know what the musical people made me do last week? They made me try on a basketball jersey, sing a song with them, and then attempt to harmonize."

"I'm sorry, but——"

"I don't even care about journalism!" he says, loudly enough that the phone buzzes a little. "Having an excuse to talk to those girls is the only reason I take that dumb class in the first place. Without the paper angle, I'm just the creepy dork who sits on the sidelines."

"So . . . you'll do it?" I ask hopefully.

There's a long pause, but eventually he mutters yes. "What about Thursday's tennis match?" he asks.

That would mean that two of the stories on my page were written by someone else. One is acceptable, two could make me look like a slacker when it comes time to count the bylines.

"I'll let you know," I say.

"Whatever," he says and hangs up before I can even say thank you.

Ten years of being a perfect-attendance nut makes faking sick on Monday a breeze. Even though I'm still on her bad side, Marcie doesn't question me when I tell her that I'm too nauseated to go to school, just sends me back upstairs with Sprite and a packet of crackers. Monday passes without incident, but when the doorbell rings on Tuesday night, I'm gripped with fear that it's Vlad reneging on our agreement. Caroline's glower when she comes up to tell me that I have a visitor doesn't help.

"James Hallowell is here," she says and then makes

a point to stomp loudly down the stairs. I've obviously violated some secret sister rule, but right now I'm too relieved to worry about it; if James is here, it has to mean that the vampires are stocked up and ready to plan. Since the "Hey! It's my birthday" T-shirt I got on my last trip to Señor Miguel's with a chocolate stain over one boob is not my most flattering outfit, I wiggle into jeans and a gray hoodie and then hop downstairs. I find him on the couch in the living room, doing his best to fend off Marcie's offers of leftover lasagna. It's never a battle anyone wins.

"I'll tell you what," Marcie is saying, her head poking out of the kitchen. "I'll put some in a Tupperware container."

"Really, don't worry abou—nope, nope, she's gone," he says and lets his head fall back against the cushion in defeat. But he smiles when he sees me. "Hey. Want to come over for some lasagna?"

Considering Marcie has been allowing me nothing but Saltines and some oatmeal that she found at the back of the cabinet, yes, I do. But I have a feeling that will hurt my case if I have to finagle another day at home.

"Using the doorbell," I say. "I'm impressed."

He shrugs. "It was time. Next, car horns."

I plop down on the cushion next to him. "So do you have a plan?"

"Sort of," he says. "There's a drive at a high school a couple of hours away, but it's not until Thursday and we need a car."

"You can take mine," I say even as my stomach twists into a tighter knot of worry. Thursday is the day of the tennis match, which means that I'll have to ask Mark Echolls to cover for me again. I try to reassure myself that there are other things I can do to impress Mr. Amado, but it's getting harder and harder to believe that I can possibly have a chance after all of this.

My thoughts are interrupted by James asking me what is wrong, and for once I don't talk about the journalism assignments—it's not like I can ask people to donate blood sooner. So instead I get up to grab my keys off the helpfully labeled hook on the doorway. "You should probably get it after nine," I say. "My dad will already be gone and Marcie spends most of Thursday mornings doing errands. But if anyone notices, I'll figure out some kind of excuse."

"Got it," he says, and then comes to meet me at the doorway. "See you Thursday?"

"You're leaving?" I ask, fighting off a twinge of disappointment as I hand the keys over.

"Marcie told me you were sick and that I couldn't stay long. I don't want to blow your cover," he says, but he leans against the door and looks around. "Your house is exactly the same. It's nice."

The low light of the front hallway is making him look very warm and touchable. I don't know if it is because I am going stir-crazy, but I suddenly wonder if I was insane not to take all of my kissing chances when I had them. Amusement flickers over his face.

Dammit. "Did you hear that?"

"Hear what?" he asks innocently, but I notice that he moves a little closer. Before I can decide what to do, however, a disgusted huff sounds from my left. Caroline is standing at the foot of the stairs, looking like she's caught us rolling around on the hardwood floor rather than standing side by side.

"Seriously?" she says. "Seriously."

This time she stomps up the stairs.

"I'd better go before your sister explodes," James says, and the moment is lost.

Wednesday night brings another visitor. I'm sitting in front of my computer, hoping for a last-minute miracle that will keep me from having to contact Mark about subbing in, when a knock sounds at my door. I open it to find Lindsay Allen with a stack of books balanced on her hip.

"I figured you wouldn't want to fall behind, so I come bearing homework," Lindsay says and then peers around the corner. "Cool room. Can I come in for a second? Sorry for not giving you a warning."

"Uh, sure. Ignore all the socks. There was an explosion." And by that I mean an explosion of boredom that led to me organizing them by print and holiday.

Lindsay walks inside, shutting the door behind her with a deliberateness that makes me nervous. "I have to ask you something," she says as she takes a seat at my desk and crosses her legs. "Did something happen with you and that guy Vlad at that party Friday night?"

Dread creeps over my skin. "Why?"

"Hmm, okay. I don't really know how to put this,

but . . . well, he was telling everybody today that you guys are dating and that you're his soul mate and that you're going to get married."

"What?"

Lindsay gives a solemn nod.

"What?" I feel like I'm in one of those teen shows where a caring friend lets her naive schoolmate know that the popular guy in school is spreading rumors about her. Of course, those usually end with everyone finding out they have chlamydia instead of a vampire husband, but the concept is the same.

"I thought it was weird," she says. "I didn't really think that he was your type. He's kind of smarmy. That's why I didn't go to his party."

"We're not even dating," I say. "What is the opposite of dating?"

"Not dating?" she tries. "I'm sorry. I didn't mean to upset you. I just thought that you should know."

It's obvious that I've made Lindsay uncomfortable. She is looking everywhere but at me, rolling a few pens around on my desk and studying an old Happy Bunny poster I tacked to the wall when I was feeling boo-hiss about the world.

"Don't apologize," I say as calmly as I can. "What exactly is he saying?"

She relaxes a little, which means she returns to her usual habit of talking in hyper-speed. "He's saying that you two hooked up. Only he's not saying 'hooked up.' He's saying that you 'sported,'" she says, complete with air quotes. "You know, I'm all for fun with vocabulary, but that's just weird. He gives me the creeps. I don't really know why, but he does."

Probably because he tried to make her his lunch. At least I can make sure that Lindsay isn't drawn back into it again.

"He is creepy," I confirm, "and you should stay away from him." Now that my caveat has been signed, sealed, and delivered, it's time to get back to the real problem. I move across the room and collapse on the bed with a bounce. "Do people believe him?"

"Pretty much, yeah," she says. "Well, those who know who you are. The others just asked if you're new or in the special classes. A few people asked if you were the person who wrote that article calling out teachers who don't care about plagiarism." She pauses. "Those kids looked kind of mad."

"But a lot of people were at Friday's party," I insist. "They should know that it's not true."

"They're saying that he dragged you and James Hallowell out of the pantry, and then kicked everyone out in a jealous rage."

There are no words for how twisted the people at my high school are. I fall backward on the bed and put a pillow over my face.

"Smothering yourself is not the answer," Lindsay says.

Lifting up a corner, I peer out from beneath the fringe. She's busy rearranging the pens on my desk into some sort of order. When she notices me watching, she colors and then tells me there's something else.

"What else can he possibly be saying? That I am carrying his love child?" I joke and then sit up. "Oh God."

Lindsay shakes her head. "Nothing like that. Mr. Amado's been asking me if I know when you'll be back. He's going to be out for personal reasons starting on Monday, so he's going to pick the editor in chief early because he wants someone who'll make sure that stupid sub doesn't accidentally erase the whole issue again," she says. "I thought it was only fair that you know."

I look at her, wondering what I would have done if our places were switched, whether I would have taken the time to give the competition a heads-up about the new deadline or about the fact that she's the victim of vampire rumor-mongering. I don't think I would have. Suddenly, I want to apologize for lying again, but she'd just think I'm crazy. So I apologize for what she'll remember.

"I'm sorry that I didn't call you back this summer."

Her eyes widen a little at the non sequitur, but she just says, "That's okay. I was busy with the animal shelter. To be honest, I smelled like dog most of the time and probably shouldn't have hung out with anyone. Anyway, I'd better get home," she says as she swoops down to pick up her bag. "My mother works late at the hospital on Wednesdays, which means my little brother is home alone. Last time I was late he watched enough HBO to make him sound like Tony Soprano." She stops when her hand is on the doorknob. "Your articles were really good, by the way."

"Yours were better," I say, and it's not a lie. Her article on James captured him perfectly, and the ones on Devon and Ashley reached some sort of Hellen-Keller-Miracle-Worker level that my articles on Violet and her love of the color purple didn't even come close to matching. She even made Andrew and his dirt bikes interesting. But Lindsay just shakes her head.

"No way," she says. I think that she's humoring me, but when I check her face for signs of sarcasm I come up empty.

"Do you want to maybe get together some weekend?" I blurt.

"Oh. Sure! There's a midnight showing of *Nosferatu* this Saturday at the Main Street Theater—"

"No!" I say sharply, before making an effort to tone down the crazy. "I mean, I don't really like vampires. Let's talk about it tomorrow at lunch."

"You'll be at school?"

I look toward James's house, wondering how the vampires are doing. Every day I sit here doing nothing is another day that Vlad chips away at my real life; I've worked too hard to let him ruin my chance at editor in chief or give me some sort of bizarro reputation. I can't miss the tennis match tomorrow if Friday's my last chance to impress Mr. Amado. I'll just keep my head down and avoid him the best I can—after all, what harm can one day do?

"Yes," I tell Lindsay, "just try to keep me away."

Chapter Seventeen

By the time I drag my feet through Thomas Jeff's heavy glass doors the next morning, I am running on one hour of sleep, bus fumes, and the three bites of cereal I managed to take before Caroline's over-the-breakfast-table scowl put the fear of sisterly retribution in me. She didn't say anything, but I knew she was mad by the way she ate three bowls of Fruity Pebbles, finishing off the box before I could go for seconds. Caroline doesn't ingest that many carbs unless she's getting back at someone. At least now I know the reason.

It only takes a few steps into the crowded lobby for me to realize that there's no possibility of getting through today unnoticed. For the first time in my life, whispers dog me through the hallways, all of which involve the words "Vlad" and "party" and "engaged." When I round the corner and see Danny Baumann bending over one of the school's anemic water fountains, I realize that this is the perfect chance to start the rumor-squashing process. I just have to get up the nerve to talk to him.

His light blond hair curls at the neck, and he is wearing the shorts that entranced me so long ago in World Geography, but I am not here to ogle. Much like the hungry lion approaches the gentle, mega-attractive antelope, I move slowly, stealthily. I catch him as he turns around.

"Hey there. I have a favor to ask you," I say, fully expecting him to ask who I am and why I am talking to him. But he just leans against the wall and wipes his mouth with his shirt, relaxed as casual Friday. When we get married, I'm going to buy him a napkin.

"Yo, Sophs," he says. "What's up?"

"You know my name."

"Sure. You told me the difference between Uganda and Uruguay. South America, man. Crazy."

I am aflutter that he remembers our special moment, but all I tell him is that I'm not dating or engaged to or involved in any other sort of relationship with Vlad. "And I was kind of hoping you could spread the word," I finish.

"That's not what he says. Dude is, like, madly in love with you."

"But *I'm* saying that it is not true. And I thought maybe you could correct people if they mention it?" I give him a hopeful smile. "Okay?"

"I dunno. I don't want to get in the middle or anything. Guy kind of weirds me out."

That gives me pause; last week Vlad was still topping the charts. But by the time I think to ask for more detail, he's already ambling away to do whatever Danny Baumanns do all day.

The next few hallways are better, and I start to think that maybe things aren't as bad as the lobby made them out to be. But when I turn the final corner to my locker, the hope dies. A large cluster of people stands before it; I see sports jerseys and cheerleader costumes, but also a few pairs of ripped tights and dark band T-shirts. Morgan Michaels, my locker neighbor, flutters around the edge in a long crepe skirt.

"I'm going to be late," she accuses when I reach the edge. "This is the fourth day."

"Did someone write 'French sucks' on my locker again?" I ask just as the circle shifts to reveal a wall of bloodred roses where my dented, magic-marker-smudged door should be. There are dozens. Hundreds.

"Do you like it?" a smooth voice asks from behind me. When I turn around, Vlad is leaning against the opposite wall, smiling with sly expectation. Sauntering forward, he taps his cheek. "You may show your thanks as you see fit."

Well, if he insists. Turning to the locker, I rip off the rose that's looped through the handle and throw it at his crotch, smiling when it elicits an undignified gasp. "Thank you," I say sweetly, "for making me late to math class."

There are a few snickers as I open my locker and bat away the roses that rain down. Keeping my head firmly buried in the jumble of old newsletters and orphaned pen caps, I concentrate on digging out my math book. I am pulling it out from underneath *Mangez avec moi*, our porny-sounding French textbook, when the tips of

Vlad's boots appear beneath the locker door. I stand up and meet his eyes, matching his scowl and raising him a glare before I remember that, while he probably can't force anything here, at some point I will either have to seduce the night crew or go home. Self-preservation kicks in; perhaps I should not provoke a hallway show-down.

"Excuse me," I say with frigid politeness and try to ease past him.

He grabs my elbow. "I thought you would like them."

"I'm allergic."

"Your eyes are not red."

"I'm sneezing on the inside."

At a loss, Vlad turns to study our circle of onlookers. When I first arrived, their faces held only curiosity. But now I'm encouraged by their obvious unease. One girl with a nose ring and Manic-Panicked hair is texting rapidly and pausing every few seconds to look up warily. I hear a few scattered "weirds."

"You all want to go to class," he booms, and while this causes a few people to hitch up their books and shuffle away, the majority stay put. He begins to look nervous, changes tactics. "Sophochka is still feeling a little out of sorts due to her recent illness," he says. "It has affected her judgment."

Oh, vomit.

"My judgment is fine," I say. "Your judgment is the one that's out of whack."

I can't tell what enrages him more; my words or the fact that there are witnesses. He grabs my free hand in a way that, to an onlooker, might appear to be a romantic gesture, but I can feel his thumb pressing down on the pulse of my wrist. I try to pull away, but he still has the advantage in the strength department. "You are embarrassing me," he hisses into my ear. "I would suggest refraining from that in the future."

"I have to go to class," I say loudly and catch the eyes of as many people as I can.

"Hey man, let her go," says a short and stocky guy near the front, while the girl who was texting earlier says that she's going to go get Ms. Kate. The murmuring increases, and for a moment Vlad simply looks betrayed.

"Very well," he says loudly for their benefit, and lets me go. He scoops up an errant rose and places it on top of my binder with a flourish. "We will continue this conversation later."

I knock it off and brush past him, but curiosity makes me look back before I round the corner. I immediately regret it. I have been on the receiving end of many heated looks in my day, but nothing compared to the one Vlad is giving me now. His back is to the crowd, his head angled down so that only I can see the way his eyes follow me from beneath his drooping bangs. They are full of such raw desire, such menace, and such hatred that my body revolts. As soon as he realizes that I am watching, he scrambles to realign them into something more benign, but it is too late. I've already seen what a mistake it was to come today.

He follows me everywhere. I come out of math, he is standing by the water fountain; I leave chemistry, and he is waiting at the corner with a cool offer to carry my books. I was crazy to think that I could avoid him for an entire day—I can hardly escape him for a minute. After a clever shortcut through the band hallway, I manage to make it to the cafeteria without a tail. Lindsay waves at me from her seat at the round table near the back. She scoots over when I approach, clearing away the papers and pens that are scattered all over the table.

"You made it!" she says. "We're using lunchtime to work on the upcoming push to get recycled napkins in the cafeteria." She points to the rest of the Green Team. Most of them are either college-prep junkies or band guys who have crushes on Lindsay. And then there's Mark Echolls, who frowns at me from beneath his shaggy brown bangs. I can't tell if the pizza sauce clinging to the corners of his lips makes him look more or less threatening.

"Thanks for covering for me on Monday," I say, but he just slides to the side. I take a seat, doing my best to arrange myself so that the cement column acts as a shield between me and the rest of the cafeteria.

Lindsay reaches over to push a few glitter pens toward me. "Do you want to outline 'Napkin' in blue? Elise is doing 'Change' in green."

I am grateful for the distraction, even if it involves glitter pens. I have just made it to the fifth letter when the sound of a familiar voice causes me to over-squeeze the tube in my hand and dot my "L."

"Sophie McGee," Vlad says. "Have you seen her? No doubt she will be sitting in a corner somewhere."

I spot the back of his pale head several tables away. If

I can see him, that means he can see me. I slide closer to Mark to conceal myself, but he pushes me away. When Lindsay notices our tussle, she follows my gaze to Vlad and then gives me a worried look.

"Don't let him see me," I say just he starts to turn around. Panicked, I duck beneath the table, holding my breath as his boots approach. When he asks if anyone at the table has seen me, Lindsay starts to tell him that I went home sick, but Mark interrupts.

"She's under the table," he says with obvious glee, but it's followed by a smacking sound that I'm pretty sure is courtesy of Lindsay. "Ow!" Mark says. "What? She is."

And that's how nemeses are made.

When I creep out, Vlad is watching me with barely controlled rage. "Sophochka does like her games."

Before I can figure out how to handle this situation, I hear the clatter of a tray being dropped. Caroline is standing behind us, trembling like someone just punched her in the stomach.

"Liar," she says. "You are such a liar."

"Caroline—," I start, but she is already running toward the door.

I don't catch up with her until she's outside the auditorium, and I have to step in front of her to stop her from moving. The tear tracks running down her cheeks stop me cold.

"Caroline, *none* of what people are saying is true."

"Then why did everyone see you having a lovers' tuft in the hallway this morning?"

"A lovers' *tuft*?"

"Yeah."

Correcting her right now would be mean . . . and would probably result in my immediate incineration from the sister death ray. "That was not a lover's tuft. That was a 'stop stalking me' tuft."

"Vlad? Stalking you?" she scoffs, and runs her eyes over my outfit, which I admit happens to be a little mismatched due to my impending forced vampire marriage. "Please," she says coldly.

Her dismissal stings. We have always had differing opinions on the amount of time and effort that should be put into designing an outfit, but she has never been outright rude. She knows it, too—for a second her disdain wavers, but then anger swamps it once again.

"You lied to me," she says. "I asked you what happened at the party, and you lied. I asked you if Vlad was at our house, and you *lied*. It was his Hummer. You've been dating him the whole time."

I grab her arms to try to get her to focus on me. "Caroline, he's a *crazy person*. Nothing he could do would *ever* make me date him. *Ever.* I am doing everything I can to get him to stay away from me for good," I say, but she slaps me off and starts to run down the hallway. I whirl around to call after her, and then freeze.

Vlad is standing at the end of the hallway, and from the way he is looking at me, I would say that he over-heard everything. As Caroline runs by him, he makes a show of watching her disappear around the corner. When he turns back to me, he gives me a mean smile that I understand all too well.

Caroline makes it to her last two classes. I know because I check, earning a nice start to my tardy-slip collection. My plan is to find her at the end of the day, explain things as best I can, and whisk her away to the safety of home, where I will convince my father to start building a bomb shelter made entirely of garlic and sunlight. When the final bell rings, I try to rush out of study hall and intercept her at her locker, but Mr. Hanfield stops me.

"You can't leave the book rack like that," he says, pushing up his glasses and crossing his arms. "It's a mess."

The book rack is always a mess. Most of them don't have covers, and all of them have at least one drawing of a penis in the margins. But I can't get into an argument, not now. "I will do it next time, I promise."

"No, I'm tired of you students treating things like they are yours to destroy." He points to the books that hang over the edges of the rack, their pages mangled. "Do it now."

I stack them up and jab them into the open spots. "There. Done."

"That's not finished," he says.

"I don't care!"

He screws up his face in disbelief. "Would you like detention, young lady?" he asks, grabbing his pad of conduct slips and starting to scribble something down.

I look to the hallway, now full of catcalls and laughs and meeting times. If I'm going to get detention anyway, might as well make it something worthwhile. While Mr. Hanfield's head is still bowed, I slip out into the mass of exiting students and head straight for Caroline's locker, which happens to be on the other side of the school.

She's not there. I tell myself to be calm. Caroline is a popular girl of habit. After school, she and her friends can normally be found in the front hallway, perched on the empty ledge that used to contain photos of National Merit finalists until the year we didn't have any. Now they are too embarrassed to fill it with anything else, and Caroline and company have moved in.

Today, however, Caroline is missing. After muttering a curse under my breath, I fight against the flow of exiting students and make my way to the side wall. When I get there, Caroline's friends are busy arguing over whether or not belly rings are trashy. Amanda looks up as I approach.

"What do you want?" she asks, brushing at her designer jeans like I am emitting imaginary traitor dust.

"Have you seen Caroline?"

"No. She never showed up."

"But she was supposed to meet you here? She never said anything about going home?"

"She wanted to spend the night at my house tonight." She waits a second for it to sink in and then adds, "Because she didn't want to see you," in case I missed the insult.

"Do any of you have last period with her?"

"Hey, Marta," Jessica says. "Where's Caroline?"

"She has geometry with me. But she skipped out early, saying she felt sick. I think she wanted to go to the mall."

It's a possibility. Caroline has been known to blow a year's allowance on boy-induced shopping sprees. But usually she takes yes-women and bag carriers. "Wouldn't she have asked if you wanted to go?"

"My dad cut up my credit cards," Marta says, shaking her head.

"I dated all the salespeople at Abercrombie and Fitch. I can't show my face in there for at least another month," says Amanda. "Evelyn?"

"She didn't ask me," Evelyn says, looking up from putting on bubblegum lip gloss. "And that's weird, because we were supposed to go together the next time and buy matching pajama bottoms for next Friday's spirit day."

Marta claps excitedly. "The ones with the pink bunnies?"

"Yes!"

"You should see mine—they are covered in broccoli and say 'Eat me.'"

"Cute! Mine have monkeys!"

"Mine have whales," I say to regain their attention, and earn three surprised looks. I will not be sidetracked by pajama pants. "Call me if you see her," I say, and then stand there stubbornly until I'm sure that they've all programmed the number I give them into their cells.

As I walk back through the hallways, I dig my phone out from the bottom of my bag. After a silent thank-you when it lights up fully charged, I dial home. Marcie picks up on the third ring, and I try to keep my voice calm and level when I ask if Caroline has come home.

"She called earlier and said that she was staying with Amanda. I asked if she wanted to pick up clothes, but she said that she would borrow something. She sounded upset," Marcie says, and I can hear the concern through the crackle of indoor reception. "What's going on?"

"Nothing. Just leftover boy stuff," I lie.

"Then why are you calling?"

One point for Marcie. "One of her friends said that

she had forgotten something in her locker and I wanted to bring it to her."

Marcie seems to buy it. After claiming that I have to get to the tennis match, I hang up and head to the side hallway, planning on doing a few laps to hunt for Caroline. I'm starting to feel silly—she's probably licking her wounds somewhere safe and warm and full of attractive men. Worst-case scenario, I'll check the boys' locker room.

I'm passing the open, chemical-smelling doors in the science hall when I hear a high-pitched giggle that I'd recognize anywhere.

"Neal, stop it," Violet says, but it doesn't sound like she wants him to stop anything. I run into a physics classroom only to walk in on Neal tickling Violet with a remote-controlled robot.

"Thanks for coming to the Robotics meeting," he tells Violet, who has leaned over to tap the robot's head with a very curious expression. "I don't know where Adam is. He told me that he would be here."

"We should name him," Violet says. She picks up a pencil and taps the robot on its shoulders. "I dub thee . . . Simon."

"Simon? Did you just name my robot Simon?"

"What is wrong with Simon? It was my brother's name."

"I didn't know that you had a brother."

Violet looks down at her hands with a mournful sigh. "He is gone now."

"I'm sorry," Neal says, immediately contrite.

"It does not matter anymore. It was a long time ago." She shoots him a suggestive look from beneath her lashes. "A long, long, long, long—Sophie!" she says when she spots me in the doorway. "You are not supposed to be here."

"Neither are you."

"We got back early! And since I promised Neal that I would come to his Robotics meeting until he had more than one participant . . . What's wrong?"

"I can't find my sister or Vlad."

Neal stops twirling Simon in a circle. "I saw them talking in the middle of last period."

My stomach lurches. "You did?"

"Yeah. I forgot my graphing calculator, and her locker is by mine," he says. "You know, 'Garville'. . . 'Garrett.' It's the curse of alphabetical order."

I try to keep the panic from leaking into my voice when I ask my next question. "What were they saying?"

"I don't know. I tend to tune her out. Most of her interactions involve really loud kissing." He stops when he sees what must be my horrified expression. "Hey, it's okay. It seemed to be a friendly conversation. I mean, at first she was mad, but then he stared soulfully into her eyes and then they walked off together." Neal rolls his eyes, as if he hadn't been doing his own soulful staring at Violet these past few weeks.

"Where were they going?" I ask.

"Um. To make out?"

"Where?"

Neal is starting to look nervous. He fiddles with the remote control, causing Simon to twirl in a confused circle. "I don't know," he says, uncomfortable. "Where do people usually make out?"

"I don't have time for sarcasm right now, Neal."

"But I really don't know!"

I turn to Violet, unable to hide my panic.

"I will go find the others," she says. "They should be at home now."

"I'll come with you," Neal says, but Violet waves him back into his seat.

"Stay with Simon. This is a family matter." When he protests, she stares into his eyes. Neal's shoulders slump and he turns around to fiddle with a few loose screws.

"Violet!" I scold. "I've never seen you do that."

She looks at me, innocent as a cartoon bunny. "What? We need him to stay! And the magazines said that we are allowed to use our feminine wiles. I do not understand your qualm."

I doubt *Seventeen* would include vampire mind-control under the "feminine wiles" umbrella, but now is not the time. When she flounces away, I try not to worry that the cavalry is skipping.

I start to search for Caroline in earnest. Vlad disappeared with her in the early afternoon—too early for the direct sun not to drain him—so it would have to be somewhere in the building, somewhere removed and isolated. I check the auditorium, thinking that he could have her holed up backstage, but the heavy red curtain is open and a group of students is taking advantage of the unoccupied stage to practice choral parts for *High*

School Musical. Next I scope out the band hallway, but it is brightly lit and filled with the sounds of tortured trombones and tubas. My search of the locker rooms—girls' and boys'—turns up nothing other than a surprised and shirtless Danny Baumann who says, "Yo, South America. You're kind of freaky, aren't you?" and pats my dazzled head before he leaves.

Think, Sophie. Think. If he disappeared with her before fourth period, he had to take her somewhere that would have been empty since approximately one o'clock. That nixes all the rooms of the front office and the teachers' lounge, and the library would have at least had the librarian and a few indentured study hallers. All that's left is the cafeteria, and when I think about it, it makes sense. Today was not a Student Council day, and so it would have been free of any desperate souls doing their best to pad their college application. The cafeteria ladies clear out mid-afternoon, and so it may be the one place in the school that would have been empty when Neal says they disappeared.

Heart pounding, I start to run, taking the corners so fast that I'm lucky the halls are deserted. I burst through the doors and into the closed-down cafeteria, my footsteps echoing across the checkerboard tile. The fluorescent lights are off, and while the safety ones hanging near the front flicker dimly, the entire back half of the cafeteria is shrouded in darkness. To the front is the alcove that contains the lunch lines and, beyond that, the swinging doors that lead to the kitchens. Is it my imagination, or is there a light on behind those nautical peepholes?

As if in answer to my question, a sound rumbles up from behind the doors. *This is it,* I think, and I take a deep breath. Then it occurs to me that if Vlad does have Caroline tied up next to the instant mashed potatoes, I have no intelligent plan of action.

A weapon, I can at least find a weapon. But what? The cafeteria switched to plastic utensils long ago. And anyway, should I be looking for something wooden? More and more, my question-and-answer session with James is proving to be woefully inadequate. Next time I am in a room with any vampire—one that does not harbor violent and/or marital feelings toward me, of course— perhaps I should spend less time crushing on them and more time asking them to list their weaknesses.

Ignoring the escalated *bump-bump*ing of my heart, I spot a cart of washed dishes next to the back wall and rush to inspect it. After a moment of deliberation, I grab the wooden spoon and a knife and do my best to file it into a point. Two thousand years of folklore can't be that wrong, right? And besides, at the luau showdown, Vlad chased after Neville with a shattered piece of door. He doesn't seem much for meta jokes.

I approach the swinging doors with as much stealth as I can manage. Pressing my ear against it, I listen for furious whispers or the struggle shuffle, but only hear a steady, persistent dripping and the low buzz of a running dishwasher. I nudge it open with my toe and peek inside—it is empty except for gleaming sinks, long metal counters, and a few large pots that must be the source of the school's mystery chili. The light I saw comes from the two windows across the way. In a flash, I realize that there's something else I should be noticing. The light is pale and gray. There is no sun.

Sliding across the tile, I go to the window. Thunder rumbles in the distance, and I can hear the tinny drops of rain hitting the aluminum sill. They could be any-where. Caroline could be anywhere. I tell myself to calm down, but my chest is constricting so fast that it is dif-ficult to think rationally. He is using her as bait, so he will not want to kill her. He still thinks I'm his ticket to the Danae, so he won't want to kill me, either. This will be fine—I just have to keep moving.

My next step should be to see if Vlad's car is still here. Tucking the spoon down my shirt and into my waistband, I jog back to the swinging doors. In my rush, I hit them with an ungainly smack and wince. When I open my eyes, the twin forms of Devon and Ashley are standing in front of me, side by side like a double statue. The low light plays tricks with their features, giving me the eerie sensation that I am looking at one face, one body, split in two by a magic trick gone horribly wrong. They move forward in grotesque tandem.

I stumble backward through the doors until my tailbone hits the hard edge of a metal counter. It vibrates beneath my fingers, setting off a high hum that competes with the rhythmic thumping of the dishwasher, which is sounding more and more like the rush of blood now pounding in my ears. "Where is my sister?" I ask as my hand searches for the reassuring hardness of the spoon's handle.

They step into the light. First I see their square chins, then their lips, leeched of color and drawn into a flat line, and finally, their eyes. They are just as dead as usual—four shiny black buttons.

"I said, where is my sister?" I ask again.

The one on the left lifts his arm, and for the first time I notice that he is clutching a crumpled piece of paper. When I make no move to grab it, they step forward again. Realizing that they will not move until the delivery is complete, I flatten the note against the counter. A line of flowers and hearts dances across the top. There is only one person I know who has the guts to turn in decorated assignments. The paper is Caroline's. The handwriting is Vlad's. Who the dark red smudge—blood?—at the corner belongs to is anyone's guess. I feel like throwing up as I begin to read.

Sophochka,
I would be most delighted if you would join me at our special place in the forest—your sister is already here and very eager to speak with you. However, please make haste. I fear I am impatient for your company, and night is coming fast.
With warm regards,
Vlad

I wad the note up into a ball and throw it toward the twin who carried the letter. He doesn't even flinch. It bounces harmlessly off his chest, which does nothing to make me feel better or scare away the tears that are threatening. Leaning back, they beckon toward the exit in an eerie parody of an opening door. Inching forward, I start to move past them, only to feel two strong hands clamp around my arms and lift me up.

Chapter Eighteen

"Let go of me, you twin freaks! I'll go with you," I yell as they drag me across the hallway and through the darkened gym, empty now that thunderstorms have cancelled all the practices and meets. We are moving faster now; the bleachers flash past to one side as we head to the exit that leads to the athletic fields that lay in back of the school. One second we are in the gym that smells of sweat and baby powder, and the next we are outside in the wind and stinging rain, trudging across the muddy soccer field as we approach the thick block of woods from the side. The ground squishes with each step, and a crack of thunder splits the dark sky overhead as drops soak my shoulders and back. The front of my shirt is still dry, and I pray that it will stay that way so as not to expose the spoon I've stashed. If we're being entirely honest, a wooden spoon is a sucky secret weapon, but for the moment it is all that I have.

We hit the line of trees, plunging us into even deeper shadow. Devon and Ashley cut through the brush as though it is nothing, but branches whip across my face. Every so often my feet scrape hard against the ground, jarring my ankles and making me feel so shaken and battered that I don't register that we've reached the clearing until they throw me to the ground. I manage to catch myself two seconds before my nose hits the sopping layer of rotting leaves, but my hands sink beneath me. I tug them out of the mud and then scramble to my feet, whirling around just in time to see Devon and Ashley's eyes focus on a spot behind me.

"I am so pleased that you could join us, Sophochka," Vlad says. He is perched on the rotting picnic table, his black shirt molded to his chest. As I watch, he crosses his legs and brings his hands to rest on the bump of his knees.

"Where is Caroline?" I rasp, searching the clearing frantically. Nothing. I stand up and turn in a circle, peering through the gaps in the trees. The rain has turned everything misty, creating a wall of fog that prevents me from seeing beyond this tiny bubble of space. Vlad waits for me to stop twirling before casually leaning to the side to reveal Caroline's slumped figure tied to a tree with a bright pink neon cord. Her head hangs forward, her curly blond hair veiling her face.

"Is she . . . ," I start, the dawning horror feeling like ants crawling up my skin.

"Oh, she is not dead. I just did not want to listen to her for one more second—she knows quite a few curse words. What is a 'lametard'?"

"Let her go," I say. "She has nothing to do with this."

"She has everything to do with this," he snaps. "If you would have but given me a second chance to court you, I would not have needed to resort to such drastic measures. But you have made it clear that you have no intention of doing this the civil way, and I do not have time to overcome your stubbornness or endure your public insults. I have tired of this place," he says, springing off the picnic table with an agile hop. "Here is what I offer. You agree to become a vampire and marry me now, and I release her. She might wonder why she has a sore neck for a few days, but otherwise, she will remember nothing."

My eyes fly to Caroline. "You didn't . . . ," I start, but I see how his gray eyes are sparkling; I see how there is color in his cheeks.

"Oh, I did not make her a vampire. Just a beverage. After all, it has been such a very long time since I indulged in fresh human blood," he says. Reaching out, he runs one cold finger down my cheek and then traces the crescent of skin exposed above the collar of my T-shirt. "Usually I have difficulty pulling back. But then I remembered that I needed her to get to you."

I slap his hand away without thinking. *How about we not antagonize the crazy vampire who holds your sister hostage, okay, Sophie?* Swallowing, I try to keep my voice calm. "I thought that you needed witnesses."

"We have them," he insists.

"Who? Squirrels?"

"No, of course not," Vlad says. "Sometimes your humor is inappropriate. I was speaking of Devon and Ashley."

"They hardly talk!"

"I admit that they are not ideal, but you have left me with little option. Still, just to allay your worries . . ." Walking over, he pats one of them on the cheek. "Come, Ashley, say hello to Sophochka."

Ashley opens his mouth and emits a dusty grunt.

"A word," Vlad insists, but I don't hear whether or not Ashley speaks because Caroline is stirring. I need to distract him.

"Okay," I say, and then repeat it loudly to cover up her groan.

Vlad turns to face me. "'Okay' what?"

"Tell me more about what will happen when we are Danae," I say, moving to the side so that his back is completely toward Caroline, who is now blinking as though trying to focus.

He smiles. "I suspected that you were not nearly as indifferent as you claimed. I am sure that they will reward me handsomely. A real house, for a start—they are said to have thousands across the world. And then perhaps a position of some import."

Caroline is now fully awake and staring at us with wide, horrified eyes. Holding her gaze, I telepath a plea for her to stay still. It fails. She begins to wiggle, and while she may be tied to the tree with a jump rope, Vlad did not count on cheerleader flexibility. However, there is no such thing as cheerleader stealth. In order to mask the rasping sound of her movements, I step closer to Vlad, checking to see if Devon and Ashley have noticed her. Nope. Their expressions are still Grade-A vacant. Still . . .

"Vlad," I say sweetly. "I do not like them watching us. It's creepy."

He looks over me to bark at the twins. "Turn away," he orders and they dutifully turn to face the trees. When he turns back to face me with a smug smile that says, "Look what I can do," I ask him what kind of position he could have.

"I do not know," he says. "I have always wanted to be a judge. High Examiner Vlad Mervaux. Yes, that has a nice ring to it."

"You would make a wonderful judge," I lie, noticing that Caroline is almost free. His face moves even closer, so close that I can see the darker ring of gray in his eyes.

Picking up my hand, he runs the pad of his thumb over my knuckles. "You know, you are not entirely without hope. We will work on the clothing."

Be still my beating heart. Now that Vlad is so close, I can no longer see Caroline. I hope that when she is free, she runs. Just runs. Then when I am sure she is safe, I will make my move with the spoon.

All this talk of social-climbing has made Vlad amorous. He moves forward, trying to press up against me, and I instinctively back up until I hit the hard trunk of a tree. His features have relaxed, and now he sizes me up with a gaze that lingers like a lazy drawl. The sound of the rain dribbling its way down through the canopy of leaves drowns out almost everything else. So many things are rustling that it's difficult to figure out if one of them is an escape rustle. I brace myself against the tree, digging my fingernails into the bark as I lift my heels to sneak a surreptitious look behind him.

But I am not stealthy enough. His eyebrows quirk downward, signaling suspicion, and his head begins to turn. I have to stop him. But how?

Darting forward, I grab his cheeks and pull him toward me. Before I can give him the kind of sexy, diverting, cheek kiss that will go down in the annals of seductress history, he turns his head, forcing his mouth against mine. His lips are cool, wet, and slightly . . .

tangy. Oh. Oh. Gross. My fingers clutch his shirt, not because I'm in danger of melting into a puddle of goo, but because it helps keep me from slapping him away when his lips begin to move sluggishly. Caroline better be running like the wind right now, the wind.

Suddenly our teeth bump and scrape. He bites my lip, sharp as a bee sting, and I gasp. Rearing back, I dart to the side without thinking—not being familiar with the ins and outs of demonic make-out sessions, I am determined to evade whatever "move" this heralds. I turn, ready to defend myself or make excuses. For a few seconds my brain refuses to process the evidence in front of me. When it finally sinks in, I only wish that it were a hallucination.

Caroline has wrapped herself around his back, her tan legs clamping around his waist as she hits him over the head with a branch. Her hair sticks to her shoulders and back in long, wet strands, and I can see a raw, bloody gash on the left side of her neck. The rain has exposed patches of skin beneath her white T-shirt.

"Stay away from my sister," she shouts after a series of zinging swaps to his neck. "And never bite me again. *Gross.*"

Vlad could toss her off him with very little effort—of that I'm sure—but right now he seems too stunned. The crook of Caroline's elbow is a surprisingly effective blindfold. He stumbles forward with his arms extended, Lurch-like, before hitting a tree. Growling, he reaches behind him, grabbing Caroline by the neck so hard that she actually squeaks.

"Hey! Let go of me. And cut your nails every once in a while, freak. You really are a—," she begins, but then starts to choke. Vlad is squeezing.

Stealth and seduction have failed. Time to move on to plan B: a full-frontal, last-ditch, completely insane attack. As Vlad holds Caroline up like a chastised kitten, I grab the handle of the spoon and pull it out. He is not looking at me, just smiling as she squirms. With painful slowness, he begins to turn in a circle, showing off his catch. A crack of thunder splits the sky overhead as I rush forward, holding the spoon aloft with both hands and yelling nonsensical obscenities at a *Braveheart* decibel.

His eyes widen when he sees me pounding toward him, and he drops Caroline, who hits the ground rolling. I touch his arm for one whole second before he captures my wrists and rips the spoon from my grasp. I hear a snap and the vibrating zing of something lodging itself in a far tree.

Grabbing my neck with one hand, he pins me to the ground, my head twisted to the side at an odd and painful angle. I watch as his other hand darts out and captures Caroline's ankle. He drags her across the wet ground, turning her so he is holding us side by side so we are facing each other. For a few seconds she coughs and splutters, her eyes closed. When she opens them, they are a bright, feverish blue.

Vlad pinches our chins and jerks them upward so we are forced to stare into his enraged face. My legs are trapped beneath his body, and my hip begins to throb. When I struggle, he presses down until I cry out in pain.

"You thought that you could trick me?" he asks.

Caroline starts to cry. Our hands are trapped between our bodies. I wiggle a pinkie finger, trying to find hers to tell her that I am here, that I understand. That I know what I have to do.

"Let her go and I will become a vampire," I say. At least then I will be an even match for him.

"And?" he says.

"And I will marry you. You will be a Mer—" I pause as something strikes me. "Wait a second, if you turn me into a vampire won't I be an Unnamed? So then when we marry you will just be Unnaming yourself again," I say, and then I realize that all I'm really doing is undermining the only reason he has not to kill us.

The eagerness in his eyes dims a little, and I start to worry. It's occurred to him, too. "You are human but you are already Mervaux," he says tightly. "The Danae will understand that you are an exception to the rule. A wormhole of sorts."

Caroline suddenly stops sobbing. "It's a *loophole*, idiot," she sniffles. I have never been more proud of her in my life.

"Shut up!" Vlad hisses. "If you say one more word then I will—"

"Do we have a deal?" I ask to draw his attention back to me.

His eyes narrow, and I feel a surge of hope—and a surge of fear. *Oh God, I am going to have to go through with this.* I shut my eyes, ignoring the rain on my face as I try to think of the best strategy. Just because I give in now, it does not mean that I have to give in forever. I will still be me, just fangy. I can still fight him. I can still stop him. And if not, I will stake myself.

When I open my eyes, Vlad is tilting his head to the side as if weighing his options. "Fine," he says and then releases our necks. "But if you do not keep your word, I will find her and kill her. And everyone else that you love."

We struggle to our feet, Vlad watching me warily all the while, as if I might bolt. Even if I was free to, I don't think that I could. My legs are shaking so violently that I nearly collapse. Caroline is now standing with one hand to her wounded neck. Something is sticking out from beneath her foot, angled up from the pressure. It is half of the broken wooden spoon.

Caroline and I have never seen eye-to-eye on anything, have never been able to read each other's minds, but now I imagine little brain waves wiggling their way from my mind to hers, telling her to find a way to give me the piece of wood beneath her foot.

"You need to go," I tell her. "But give me a hug first."

Beside me, Vlad rolls his eyes and then sets to studying his fingernails. "Make it quick. I am eager to be done with this," he says as Caroline starts to step forward. I lift my fingers to tell her to stop and then make a point of flicking my gaze down. She stops, her mouth forming a little "O." Before her face can give anything away, I wrap my arms around her shoulders. Suddenly she lets out a wail and drags us to the ground.

"Oh, stop. You are always so overdramatic," Vlad says as Caroline fakes heaving sobs, all the while wiggling the spoon out from beneath her foot. She yells at him to shut up, even while she's tucking it in my waistband. The point where it snapped is sharp, shardlike. After she is sure that it is concealed by my shirt, she stands up and backs away.

"I'm sorry for not believing you," she says and starts to cry anew. "I'll come back."

"Don't. Please."

"But what will I say?"

"You'll think of something." I manage to offer her a grim smile. "You're good at that. It's okay, Caroline," I say. "I swear. Go."

She remains still for one final second and then takes one step backward, and then another, and another. I watch her vanish into the wall of woods, listening to her footsteps dwindle as she gets farther and farther away. The tip of my makeshift stake digs into my side, but I don't mind the pain. The pain is hope.

"Now," Vlad says. "Where were we?"

Chapter Nineteen

He advances toward me, and I instinctively take a step back. It's difficult not to lunge at him again with the stake, but I know that a frontal attack is doomed to repeat failure. My only chance of success is if I wait until he is distracted.

"Once it is done, how will we contact the Danae?"

Vlad sneers. "For all of their 'secrecy,' it is not difficult to figure out who among the families is a part. I will contact them with word that I have information on Neville and then use that to explain—" He stops. "You do not care. I will not let you stall any longer."

He moves forward again, and I retreat until my back

is against the tree. My mind wildly wonders if it is the same one as before as he stands in front of me and forces my head up.

"Is this really worth it?" I blurt. "You've alienated all of your friends."

"I will have new friends," he says. "It is as they say—to make an omelet, you must crack a few heads."

"Eggs," I say. "Crack a few eggs."

"That does not make any sense," he says impatiently, and then without even a three, two, one, he bends over and buries his fangs in my neck.

Like before, the pain is like a sudden fire as Vlad's thumb digs into the hollow between my neck and collarbone. But whereas before it was over like a lightning flash, now it seems to go on and on, until none of my senses are acting like they should. I see oceans of dull red and deep indigo. I smell junkyard rust, thick and undeniable. My fingers feel as though they sparkle.

Fingers, I think through the gasping shock. *I am supposed to be doing something with them.* Even though my muscles feel like cotton, I manage to lift my arm to my waist, wrap my palm around the handle, and tug it from my waistband. As I'm testing the point with my thumb, Vlad jerks at my shoulder, and I press down hard enough that I know I've torn it open, and here when I have no blood to spare. He's grunting at my neck like a piglet, and even though my mind feels like a balloon that's escaped its owner, I would like to laugh at him for losing his perpetual air of civility; this is as distracted as he will ever be. Slowly, carefully, I ease the jagged handle between us. I know that I will have one chance, only one chance, and I can't even check my aim.

The color begins to leech from the sky, and for a second the edges of my vision turn gray. *No. No, not yet.* Any second now Vlad will be pulling his head back, mouth smeared with blood, and offering me his own, and I will take it because the only other choice will be to die and let him have free reign on the world I've left. *One upward thrust,* I tell myself. *One upward thrust and then you can go to sleep.* Closing my eyes, I take a ragged breath, picturing all the remaining energy in my body flowing upward, flowing to my arm, flowing to my fingers, flowing through the very wood.

I attack . . . and I feel flesh give. But nothing happens.

I missed, I think, *I missed.* The only thing left to do is hope that vampires can't exist without a liver. But then Vlad starts to choke, his fangs digging deeper and deeper with every heave until finally he tears his head back and looks me in the eyes, blood dripping from the corners of his mouth in a grotesque frown. And then everything is gray, gray forever, gray raining down on me, covering me in ash until my eyes burn and my skin itches.

"There," I say to Devon and Ashley, who stand before me, impassive, just before my legs buckle beneath me. Staring up at the dreamy pink sky, I think that I have never felt so weak in my life. Not even after people made me run. *Wait, should I be thinking deep thoughts?* My lashes flutter closed, and the *pumdrum* of my heart slows until I feel like eternity can fit between the beats. I start to hear things, a kaleidoscope of familiar voices. My dad. Marcie. Violet. Neville, which surprises me, because while he's okay and everything, I don't really think we were ever that close. And then James. James. I think I smile. I want to smile.

The ground expands beneath me, becoming pillowy, soft. It is a featherbed from which I never want to get up, and the further I sink, the less the cold bites my fingers and toes. If rain still falls on my face, I don't feel it.

At this point, I am not sure that I still possess a nose or lips. I am a nude Mr. Potato Head. Don't get me wrong, it feels nice. It feels gentle, it feels peaceful, it feels . . .

Smack!

I hear it first, and then feel it eons later, like thunder after a lightning strike. There is a dull buzz in my ears, the cry of an exotic bird on repeat. It crescendos, sets a pattern. *Ohfeyohfeyohfeyohfey* and then a guttural whir of *Godododod.* I should have learned more about birds. . . . Then I could tell it to shut up in special bird language so I can sleep.

"Sophie! Sophie! God," a voice says, and I realize that the sound has exploded into my name. "Sophie!"

This last bark is accompanied by the dull prodding of what can only be fingers on my shoulders and cheeks. I wince, and even that tiny movement is painful. I want to feel my cheeks to make sure that they haven't split at the seams.

The voice calls my name again excitedly. "You need to drink this," it says.

Why?

"Because I want you to stay here," the voice insists. "Now drink. Please." The final plea is accompanied by the sensation of something wet being dribbled onto my mouth. *Geez, okay,* I think, opening my mouth to let in something that feels like syrup. From above me comes a relieved sigh, and then I am drowning in the liquid, drinking it in. I am an old pro at this; when I was little I used to stand beneath rain showers and try to catch as many drops in my mouth as possible, and I do that now, only this is a monsoon and I have lost count. All I know is that with every second I do this, I regain the feeling in my toes, my legs. I feel stronger. I feel like I have a nose again. I feel like I have two noses. Five noses.

When I can feel my eyes again, I open them. James is leaning over me with only one nose. But four eyes—no, wait, two.

Welcome back, James says, his mouth stretched into a grin. *You suck at chess.*

How did you get here? I ask, the world still spinning a bit.

I came to see you as soon as we got back, and you weren't home. So we came here and found Violet on the way. She told me about Caroline.

Nice. You know, I don't think I'm actually moving my lips right now.

You aren't. It's a perk of your new condition.

What new condition?

A shadow crosses James's face. He stands up, escaping my line of sight. I pull myself into a sitting position, feeling as though I could run a marathon. I have never felt as though I could run a marathon . . . and then it hits me.

I look to my right where the rest of the vampires watch the proceedings with solemn faces. Marisabel is hugging herself and looking a bit sick, although that might be because she is staring at the dust that used to be Vlad. And Violet . . . well, Violet is clapping her hands. She runs toward me and throws her arms around my neck, smelling of floral perfume and dirt.

"I am so happy that you are one of us now!" she cries into my shoulder.

"A vampire?" I say. Or ask. My thoughts are whirring so fast that I can no longer tell.

"You are! And we are going to have so much fun!" she crows before releasing me and bobbing back to the group. I look to James, who has crossed his arms and is now staring at the line of trees as though he has just noticed them for the first time.

What did you do? I ask, saying it internally without even thinking. He doesn't respond, but the funny thing is that I can feel his mind there, the thoughts like lights through stained glass. I can feel the others' minds as well—dimmer, not as distinct, but there. And those are not the only lights I see. Tiny patches of heat weave through the undergrowth in a lazy, sporadic pattern. Slowly they take on the shapes of animals—a group of huddled mice, the compact figure of a bird taking shelter from the rain.

"I'm a vampire," I say again, and then repeat it several times, each more accusatory than the last.

"It was the only way to save you," he says softly. "Vlad took a lot of blood."

"You were supposed to ask me," I say.

Being a vampire is better than dead dead, he says, anger flashing in his eyes. *That's what you told me. You said that there were worse things. I thought—*

He stops when I stand up abruptly. I want to say that I would have rather died, but that's not true, not really. I would have liked to have not had to make a choice at all. "I think I'm going to go home now," I say, doing my best to ignore James's distressed stare or the way he tracks my every movement. I try to walk past him, but he reaches out and catches my wrist.

"What are you doing?"

"Sophie, you shouldn't go home right now. We need to talk about how you are going to handle this. Your family . . . they can't know."

"No! I am going home and I am going to see my dad and Marcie and Caroline."

"Not yet," he says, tugging at my wrist. I let myself be dragged in for the embrace. The material of James's T-shirt is soft against my cheek. Listening to him, it almost feels like it's going to be okay. If he just keeps talking, if I don't ever have to think about the next step, it will be okay.

But then James pushes me away and stares at my chest. Before I can ask what is wrong, he presses his hand over my left breast.

"Hey!" I slap at his hand, but he ignores it and presses harder.

"Your heart," he says in wonderment.

"Yes," I say slowly, "it's there." I don't know where he gets off acting like he's the one who has been drained and refilled today.

He meets my gaze. "It's beating."

"Yes, it is."

Grabbing my wrist again, he clamps both thumbs across the purplish ghosting of veins. "Sophie," he says louder. "It's beating."

"We've established that, James."

"Sophie—," he repeats, but is cut off when Neville's voice rings out behind us.

"Vampire hearts don't beat." He nudges James's thumbs out of the way, and then looks at me with identical wonder. *No one could still be human after that exchange. I have seen people turn with half that amount.* He gives a short laugh. *Vlad was right.*

Ripping my wrist away, I put fingers to my neck to test it. It's true. My skin bumps against the pads of my fingers in a happy, gentle rhythm. I could sing. I could dance. I could do a freaking cheer. And then I come to another realization: My skin is smooth, unblemished.

"You healed," James says, answering my question. "You heard my thoughts. I've watched your eyes follow the animals . . . But you are breathing. You are alive," he says aloud, but is followed by something that I know— I know—he would never want anyone to hear.

It's not fair.

An awkward silence falls, a silence that lasts until the sound of approaching footsteps make everyone tense.

"Where are Devon and Ashley?" I snap and instinctively crouch down, feeling a new strength coiled and waiting in my muscles.

"Beneath your feet," James says.

I glance down, stepping back when I realize that I'm standing in what looks like the remains of two giant campfires. Gross.

"We took them out first," Violet chirps and then nods toward the picnic table. "When you were sleeping on the ground.

I am saved from having to find anything intelligent to add by Caroline bursting into the clearing. Her hair is a mess, her clothing is more torn than not, and she's clutching what must be the biggest stick she could find in the woods. She drops it when she sees me. I am enveloped in another hug. Today may not have turned me into a vampire, but I am apparently now a hugger.

"I got in my car and drove halfway home before coming back," she says in my ear before raising her head. "Wait. Is everything fine?"

"It's over," I say, not liking the note of uncertainty in my voice. "Well, the Vlad part."

"I was so scared. I felt horrible," she says.

Thank god I don't have to explain things to Mom and Fred.

The thought comes out of nowhere. I blink and look at Caroline, who's still smiling at me with genuine relief. As much as I'd like to think it was my imagination, I have the sinking feeling that I am going to have to get used to the unedited version of people's thoughts for at least the near future.

"Let's go home," I say, turning to find the others. James has moved away and joined their group. They are busy discussing particulars—how to get Vlad's car back to the house when his keys "dusted" along with him, among other things. Caroline tugs at my hand, pulling me toward the trees. And after a few more seconds, I let her lead me.

Chapter Twenty

Caroline drives us home. She has questions—But why did Vlad want me? Was James like them?—and she deserves answers. After all, she is taking this vampire hostage thing like a pro; and a part of me suspects that it's because it answers all of her questions about why her relationship with Vlad failed. Too exhausted to find a starting point, I promise to tell her later, and after a few failed attempts to prod the story out of me, she gives up and focuses on the road. It is difficult to keep from staring at her neck. Not because of the wound, which has finally ceased to bleed, but because I can see the gentle glow of light winding out of her collar and traveling up her neck. I try to blink it away, hoping it will disappear like the after flash of a surprise picture, but it remains.

When we pull into the driveway, she uses the rearview mirror to arrange her hair over the bite marks and then reaches into the backseat. Tossing a blue shirt in my lap, she starts to pull off her own.

"Why do you have several changes of clothes in the back of your car?" I ask.

"You don't?" she says after she's pulled off her own switcheroo. "Maybe you should."

I cast a rueful look at what was once my favorite shirt. "You know, maybe you're right." I change into the navy polo and then study our front door and its folksy, suburban wreath. "What are we going to tell them?"

She smiles with some of the old bubble. "Please. Leave it to me."

And so I do, nodding every time there's a pause in Caroline's story about how I found her at Amanda's and there was a flat tire, and that's why I'm all grimy. I am distracted by the way I can feel the concern rolling off of my father. By the time I pick up Caroline's random *They are so buying it*, I'm rattled enough to beg leave to go upstairs, where I take an hour-long shower. I feel safe there, where the tile is bright white and unchanging, and where I am free of all thoughts but my own.

I check my pulse a lot in the days that follow. I check in class, I check at the dinner table, I check at stoplights. Sometimes I wake up in the middle of the night with my fingers already at my neck or on my wrist. There is always that moment of panic when I can't locate it, when I think that the fluke is finally over and that I am going to suddenly feel the points of fangs jabbing at the corners of my mouth. But then I find it. I always find it, beating fast and strong and human.

My "side effects" don't go away. Whatever balance was tipped by James's impromptu blood transfusion does not find its equilibrium. My family, teachers, and classmates now glimmer like glowworms, even under fluorescent lights, and I am still a satellite for stray thoughts. I know that this is not normal; I know that I should be looking into what it means and who (and what exactly) I am. Sometimes I watch my father as he putters around the house, wondering how much he knew or knows and finding it hard to believe that a man who owns a snowman tie could have ever been wrapped up in anything remotely supernatural. Occasionally I even try to listen in on his thoughts, before guilt makes me stop. I wonder more about my mother in this week than I have in the last five years, but I am still not ready to crack it open. I tell myself tomorrow, and then tomorrow I tell myself next week.

Mr. Amado doesn't choose me as editor in chief. While there's a moment where it makes me want to pick up and hurl something at the wall—or at least stake Vlad all over again—I know that Lindsay deserves it more than I do, if only because she played the game fair and honest the entire way through. She's already promised me that she'll include any investigative article I want to write. I am tempted to test that with vampires, but I think I'm vampired out. Or at least that's what I'm trying to convince myself of these days.

James does not come to school in the next week, nor does he appear outside my window. I try not to be disappointed, but I won't say that seeing the empty chemistry stool isn't a kick in the gut. Every night I try not to squint at his house, and every night I fail. A part of me longs to confront him, but after my shocked words during the brief time that I thought I was a vampire, thrusting my mortality in his face now seems like the ultimate insult.

But then one night I'm up late working on my French homework, trying to figure out how to tell Pierre, who is always lost, how to get to the *boulangerie* when I catch a small glow of light in the corner of my eye. Holding my breath, I peer out the window, the tiny flicker of hope shrinking with every second that passes. *Come on, come on,* I think, willing it into existence. My face is mere inches from the glass when it flares again. I am out of my chair so fast that I stumble over the legs, knocking my knees against the armrests. Lately I've been misjudging the time it takes to complete actions, to get from point A to point B. Right now, however, I don't care. I thunder down the stairs with no regard for who I might be waking.

The night air is cool, crisp; fall has sprung. Kicking up leaves, I cut across the yard and duck through the hole in the fence, expecting to find James waiting for me on the porch, but the porch is empty. Confused, I walk to the side of his house and check the window only to be met with the same infuriating lack of James. This is the proof I've been waiting for. Tomorrow I will call the asylum. "I am losing my mind," I say aloud to no one in particular.

"No, you're not," James's voice says from above me. I look up again to see his face hanging over the eaves of the highest window.

"You're on the roof," I say, stupidly. It's nice to know that whatever other changes I have experienced this past week, my powers of stating the obvious are still intact.

He smiles and holds out his arms. "So I am."

"Are you going to come down?" I ask. I should be much more annoyed with him than I am. I promise to start as soon as my brain stops going *happyhappyhappyhappy-happy*.

"Nope."

Or I can start being annoyed now. "Well, as fun as it is to stare up your nose, I have French homework to finish."

"I think that you should come up," he suggests.

"And I think *you're* losing your mind."

"Try it," he insists, walking to the corner of the house and pointing to the roof of the covered porch. "Grab the ledge and then boost yourself up."

I stare at the item in question, which is a good four feet above my head. "I think you overestimate my jumping skills."

James's only answer to that is to smile.

I decide to humor him. Crouching down, I attempt to leap toward the gutter. No one has ever been more shocked than I am when I feel the ridge of metal beneath my fingers and hear the creak of it bending beneath my weight.

"Now pull yourself up. Er, quickly please. You're kind of destroying my house."

Still in shock, I manage to swing a leg up and then crawl onto the roof of the porch. Brushing my hair back behind my ears, I peer over the edge.

"One more to go," James says, and this time I trust that I can make it. It turns out that this is a misguided instinct.

"Can I get a little help here?" I say as I hang with one heel on the roof of James's house and the other one dangling in the breeze.

He grabs my arm and hauls me up, hard enough that I bump into his chest. For a second his arms rest at my waist, and my heart beats fast between us. But then I get a flash of thought—*so alive*—and I pull back, embarrassed and uneasy. James was right; this new vampire thing is kind of a bitch.

James clears his throat and takes a seat on the highest point. "It will get easier."

"Jumping onto roofs?"

"Sure. That and everything," he says, and I realize that the reassurance wasn't just meant for me. It was meant for him as well.

We sit in silence for a few moments, and I study the neighborhood from my new bird's-eye view. The streets are quiet. Every once in a while a car passes with a gentle *whoosh*, but for the most part we seem to be the only ones awake. The moon is a pale sliver.

"I am sorry for what I said in the woods," I finally say when I work up the courage. "I am glad that you saved me, and I would've been glad even if it did turn me into a full vampire. I was just in shock. And I'm sorry because it *is* unfair, and you have every right—"

"Stop," he says.

The shortness of his interruption makes my stomach sink; it was too soon to come over here. I peer over the side of the roof as I try to figure out my exit strategy.

It's still a little daunting to think that I should ever just leap off a roof. "Maybe we should talk later," I say, but before I can do anything, he grabs my hand.

Idiot, that's not what you meant. The thought cuts into my own, and it takes me a moment to realize that's not my thought—it's his.

"Then what did you mean?" I ask, and I can tell that I've thrown him.

"Okay, that really is kind of annoying," he says before his face turns serious. "What I meant to say is that you shouldn't apologize. I was jealous, but that doesn't mean I'm not happy that you're alive. *Never* apologize for that."

I look at him, not knowing what I could possibly say through the well of emotion that has decided to gather in my throat.

"And if I ever act like you should," he continues, "you can totally throw things at my head."

I manage a shaky laugh. "Just then?" I joke, but it has no edge at all because I am too busy looking at him. After all these days of being surrounded by slightly neon people, it's nice to be next to someone who is nice and non-shiny.

"You, on the other hand, look like a weather map," he says.

It's all I can do not to pull my hand away; this is not something that I am going to get used to, not the mind reading or the idea that James pictures me as a warm front. "Really?" I ask, more disappointed than I want to be. *At least he didn't say that I'm the color of a baboon's butt.*

He snorts, and I realize that he's still tuning in.

"Stop listening!"

"Sorry," he says, not sounding sorry at all. After a while he says, "I wasn't being serious. There's just a slight glow."

"Why can't I hear you as well as you can hear me?" I ask, because it's true. I only seem to hear him when we are touching.

"I don't know," he says. "Maybe it's because you're not a full vampire."

Maybe. For all my attempts to drown myself in normalcy, questions are starting to seep in. Lately, I've been trying to remember all of the things Vlad ever said and trying to sort the legitimate from the delusional. I should have taken his dumb book when he offered it to me.

"Then what am I?"

"You're Sophie," James says. "That's all that matters to me. That's all that matters to anyone."

"Do you think the other vampires will stay?"

"Marisabel is already gone."

"What?"

"She left a few days ago. She said there were too many memories here, and she wanted to try things on her own for once."

"But where will she go?" I ask.

"She said that she'd figure something out."

"So Violet and Neville are staying?"

"You couldn't pry Violet away with a stick. And Neville apparently has some part in the musical. Troy or something? I don't know. He's very excited."

It's a little strange how happy I am to hear that Violet will be staying, even though it means that the Neal problem is still . . . well, the Neal problem.

"What about Vlad?"

"He's dead, Sophie."

"I know that. But aren't people at school going to wonder where he went?" I ask.

"There never were any records. Vlad used his powers to convince people that he should be there, I'll be able to convince people that he shouldn't. And after all, there aren't any parents to report him missing."

"So you're staying?" I ask, because while all signs point to this, I just need for him to say it.

James looks at me, his eyes dark with emotion. So is the rest of his face because, you know, it's the middle of the night. But his eyes are darker. I swear.

"Where else would I go?" he says softly.

"I don't know. I thought you might want to get away from . . . reminders."

He looks up at the sky, at the stars above. "When I came back I thought that living in my old house would make everything feel . . . I don't know, corrected somehow. I thought I would feel like nothing had changed. And then when it didn't feel like that, I hated it. I hated every single brick and shingle. But it doesn't matter anymore."

"Why?"

He looks at me, gaze intent. "Because when I'm with you, I still feel like me. And maybe that's enough."

His words elate me—there is no other good way to describe this—and it causes severe technical difficulties between my brain and my mouth. But maybe that's because I'm not supposed to talk. This time I have no trouble closing the distance. My kiss lands southeast of its target, but he corrects my tactical error. It's not perfect. Sure, his lips are cooler than the average guy's and I think that I may be sitting on his hand, but under the very strange circumstances I think this is a happyish ending.

And you know what? Kissing on rooftops is kind of awesome.

Acknowledgments

Vampire Crush wouldn't be here without the help of a crew of amazing people, including Cristina Hoepker, its earliest cheerleader and official godmother; Meghan Deans, who is not only a critique-giver extraordinaire, but who also wins the prize for enduring more lunches where the main discussion topic is "Vampires and Writing About Them" than anyone, anywhere; Lindsay Ribar, whose enthusiasm has been invaluable; Preeti Chhibber, future publishing star (just you wait); Amy Spalding, generous giver of many Google chat pep talks, and Jenny Jackson, without whose patience and understanding this book would never have been finished. Not to mention the other wildly intelligent readers of early drafts: Laura Brett, Tina Brilej, Lindsey Cuddeback, Mara Dabrishus, Emily Giglierano, Marjorie Hakala, Marisabel Hoepker, Molly Jacobs, Alaya Johnson, Laura Lancaster, Chris Lough, Robin Keller, Liz Kies, Chrissy Marcum, Jessica Sison, and Nikki Wood.

My eternal gratitude to the team at HarperTeen:

Erica Sussman, the most talented editor anyone could ask for; Tyler Infinger, who I'm sure has helped in more ways than I know; Alison Klapthor, designer of the kick-ass cover; and Jessica Berg, crackerjack production editor. At Levine Greenberg, thanks should go to Beth Fisher, who helped get Sophie to Germany and Russia, and Victoria Skurnick, the world's best first boss and an even better agent. And, finally, a million billion thank yous to Sue Robinson, aka Mom, who is not only endlessly inspiring, but who patiently wrote down my stories when I was four and never once edited out the exploding Christmas geese, and to Gary Robinson, aka Dad, who not only read my teen vampire romance, but who finished it first.

You guys are great.